AJITA

K. Sridhar is a particle physicist with a passion for philosophy, art and literature. He carefully follows classic rock music and the Hindi film song. In recent years, he has evolved into a keen pedagogue. Each of these interests have led to academic, quasi-academic and popular writings.

His first fiction book, *Twice Written*, was published in 2011, followed by a critical edition of the same in 2019. *Ajita* is his second novel.

Sridhar has lived and worked in Bombay for most of his life. He now lives in Bangalore with his wife.

AF520212

Advance praise for *Ajita*

'An epic experimental narrative that teases at the boundaries of time and the possibilities of language, even as a heartfelt story unfolds. A very enjoyable and enlightening read.'

PRAYAAG AKBAR, author of *Leila* and *Mother India*

'In an engrossing form that makes the reader a necessary participant in the novel, *Ajita* has the delightful voltage of being inside a maze.'

SUMANA ROY, author of *How I Became a Tree* and *Provincials: Postcards from the Peripheries*

'Written with all the flourish of a metaphysician who entices the reader's imagination to glimpse ouroboroi in Möbius strips, Sridhar's *Ajita* is an exquisitely crafted play of and on language. The story of Ajita in ancient times and Moksh in modern times delicately bombard each other only to become that river of fire, the conceptual confluence innovatively irradiated by Sridhar's deep explorations.'

NANDINI BHATTACHARYA, academic and the author of *Love's Garden*

K. SRIDHAR

AJITA

A Novel

Published by Westland Books, a division of Nasadiya Technologies Private Limited, in 2025

No. 269/2B, First Floor, 'Irai Arul', Vimalraj Street, Nethaji Nagar, Alapakkam Main Road, Maduravoyal, Chennai 600095

Westland and the Westland logo are the trademarks of Nasadiya Technologies Private Limited, or its affiliates.

Copyright © K. Sridhar, 2025

K. Sridhar asserts the moral right to be identified as the author of this work.

ISBN: 9789360451912

10 9 8 7 6 5 4 3 2 1

This is a work of fiction. Names, characters, organisations, places, events and incidents are either products of the author's imagination or used fictitiously.

All rights reserved

Typeset by Jojy Philip, New Delhi

Printed at Thomson Press (India) Ltd

No part of this book may be reproduced, or stored in a retrieval system, or transmitted in any form or by any means, electronic, mechanical, photocopying, recording, or otherwise, without express written permission of the publisher.

Author's Note

The characters in this book are imaginary—all twenty-six of them. But when they come together—and even when, like in this book, all twenty-six of them never come together at the same time—they create worlds probably more real and certainly more eloquent than our own.

The chapters in this book are marked with a number and an alphabet. The alphabet marks its own absence in the chapter whereas the number is a more conventional ordering. And, in embarking on this book, you are invited to follow either the numbers or the alphabets and you will still be reading the same book.

The form of the book, where the last chapter loops back into the first, brings to the mind an ouroboric image but it is, in fact, a Möbius strip, as it twists and loops back. The deployment of these formal games in this book is my tribute to the remarkable literary movement, Oulipo, of which Raymond Queneau, Georges Perec, Jean Lescure, Italo Calvino and others were a part. The movement is best described by Queneau: he described Oulipians as being similar to rats which construct the labyrinth from which they plan to escape.

A good part of this book uses a confident voice in which a 2,500-year-old history is presented but that should not deceive us into believing that this fictional account is true. It is a style that allows the writer to take the reader along very briskly through a definite narrative. The writer is like a guide taking tourists along the main street of a historical city and showing them the important monuments without passing the alleys, with small homes and shops, or the slums and shanties of the city that are best hidden from sight. It is the presentation of history as fact that makes it easy for the touristic gaze of a reader. Except that what is consumed as fact may not be fact at all. History distorts facts in several ways and fiction even more so, if in more interesting ways, but the 'state of affairs', even when it was described in the past, is a mess of conjecture, speculation and falsehood. So, it may well be that only the side-streets, the slums and the shanties exist and the main avenue is an illusion.

And while the ancient past that the book deals with is now the stuff of fiction, so is the more contemporary time that it portrays. To somehow pretend that all this is not illusory, I employ a timeline that leads you through the chapters, in spite of the fact that time itself is the greatest of illusions. Even in that artifice of time-keeping there is a pretence at distinguishing the past from the present, using seasons to mark the past and months to mark the present. And, in a departure from standard BCE and CE conventions, the years before Christ are denoted with a minus sign.

1. B

Summer – 524

Ajita was lying flat on his stomach on the ground along the wall of the kitchen. The seven-year-old had spent all morning in the garden following the trail of red ants who had now found a way through a tiny hole in the wall straight into the kitchen. It was a long trail. There were so many ants and there was so much happening that young Ajita could not contain his excitement. He was particularly interested in two of them and was trying to follow them with his eyes to figure out how they were taking food from the kitchen and carrying it to their home in the garden.

'There they are, Gura and Dhura,' he muttered. 'Someone has told them to make sure the food is collected and put safely and quickly in the anthill. That is why they are moving so fast.

'I wonder what language they speak to each other. Is it a language I don't understand? Or even sounds that I don't hear? I am sure they can speak, or else how would they know where the food is? That they have to follow this line and reach the kitchen? I wish I could hear them and understand what they are saying to each other.'

Even as his mind raced, Ajita made sure that his eyes were trained on Gura and Dhura. He did not want to lose them. At one point, he wondered if they could see him, like he could see them.

'Or am I so huge that they can't see me with their tiny eyes?' he thought. 'Do they see tiny things with their eyes? Creatures so small that they are for Gura and Dhura, as small as Gura and Dhura are to me!'

Ajita recollected his visit to the grand market in Vaishali on the first day of Margasirsah. His father often went to Vaishali and that day he had taken him along. It was not Ajita's first visit to Vaishali: he had visited the city quite often when he was younger. It was just that he was seeing it now as a curious and awestruck seven-year-old and he was savouring the city to its fullest. As they entered the marketplace, Ajita had tightened his grip around his father's index finger. The expanse of the space and the sea of humanity around him were overwhelming, even if he was enjoying it all. He looked up sideways to see his father. Govinda was a tall man whose erect posture made him look taller. From that angle Govinda looked like he was the tallest person around. For Ajita there was no one quite like his father.

Ajita had noticed how, in spite of the crowds, there was an order in the way people moved around in the marketplace. People who were walking up the street stayed on the left and the ones coming down moved on the right. They walked past a fountain and the line of people naturally curved to go around the fountain. He was really impressed with the fact that everyone knew what they should do to help maintain the discipline of the market. A huge cart laden with goods got stuck in the middle of the street, causing some disorder.

However, people appeared, helped move the cart, and soon order was restored.

As he saw the ants move in and out of the kitchen, their discipline reminded him of the people in the market and how orderly they were. If anything at all, the ants seemed to follow their queues in an even more regimental manner.

He placed a small stone somewhere along their path, making sure that he did not injure or harm any of the tiny creatures as he did so. Chaos followed. The neat order that the ants had set up was destroyed and they ran around confusedly. However, all this lasted only for a few moments and soon order was restored as some of them seemed to take charge. A new line was formed quickly: moving around the stone just like the people in the market had moved around the fountain.

'Do you think there are tiny creatures that we cannot see?' he asked his father later in the day.

'What tiny creatures, Aju?'

'Creatures that we cannot see. Like very, very tiny ants? Or … perhaps … sounds that we cannot hear?'

'Well, it's hard to say for sure though I don't see why not,' said Govinda. 'Why do you ask?'

'I think there are creatures smaller than even tiny ants. Small ants can see very small ants and the very small ants can see the very, very small ants and so it goes, you know,' said Ajita, in the way of an explanation.

Govinda laughed. 'I don't know.'

Ajita seemed convinced of his idea. 'And sounds?' he persisted. 'Do you think ants talk to each other so softly that we cannot hear them?'

'I don't think they can talk.'

'Then how do they tell each other what to do, where to go, where to find food …?'

'That is niyati: the order in everything—in things living and non-living. That is how ants know what to do. That is how a stone knows how to fall and the night knows when it is time for the full moon.'

'And people in the Vaishali market?'

'What of them?'

'When they walk in the market, is that also niyati?'

'That is different. We have minds. We can use that to think and do things. We can talk to each other and understand each other. We live together, make our own customs and laws which help us live together, and we follow those laws,' said Govinda with a sigh. Ajita's questions were never-ending.

'And the ants? They don't speak to each other or make their own laws?'

'I don't think so,' said Govinda, smiling. 'You know, we plan to send you next month to a gurukula where you will start your education. And there you will find all your answers.'

The young eyes widened. 'I will learn all this there?'

'Yes, in a few years you will. First, you will learn to ask the right questions and then find the answers.'

'A gurukula?' Ajita said to himself. 'It sounds so interesting.'

For the rest of the morning, he imagined the kind of things he might learn at the gurukula. It was only when he cuddled up to his mother for his afternoon nap that he realised that he would have to leave home, his parents and all that was familiar. He huddled closer to his mother as the thought crossed his mind. He decided he would divert his mind and return to the question that had haunted him all morning.

'Do you think there are very, very small creatures like very small ants, Maye?' he asked.

'No, I think not.' His mother's answer was clear and unhesitant.

'Tath said he was not sure. Why are you so sure there are no such creatures?'

'If we can't see them, they don't exist.'

'Hmm. The other day Tath said that even if we can't see the wind, it exists. He said that to explain to me that the gods are there even if we can't see them.'

'That's true. We cannot see the wind, nor can we see the gods. However, we know that the wind is there when we feel it hit our face or our skin. Your teeny-weeny creatures, on the other hand, we cannot touch or feel them. So, there is no way of knowing they are there. I think it is the same with the gods.'

'That is not what Tath says ...'

'I know. I am telling you what my Tath told me when I was a small girl. We lived in the mountains, Aju. We had to walk long distances uphill to get water, food or wood. And all of us in the house had to do that so that there was enough for everyone. My father or his father never found the time to do yajnas and invoke the gods.

'Your Tath has grown up in the plains near the cities. Life is much easier here. Look at our home. We get water from the stream which is so close to our home, we grow our food in our garden, and we can also get what we need from the market, which is not very far off. When your father performs yajnas for other people, they give him things that are useful to us at home. He can afford to spend all day with these rituals and, in fact, it helps him take care of our needs. My own feeling is that when you do these rituals all the time, then the gods whom you invoke start appearing very real to you.'

'What does that mean?'

'It's like this. You know the wooden elephant I got for you from the fair? It is only a piece of wood which is shaped like an elephant. It is not a real elephant till you start playing with it.

Once you get involved in the game and you have made yourself a king out on a hunt and you set out with your soliders and horses then this piece of wood does feel like an elephant. If in the middle of your game I tell you it is only a wooden toy, will you agree with me?'

'So, you are saying that the yajnas are a game?'

'Like a game. Anyway, you should sleep now. You are sounding very tired.'

'Maye, I am scared. I don't want to leave you.'

'Oh, did your Tath tell you that we are sending you to the gurukula?'

'Yes, Maye.'

'I will miss you so much, my dear one. I am not sure I want you to go at all. Having said that, you are our child. Strong and fearless.'

'I will miss you when I sleep.'

'I know. Though soon you will get used to sleeping on your own. And there are other students there in the gurukula, so you should know that you are not alone there.'

'I am not scared of sleeping alone, Maye. I am scared of sleeping. That is why I hold you and sleep.'

'Scared of sleeping? I have never heard you say that.'

'Yes, Maye.'

'Why on earth?'

'When I am sleeping, I don't know where I am. It is all so dark and I feel like I am out in the night going to some place I don't know. So, I worry that I will wake up in a new, strange place, without you and Tath. Where I don't know anyone. How do I know that I will always wake up in our home next to you?'

'You worry too much, my little jewel. Your mind is so full of questions. When you try to sleep, gently pat your questions to sleep too. Let them lie still. Then, just as you close your eyes, think that my Maye is with me. Your Maye is always with you.' Saying this, Dhvani pulled her son closer to herself.

The day Ajita had to leave for the gurukula arrived sooner than it should have, or so Dhvani felt. She had tried hard not to let anyone guess the emotional turmoil she was going through, least of all her little son. She had managed to get some strength out of the fact that Ajita himself seemed to look forward to the gurukula with great excitement, and in his little joys she always found the greatest comfort. Ajita had woken up with the sun that morning. While he was looking forward to the new world that lay ahead of him, he also wanted to touch and feel his home, his parents and his friends.

He ran into the garden to greet one of his newest friends: a tiny mango plant. He had dug a hole in the ground with his friends Surjan and Ratna, and had planted a mango seed there not long ago. He was overjoyed when a small plant emerged out of the soil one morning. He had tended the plant with the utmost care and he knew he would miss it a lot. He had asked Ratna to look after it while he was away. He was still in the garden when he heard his Tath calling him. He had forgotten completely that it was time for his morning prayers. It was only two weeks ago that he had got his sacred thread and with the thread came the duty of praying thrice a day: in the morning, at mid-day and in the evening. Though, today he hoped his father would not keep him long at the prayers for he wanted to run down to the pond to meet his friends.

His friends were waiting for him near the pond when he finally made his way there. It was where they met every day, played and ran around, swam and swung from the trees to pluck the ripest fruits. Today there was no time to enjoy the pond and splash around. Ajita didn't feel like it either: when he saw his friends the full realisation of his departure dawned on him. It was a teary farewell and Ajita realised that it took longer than it should when he heard his father's voice calling out to him from a distance.

'We have to leave now, Ajita,' said Govinda, as he came closer.

As they walked home, Govinda said, 'You will find that the ways of the Gurkula are very different, Ajita. Though I am sure you will get used to them very soon. You will not have friends like Ratna there. It was alright for you to have him as a friend when you were small. Now you have grown up and you will have to move forward. You will have new friends there.' Ajita did not say a word. He had always known that his Tath did not like him spending time with Ratna, though he had not tried to find out why.

When he finally set out with his parents on his long journey to the gurukula, Ajita turned to look in the direction of the pond as the cart passed it. The area was empty, his friends had left and Ajita again felt something tug at his heart.

It was planned that, on their way to the gurukula, they would go first to Dhvani's maternal home, so that Ajita could meet and spend time with his grandfather and his uncle's family. Owing to his indifferent health, his grandfather had not attended his thread ceremony and that was another reason to meet him. The journey was a long one: the fact that they went up the hill to his grandfather's house on mules was the high point of the journey for Ajita.

Ajita only had a few faint memories of his grandfather's home. So it was on this visit that he would get the chance to really know this home. His grandfather's home was quite different from his parents' home, though it had a charm of its own. It was when he ventured outside that Ajita felt the sheer power of nature overcome him: the huge rocks, the views of the mountains in the distance, the tall trees and, most of all, the silence of the woods.

He sat down under a large, shady peepal tree. 'I wish I could live here forever,' he thought to himself. 'I would have so many friends here—these trees, these creepers and I can't even imagine what animals I will find in this place.' He thought of the mango plant in his garden and he wondered whether Ratna would take care of it. His thoughts then turned to Ratna and Surjan and he realised once again how much he was going to miss his two friends. This flow of thoughts was interrupted when he saw his grandfather sit down next to him.

'I am very happy you are going to the gurukula, Ajita,' his grandfather said. 'I hope you will study well and make a name for yourself.'

'Did you go to a gurukula, Aiyya?'

'No, I did not. My father moved to these hills when I was very young. I was not even a year old when I came to this place and I have lived here all my life. My father was a very learned vaid, did you know?'

'What is a vaid, Aiyya?'

'A vaid is a person who cures illnesses and makes medicines. We are a family of vaids and have practised medicine for several generations. My father was, however, more interested in studying medicinal plants that grow in these mountains. So, he decided to come here and spent his life studying leaves and plants. He knew so much—in one glance, he could distinguish the good medicinal plants from the poisonous ones. So many vaids from the plains used to come up here to consult with him and take his potions and preparations. He was a very generous man and shared his knowledge and his medicines freely, never demanding anything in return. Some people would offer him something of their own accord; he would then accept it graciously. Though I have seen quite a few vaids who only took from him, he never had a complaint on his lips. He was a great man.'

'I wish I could have met him. I could have made friends with so many trees and plants with him around.'

The old man smiled and said, 'I am sure he would have also loved to share all that he knew with you. That is what my education was—walking through these forests with him and learning from him. Of course, he had much more to offer than my mind could deal with.'

'Why can't I stay here with you and learn from you all that your father taught you? Why can't I make this my gurukula?'

'No, Ajita. You are on your way towards greater things. You will learn a lot in the gurukula and you will learn very well, I am sure. Years later when people speak of you as a famous agnihotri and you are called upon to conduct the great fire rituals, I will feel great pride.'

'Aiyya, don't you do any fire rituals?'

'Some small ones … well, no. Not really. Growing up here and living here in these mountains means you have other things to attend to and you cannot spend time performing rituals. We have to do everything here on our own. It is not like living in a village like yours where you can get help for everything. Last year, there was a great storm and a part of the roof of this old house got damaged. Your uncle had to spend a whole week working on it to get it restored.'

He paused and then continued, 'My father was properly trained to perform rituals. However, after he had spent time here, he also did not do any of them regularly. He told me often that the forest was our altar and the trees were our fires and that we had no need to perform sacrificial rites. I grew up with that way of thinking.'

It was getting a little cold outside so they decided to move in. As they got up to go, Ajita's grandfather said, 'In the end, Ajita, it does not matter whether you are a great agnihotri or a simple vaid. What matters is to have a deep sense of what you are doing. It is not so important to do great fire rituals as it is to understand their significance. And when you understand that, you will find there are so many other ways of finding that same meaning. You may find it in the mighty mountains or in a tiny leaf, you may find it in chants or in silence or, like a very old friend of mine, you may find it in singing.'

It was with a heavy heart that Ajita left the hills to go down towards Vaishali. When it was time to get into the cart, he started weeping. He was going away from his grandfather and his home, and the hills and the forests. He was also leaving his mother who was not going to accompany him to the gurukula. Ajita wouldn't stop crying, and Govinda had to carry him to the cart so that they could leave quickly.

It was a few hours into the journey that Ajita composed himself. However, he was still thinking of his Aiyya.

'When Aiyya speaks to me, I feel I can understand every word he says,' he thought to himself. 'And it is the same with Maye. Tath is very difficult to understand, though. He uses words like niyati which I cannot fully understand.

'I need to go to the Gurukula to study. I will not just understand what Tath says, I will speak like that myself.'

He looked out of the cart, felt a gust of fresh air caress his face. He closed his eyes and inhaled deeply.

2. D

February 1983

Moksh is waiting near the gate of his school for Vithal Uncle, one of his father's closest associates. He is somewhat anxious because he has to pay his examination fees in the school office in the next half an hour.

'I was wrong to not have met him earlier this week for the money,' he tells himself. 'It was silly to put this off to the last moment.' When his father was alive, he took care of all these things for Moksh. When he remembers his father Moksh's eyes well up with tears.

He looks at the examination form again to see if he has got everything correctly written in. A few minutes later, Vithal Uncle shows up with the money much to his relief. He completes the formalities necessary for him to be able to appear for the final exam.

As he steps out of the office, he remembers his first visit to school with his father twelve years ago.

Moksh is barely being able to see above the top of the table which is about as high as he is. The clerk turns to his father with a questioning look.

'Moksh Malhar? Malhar? That is a strange family name.'

Moksh's father explains patiently: 'Yes, that name was given to my father, who was a singer. He was so famous for the Malhar compositions that he sang that it became our family name.'

'He sang Malhar, so his name became Malhar! That is an interesting story. You also sing, sir?'

'No, no.' Sanjay Malhar's irritation is slowly becoming obvious.

'What was the family's name before that?'

'I am not sure I have to tell you that.'

'Hmm, what about religion? You have left that column empty.'

'We are atheists so I left it blank.'

'Atheists?'

'Yes, non-believers.'

'But, you must have been born into some religion. It is not about what you believe, no, sir?'

'I am sorry. I have no religious affiliation. My son has no religion either.'

'But you have to write something in the form. I can't process it all blank like that.'

'I am sorry but I refuse to write anything.'

The clerk is somewhat taken aback by Sanjay's vehemence. 'Okay, wait a minute. I will just talk to the principal.'

A little later, the principal comes out of his office. 'Mr Malhar, thank you for waiting. I apologise for the confusion but it is perfectly alright if you want to leave the religion column blank. Most people, even non-believers, fill up the column with some religious group or the other, for the sake of convenience. So, our office was not sure how to process the blank entry, but we will accept it as it is.'

His inability to look above the clerk's table, his father's presence, the gentle, smiling principal are almost fresh in his memory. He was too young at the time to follow the conversation but this was one of his father's favourite stories which, through several retellings, became a part of Moksh's memory. It also became a way of telling people that religion was a blank in the Malhar home.

But that wasn't quite true. Moksh's mother was a religious person, at least as far as her quiet, personal practice of religion went. The lamp, flowers, incense, religious images were all a part of the corner of the house that Moksh remembers as his mother's. (*This is what homes in Bombay are like. A 13 ft × 11 ft room for sleeping or two such rooms if you are lucky, a 10 ft × 8 ft space for cooking, a luxurious 14 ft × 18 ft room for living, whatever that means, one or two 6 ft × 8 ft spaces for ablutionary functions … Wait! By now this house is worth more than two lakh, or even four if you are in one of the not-so-suburb suburbs. So where in this house can one fit in a corner for praying? How big is that going to be? 3 ft × 5 ft? A little bigger? A Bombay architect's primary problem is theological—that of fitting in all of omnipotence in 15 sq. ft, in short, the problem of containing in a tiny space that which contains everything.*)

Moksh remembers he was barely fourteen when he saw Meghana, his mother, sitting in her corner, crying. His attempts to figure out why got him nowhere, at least then. He soon learnt that a cancer was growing in her intestines. She was gone before he was fifteen but he never forgot her, or her pain. Now that she was gone, he came to associate the place of her worship with suffering. He felt the objects kept there provoke anger in him. The aversion that he still feels to the smell of incense—or anything that smells vaguely of religion—comes out of this place.

Yet, he is upset when he sees his father remove the religious stuff from that corner to clean it up, while Meghana's ashes are still warm. Sanjay let Meghana have that corner to herself when she was alive. Now, with her gone, there is no reason, no space for anything religious. But what Moksh will not know is that with her, a part of Sanjay has gone too; he is not himself anymore. The sense of urgency with which he goes about emptying the corner that his wife chose to consecrate will be the first sign of Sanjay losing his grip over himself.

In fact, Moksh remembers that moment quite clearly. It is after his mother's cremation; the sort of afternoon which, having come after a night of little sleep, fills him up with overpowering exhaustion. But, more than the exhaustion, it is a feeling of overwhelming emptiness that threatens to swallow him up. It is not something that Moksh knows how to come to terms with. The house is full of people who have come to grieve, to help or to simply make an appearance. Moksh cannot even recognise a few of them; he has never seen them before. Some of these people will not leave him alone. He wants to tell them that he is not seeking the expressions of commiseration that they are so eager to offer but cannot. He moves to the only quiet corner in the house—a small alcove near the balcony just opposite Meghana's prayer space.

It is a little while later that he sees his father enter the room. Sanjay is carrying a bag in which he starts emptying the objects that occupy a corner in the prayer room: the photo frames, the prayer books, the boxes of camphor, the rolls of incense sticks, a tiny pot of water apparently from the Ganges. It takes Sanjay only a few minutes to take apart an entire pantheon. The violence of his father's actions upsets Moksh so much that he will never forgive him for it, but when he thinks about it years later he realises that, ironically, it is in this moment that his own atheism took birth—an atheism that is born out of emotion rather than reason. But, as he clings to his mother's memories, some bit of her faith also stays with him. His atheism, therefore, is no reflection of his father's. His father is an unbeliever; his is a believer's unbelief.

Sanjay's behaviour after Meghana's passing away worries Moksh. He returns home late one evening after a game of cricket to the news that his father is in hospital. He hears about it all. Sanjay, with a few of his associates, sets about the task of exposing a guru by showing his gullible followers that the miracles that the guru was claiming were nothing more than chicanery. Some of the followers are not quite as gullible; their allegiance to the guru is because of interests that are not spiritual but material. Sanjay is the only one in his group totally unwilling to see their point of view, upon which they beat him up severely. It takes Sanjay several weeks in hospital before he can walk again.

While Sanjay is still in the hospital, Moksh goes to meet him. He listens silently as Sanjay talks about the political situation in the country. Moksh's lack of interest is apparent. When Sanjay—finally noticing his son's silence—stops talking, the tension in the room is palpable.

'You have to stop all this… ' Moksh stammers out finally.

'What?'

'What? You know what. Fighting superstition on the streets, picking up quarrels with anyone who says anything about religion. That's what!'

'But… '

'No, Papa! This is really enough. I've lost Ma but I can't lose you. I can't.'

'Nothing will happen to me.'

'Look at yourself! You are in a hospital with your legs broken. But you still say nothing will happen to you!'

Sanjay is silent, while Moksh is unsuccessful in fighting back his tears. 'Okay, I promise. I will not involve myself in anything that can harm me. Or you,' says Sanjay at last.

A promise seeks to fix the course of one's actions in a future so far that no one actually has any control over it. It is like the man who, having seen his reflection in the river, goes further along the bank seeking that same reflection. The river flows, the light changes, the rocks in the river are now in a new arrangement. The man himself is no longer the same, yet he seeks the same reflection. 'He kept his promise,' they will say. 'He is the same man he always was. He is not one to change.' By staying true to his promise, he recovers a sense of an unchanging self in the flux of things—a buoy that anchors his reflection to one point in the flowing river.

But the flow sometimes allows for no fixity. With time, promises are forgotten.

One evening, about three years later, Moksh returns home from school to hear his father speaking on the phone. He notices Sanjay lowering his voice when he sees him. Moksh knows something is up—but what? Sanjay will clearly not let him in on whatever he is up to. Moksh worries. He knows that his father is back to fighting for causes he cares about. Over the next week, Moksh figures out that Sanjay is planning to take on a swami in the course of his public talk. The swami is proposing to argue in favour of the caste system by presenting 'its consistent, internal logic', as per newspapers. Moksh can see why his father is upset with the swami but he is also sick with worry about his father's safety. He cannot stop his father, so he can think of no better plan than to go for the talk himself.

A week later, Moksh arrives at the venue which is overflowing with people. The number of policemen there make it look more like a political meeting than a religious gathering. He smiles to himself, thinking how his father might argue that religion is, in fact, nothing but politics. He cranes his neck to see if he can spot his father somewhere but the floor seating makes the task almost impossible. The swami appears on stage, in front of a reverentially quiet congregation. It is when the swami begins his speech that Moksh sees Sanjay in one corner of the hall. Nothing in his manner or look suggests that he is there with a plan.

The swami is quite a captivating speaker. Almost everyone in the hall is listening to him with rapt attention. Moksh realises how charming the swami is, how beguiling his sermon.

The swami moves to talking about the caste system.

'You see,' he starts, using his characteristic pause at this point for effect, 'it is true that everything is ultimately the same—Brahman. It is like saying all fire is the same which is, in fact, true. All fire is the same; all fire burns. But, tell me, what is the fire you cook on? The fire in your kitchen, the fire from your stove. If I tell you to cook on the fire in a cremation ghat, will you agree? If I tell you all fire is the same, will you agree? You tell me! No, you will not! You will say this swami is talking nonsense. So, all fire is the same at some level but also not the same at another level. Similarly, all human beings are the same—that is what our religion says. That is beautiful, but you have to know at what level that is true. Not at the level we live our lives. At that level, all human beings are not the same. Some are like the fires in the kitchen, the others are like funeral pyres. That is why we have the varnas.'

He pauses again but this time it is not intentional. He has been hit by a stone—one of the few that were flung at him. Moksh looks up to see Sanjay hurling more stones even as he is shouting at the swami at the top of his voice. Three policemen swing into action, losing no time in grabbing Sanjay by his neck. But this is not before the gathering turns chaotic, with people running helter-skelter. Moksh scrambles to a safe corner. Fifteen minutes later, Moksh emerges from his refuge to realise that Sanjay, along with his associates, has been taken to the police station.

It is late next afternoon when Sanjay returns. He is home but with a few others, among them a gentleman whom Moksh has not met before. His name, he learns soon, is Jagannath Lotvala. He is a wealthy mill owner, but is strangely sympathetic to the communist cause. Moksh also learns that Lotvala finances much of the activities of Sanjay's revolutionary group. It is his money that got Sanjay out on bail. Lotvala's appearance betray his class: the silk Nehru jacket, the cufflinks on his shirt sleeves, the ring on his finger are all clear markers of his wealth. But his manner is gentle, showing none of the arrogance that Moksh associates with wealth.

Lotvala listens intently as the others talk amongst themselves. He finally gets up, saying, 'Sanjay, I have to go now. But I will call you later. You take care of yourself. Lie low for a bit, if you know what I mean.'

When the others leave, Moksh is silent. He has been having several imaginary conversations with his father—about his promise, about whether Sanjay loves him at all or whether he cares only for his activism. But now that he is alone with him, Moksh feels like a log caught in a river current. He feels unable to resist the flow, now that he is in the river.

One morning, two weeks later, when Moksh is walking to the school bus stop, he sees Sanjay at the top of the lane returning home after his morning walk. He thinks he will wait for him before he walks to the bus stop. As he watches his father walk up, Moksh cannot help noticing that Sanjay's posture is bent as though carrying a weight on his back. It is a change he has been noticing in his father over the past week. At that very moment, a motorcycle, with two men on it, comes up the same way. As it comes closer to Sanjay, Moksh realises that something is very wrong. He shouts out to his father. Almost simultaneously, the man sitting on the back seat of the bike pulls out a gun, firing several bullets at Sanjay. Even as Sanjay falls, clasping his chest, the bike, making a U-turn, moves out of sight.

Or rather this is how Moksh remembers the tragic morning much later—as a reconstruction into a series of sharp images of raw stock that was a sort of blur. Neither the ache in his heart nor the tears in his eyes are of any help in lessening the mistiness of the scene. It is in the countless recountings to himself that he recovers a narrative which he then takes as real.

But his recollections of what people were telling him over the next few weeks are correct. 'You're not alone' is what he remembers many of them saying. Each time he hears it, that line pierces him sharply. He realises they will not let him forget how alone he is. Yet, they aren't saying this out of any real concern, he feels. Once, however, what follows the 'You are not alone' is 'We are with you'. Moksh looks up to see the same man who was in the house with his father less than a month ago—the man who got Sanjay out of prison.

There is something about Mr Lotvala's manner that makes Moksh want to pay attention to him.

'You must not think that you are alone. We are all with you,' he says, gesturing to Sanjay's co-workers who are also there with him. 'Your father gave up his life for the party. We won't forget it. The party will take care of you now. You have nothing to fear. We will take care of all your expenses. Your father's sister will stay with you. I spoke to her this morning to make sure that she will be here next week.'

He pauses, looking at Moksh's searching face, then goes on: 'Also, this is not a favour—I will not like it if you think that. We know you are a very intelligent boy. If you help us in the party's work, we will all be very happy.'

Vithal Uncle joins the conversation. 'Yes, sir. He is a very best boy. He is a scholar—always got first rank in class. He can help with our pamphlet work, any writing, all that.' Then turning to Moksh, he says, 'Moksh, not to worry about anything. We are there, no? We will take care of you. Money is also not a problem. Not to think you have no father, no mother. You are the son of the party from now on. What, Lotvala Sir? Am I not right? He is now the son of communism.'

Lotvala's face breaks into a smile. 'Yes, Vithal. "The son of communism." I quite like that.'

Even as he realises how bizzare this conversation is, especially at a time like the present, Moksh can see it comes from a place of genuine concern. These were the people closest to his father, he feels secure in their presence. The image of Sanjay being shot at comes back to him. He feels a shiver run up his spine. The realisation that these are the only people he really has sinks in. He agrees to go along with their suggestions even if he knows that he will have to sacrifice some of his time after school to be able to work for them.

So, Moksh, just about seventeen, becomes a regular at the party office—a small office in one of the bylanes of the Fort area. The office has little ventilation or natural light. Moksh is given a small work table beneath a bleak light bulb which contributes significantly to the worsening of his myopic eyesight. A table fan on a shelf next to him is barely effective, so much so that it is not easy to cope with the heat or the stale smell that overpowers the room. The party brings out a monthly journal which carries a couple of analytical pieces on economics, politics, philosophy… along with several news items from across the country pertaining to workers' activism, strikes, struggles or wage settlements. Mr Lotvala takes care of the publishing expenses but the person whose lonely efforts make sure that the journal is brought out every month is Yusuf Attarwala. Yusuf Chacha, as everyone in the office calls him, is a large man with a larger store of stories. He is the sort of person who knows everyone—politicians, paupers, rajas, rickshaw-wallahs, saints, stars are all a part of his circle. His working hours are largely spent telling his office mates stories of these people over cups of chai that the maharaj from the shop across brings in. It is only after everyone goes home that Yusuf Chacha's work on the journal starts. He manages the writing, the corrections, the page layout all by himself. In Moksh he has, for the very first time, an assistant. Moksh's primary task is precis writing: making short news items from longer pieces taken from various sources. Much of this is boring so he goes about in a mechanical manner. It is only when he gets to work with the analyses that his eyes sparkle with interest. Realising Moksh's precocious talent, Yusuf Chacha resolves to encourage him. Thus starts Moksh Malhar's engagement with Marxist literature: something that is going to remain by him even after he leaves the communist party.

It is the time at home, after office, that is tough. Sulagna Maasi, Meghana's first cousin, was living alone in Pune for years with only her melancholia for company. It is her own memory of the times she spent with Meghana when they were young that makes her feel that she is responsible for Moksh's care. So when Sanjay's associates reach out to her in the aftermath of his assassination, to help take care of Moksh, she makes a mammoth effort to overcome her own misgivings before agreeing to come to Bombay. She is efficient in taking care of the house but she cannot get over her own gloominess to be anything more for Moksh. Her presence is no help in coming to terms with his grief; that is a struggle which is very much his own. For months, he cries himself to sleep but one morning he wakes up with the feeling that he has to move on with his life. He only knows that he has to cope with the situation, but while he is making all efforts to manage his grief he cannot see that he is putting away his grief in a storage space which will open for him much later in life.

3. C

Autumn – 515

Ajita was panting when he arrived at the top of the hill. He had run all the way up without pausing for even a moment or losing speed, and was at the base of a massive boulder with a flat top that stood at the peak and rose defiantly towards the skies. In these last nine years, this was his shelter when he wanted to get away from the Gurukula. Most often, he would go there when he missed home but today it was to vent his anger. He was fuming.

He lay down on the boulder and looked up at the evening sky that was just beginning to fade off from sight. The sky had opened up that afternoon after two days of heavy rain.

From where he stood, the view of the sky and the sunset was stunning. But Ajita paid no heed to it. He simply stared at it as he waited for his anger to subside and his breathing to return to normal. It was getting dark now and he heard the birds twitter as they flew home to their nests. The gentleness of the twilight, the light breeze that was blowing and his own exhaustion were making him drowsy, and he struggled to stay awake. He was well aware of the animals that roamed these parts after dark and he knew he had to be alert. He was just beginning to wonder if he should return to the Gurukula when he sensed something move below. He sat up with a jerk and peered down. It was his friend Kairav looking up at him from the base of the boulder.

'Gurudeva was asking for you. I looked for you all over and then realised you will be here,' Kairav said, as he gingerly made his way up.

The anger reasserted itself in Ajita's eyes. 'Gurudeva!' he said, in almost a hiss.

'Why are you angry, Ajita? Gurudeva seemed very pleased with you today.'

'He only appears to be. The reality, however, is that he thinks only of himself.'

'Why do you say that? He loves you. You are his favourite student.'

'None of that is true. Not a bit. I have been feeling this for a while but today it was totally obvious.'

'Will you tell me what happened?'

'You wouldn't know. You were busy helping with the yajna today.'

'True. I did not have a moment's respite today from making arrangements for the yajna. But, tell me, is your anger to do with the flooding of the river?'

'Yes, when a river overflows and floods the banks, it is telling you it has had enough.' Saying this, Ajita got up to go.

Jeevananda of Kashi was a pandit of great renown and when they learnt that he would be visiting the Gurukula for a few days, the students were eager to meet him. Jeevananda belonged to a reputed tradition of pandits whose mastery over rituals, otherwise forgotten, was the stuff of legend. Gurudeva had got to know him well when he had spent time in Kashi in his youth. When he learnt that Jeevananda was visiting Vaishali at the behest of a nobleman, he sent him an invitation to visit them.

Jeevananda agreed to spend a few days at the Gurukula. The servants and the students were all put to work to ensure that he would be well looked after. On his arrival, though, the boys were amused to see a rather unimpressive man: short and pot-bellied. He was hardly like their Gurudeva, who was a tall man with broad shoulders and sharp features. His long, greying hair made him look very noble. Now, when he stood next to Jeevananda, he virtually towered over him. That is why the students did not understand Gurudeva's deferential attitude to Jeevananda.

'Our Gurudeva is far superior to this man,' one of them said, when they talked amongst themselves later. 'Why does he have to bow to this pot-bellied pandit?'

'He is supposed to be very learned,' said another.

'Ah! Are you saying our Gurudeva isn't?'

But when Jeevananda assumed his seat at the dais or at the altar, there was no doubt about who the master was, not even in the minds of the most loyal of Gurudeva's students.

For several months before Jeevananda's visit, Gurudeva had planned to organise a grand mahayajna that he wanted Jeevananda to lead. The intonation of the mantras for this yajna had several subtleties that only an expert like Jeevananda would know and Gurudeva was keen to learn from him. The favourable time for doing the yajna was deemed to be the first day of the month of Ashvin, the day after the full moon. Like most people who are arrogant about their knowledge, Jeevananda was very demanding and soon had the whole

Gurukula set in motion around preparations for the yajna. Gurudeva was willing to agree to every demand of his.

Two days before the full moon, the sky darkened.

'Do you think it is going to rain? Does it rain here at this time of the year?' Jeevananda asked his host as they sat in the open grounds outside the Gurukula that morning.

'No, no. The rains usually last till early Bhadrapada. It is almost Ashvin now.'

'Yes, so it is in Kashi. But I have been observing that over the last few years the rains have been irregular. Why, it rained in the month of Kartik a few years ago in Kashi! It has been said that when adharma rises and men lose sight of what is right and wrong, nature retaliates. These off-season rains are a sign of the times we live in.'

Gurudeva nodded in agreement. He looked up at the sky again and grudgingly noted that it looked darker than it did earlier.

'Let us move indoors,' he said to Jeevananda, but even as he was saying this the heavens opened up and it started raining quite heavily. 'Don't worry. I will make sure that the rains will not interrupt our yajna.'

The next morning it was Gurudeva who was worried. It had rained all day and all night, and even now the rain was not showing any signs of letting up.

'Ajita,' he said, when they were together. 'You will not sit in the yajna tomorrow.'

'But I—' Ajita stopped when he saw Gurudeva's expression.

'I've made up my mind,' his guru said, with an air of finality.

'Yes, Gurudeva.'

Gurudeva looked at Ajita and saw how distraught the boy looked. Softening his manner, he said, 'Ajita, I don't have to tell you that I trust you with the most important tasks in the

Gurukula, as I know that you will do anything you are assigned and you will do it well. I wanted you to be at the yajna more than any other student. But I am worried about the rain. It has been pouring for the last two days and I am afraid it will be the same tomorrow. If that is so, we will need you and two others to make sure the supplies of firewood, ghee and food are delivered properly to the altar. I want you to make sure all this happens smoothly, in spite of the rain.'

The yajna was to start at an early hour so the inhabitants of the Gurukula were up and busy before dawn. It had rained for the best part of the night and the firewood was not quite as dry as Gurudeva would've wanted it to be. Ajita and a fellow student were trying to sort out the firewood for the yajna. When Ajita looked up from his task, he saw three human figures out in the open. It was still too dark, and from where he was standing it was hard to make out who they were. Stepping out, he saw that the three were fishermen who lived up the river. The stream that passed by the Gurukula was a small tributary of the river that flowed southward. These fishermen lived near this fork in the river. Ajita saw them often when he walked up the river bank or went for a swim. The men looked very worried and asked to speak to Gurudeva. Ajita hesitated. He was somewhat nervous about disturbing Gurudeva when he was getting ready for the yajna but the men's manner betrayed a seriousness he thought he should not ignore.

'What is it?' asked Gurudeva, when he was in the garden in some time, after Ajita had managed to get his attention. He was annoyed but he was speaking in a whisper. It was obvious that Gurudeva had also sensed the gravity of the situation.

'Swami,' one of them said, 'the tributary is in full spate and the water is overflowing onto the banks. We are trying to dam it near the fork so the flooding on our side of the bank may be stopped. We will have to do that and also hope that the rain stops.'

'Yes, please do that. I will pay you for this work with grain and meat.'

'Swami, we are already working on trying to dam the rivulet. But some of our people have gone on a pilgrimage and have not yet returned. There are only a few of us here. We will need help from your Gurukula.'

'That will not be possible. My students and helpers are busy with the yajna that we are doing here today. There is a lot of work to be done and I will not be able to spare anyone.'

'Swami, the water level is rising and we have very little time on our hands. That is why we are asking you for help. Please don't turn us away.'

Gurudeva looked at Ajita. 'Ajita, I entrust you with this work. Take two more boys with you. Find the ones who are as strong as you. This is not going to be easy.'

'But, Gurudeva, the supplies for the yajna?'

'Don't worry about that. I will get three other boys to handle it.'

So even as one yajna was readied, the stones and firewood arranged and the great fire kindled, another one was being set up where boulders and trunks of trees were piled up to propitiate the other great gods: water, air, earth and sky. Water was the primary deity in this yajna and, unlike the fire that is allowed to grow bigger in the altar, this ritual sought to diminish the power of water, to make it yield to the power of the ritual and find rest. And the sky and the wind were being propitiated too, to yield and show gentleness. The earth, as always, was the support bearing the burden and now she was again yielding only to the ritual, but not to the intensity of the other elements. The altar for this yajna was prepared with mindfulness, its geometry helped exert power over water and tame it. Like any other yajna, this one also used the power of sound. The intonation of a definite set of sounds helped attain identified material ends: power alone was not enough to move a huge boulder from land and deposit it into the river; it was the singing of a mantra that helped bring all the strength together. All this knowledge was the end result of many years of study and was transmitted from guru to shishya. The dramatis personae were not the shastris, the swamis and the hotris but men who intimately understood the water that their lives were based on. They knew the power the elements had: to bestow and to take away, to sustain and to destroy.

Ajita and his friends worked with the fishermen till late in the afternoon, helping move stones, boulders and tree trunks into the river. It was around noon that it stopped raining, the flow of the water in the river ebbed and when the sun peeped out a little later it brought huge relief to all of them.

When they returned to the Gurukula, they found Gurudeva sitting in the garden by Jeevananda's side.

'So, here you are, finally,' Gurudeva said to them. 'It is late and you boys should go and eat. I am sure you are famished. But are you all not impressed with the power of the yajna we performed? Jeevananda told me that the yajna will make sure that the river will not flood our Gurukula. When you boys were out there, we did the rituals with the devotion that is needed to exert power over the river. So strong were our mantras that we knew the rain will not harm us.'

Ajita looked at Gurudeva in disbelief. *What was he saying!*

'Gurudeva, we worked very hard today, right from dawn, to dam the river. And then too, we only helped the fishermen. They understand the river and knew what was needed to be done. They did most of the work themselves, we only helped them. If the river moved away from our side of the bank, it is them we have to thank.'

Gurudeva glared at Ajita, displeased at his gall, but somehow stopped himself from exploding.

'You speak ignorantly, Ajita. I thought you would know better after all that I have taught you. It is foolish to attribute great meaning to the petty work that small people do. They did what I told them to and I will reward them for it. But I want you to understand that nature and its gods do not pay heed to these trifling deeds. We were here, far away from where you were working, doing whatever was needed to tell the river to find a new path. And it did. This does not happen by throwing stones and trees into the river. And what about the rain? How did that stop? You are not going to tell me that the fishermen did that too! It was us. We stopped the river and the rain. We made the sun shine. And yet that, for the great task we have performed, was a trifling matter in itself. What we did will exert its power in several other planes and in many realms. For us, the flood was really a small issue to deal with. Anyway, I think you should go and eat now.'

As Ajita finished narrating the day's events and the reason for his anger, he looked at Kairav who looked at him solemnly for a moment before bursting into laughter.

'Ajita, you are making a big deal out of nothing. I think you have worked too hard today and are too overwrought to be reasonable. I think you should sleep over this matter. You will feel alright tomorrow.'

'What are you saying, Kairav? *I* am not being reasonable? There is not a wee bit of reason in what Gurudeva is saying. He was talking nonsense.'

'Don't speak about him that way. He is our guru.'

'You know, I have always followed everything he has told me. But now I wonder if I was too young and did not know any better. Suddenly, I see him as being devoid of reason, selfish and arrogant.'

'Oh, My Lord! You are making a mountain out of a molehill. You worshipped Gurudeva then and you worship him now. Think of how you have been with him all these years. Think of all that you have learnt from him, how you held on to every word he uttered. Are you going to disown all that for something as silly as what happened today?'

Later, when the two friends had returned to the Gurukula and Ajita lay down in bed that night, he wondered whether he was judging Gurudeva too harshly. He still did not doubt that Gurudeva had been wrong. But was it right to say he was unreasonable, selfish and arrogant? Where were these feelings against Gurudeva emerging from? If he was being honest, it was not just this one matter. Over the last few months, some of these doubts were growing inside him but today they had burst forth. Maybe he *was* being too harsh. There was no need to talk about Gurudeva the way he did today. Ajita turned to his side, sleep far from his eyes. It was never an easy relationship with Gurudeva. There were times when he felt a strong adoration for Gurudeva but it was never an unquestioning devotion to him. Maybe he was just not given to that kind of devotion, Ajita thought. He had felt it rarely when he was younger and over the years it had only diminished.

He remembered his very first meeting with Gurudeva when he had just arrived in the Gurukula nine years ago. It was late in the afternoon when they arrived, tired and hungry after their long journey. Gurudeva waited to meet them till they had finished their meal. He greeted Govinda warmly, or so Ajita thought.

'Govinda, my dear friend. It is so good to see you after all these years.' Looking at Ajita, he went on: 'So, this is your little boy? Ajita?' He paused. 'Ajita, do you know that Govinda and I studied together in the same Gurukula? Those were good days, weren't they?'

'Yes, they were,' said Govinda, but Ajita felt his father was not his usual self.

'So, Ajita, you want to live here and be my student?'

'Yes, Gurudeva,' little Ajita had said meekly.

'And what do you want to learn the most about?'

'I like animals. And plants.'

'He has been spending a lot of time with ants,' said Govinda.

'Ants? What do you know about them?'

Ajita was not sure why Govinda had so readily told Gurudeva about his interest in ants.

'I just follow them and see how they find food and store it.'

'There is a lot to be learnt about ants. One way to find out about them, Ajita, is to follow them as you have been doing. You will learn a few things, sure, but that might be limited. The other way is to first find out what has been said about them. In the Vedas and the Brahmanas, for example. Do you know that ants are able to dig very deep holes in the ground and they always dig in regions where there is water deep underground even if the soil on top looks dry?'

Ajita's eyes lit up. How did Gurudeva know this?

Gurudeva did not miss the spark in his would-be student's eyes. He went on: 'You must be wondering how I know this. Did I spend time sitting out in the sun in an arid desert to find out how ants behave and what kind of holes they dig? No,

I found this out from the Atharva Veda. The Atharva Veda tells us a lot about ants—the wonderful abilities they have, how they build anthills and how snakes live near these anthills. There is an immense amount to learn. But for that, one must know where to start and what to learn and understand. And, most importantly, one should have the right guru.'

He paused at this point in his monologue, then said: 'I am happy to take you on as my student. But I want you to work hard.' Then turning to Govinda, he said, 'I hope he is a better student than you were, Govinda. It was not easy for you to learn anything, I remember.'

Govinda looked down and avoided looking at Ajita.

'I hear from friends that you are not doing too badly,' Gurudeva went on. 'It seems you do get invited to perform some rites. I am sure that is good enough for you.'

Ajita looked at his father. He felt ashamed to stand there and listen to Gurudeva patronise his father. When he was alone with his father later, he held his hand and said, 'Tath, I don't want to live here. I want to go home with you.'

'No, my son. No, please.'

'Tath, I don't like that man. I didn't like the way he talked to you.'

'You mustn't think that, Ajita. He is very learned and knowledgeable. He probably looks at me from his position and I look very ordinary to him, perhaps. That is the order of things, my son. Some people are better than you, some more famous, some wealthier. I am happy to just be a good person loved by my wife and son.'

'But if he speaks like that, I don't think I would like to learn anything from him.'

'You are not here for him, Ajita. You are here to seek knowledge and the path to truth. You will need to be guided on that path for some time. Pay attention to the destination, not to the lamps that light that path. Be grateful to the lamps for illumining your way but revere only your destination. That way you will never go wrong.'

He put his hand gently on Ajita's head and said, 'I will be very happy if you study well and make Gurudeva remember me as your father and not you as my son. You should be the best student he ever had.'

'He will be a very good student. And you don't worry about him. He will be fine here,' they heard someone from behind them say. They turned to see a woman at the doorstep—Gurudeva's wife, his Guruma.

Govinda spoke to her with folded hands. 'He is our life. And we are leaving him here with you. I know that he will be very well looked after.'

The moment he saw her, Ajita knew he would share a bond with her. Her gentleness revealed itself in her kind manner and quiet smile. Through his years at the Gurukula, Guruma would be the one person he would turn to whenever he felt lonely.

When he thought of his father now, Ajita realised that he had to stay in the Gurukula. He resolved to put the events of the day behind him and get over his feelings of anger and resentment.

The first thing that Ajita wanted to do the next morning was to seek out Guruma.

'I need to speak to you, Guruma,' he started, abruptly. He told her about the flooding of the river, their work on building a dam and then what Gurudeva had asserted about the yajna and how that had angered him.

'I should not have felt that way. It was wrong.'

'It is fine, son. All of us feel anger at times. That, in itself, is not wrong. But it may be not so good to extend it. It is best to feel it intensely and leave it behind. I will also speak to Gurudeva when he is free. I am sure he will understand your feelings too. But now, put this behind you and look forward to a new day. You will feel better then.'

Ajita felt relieved. Guruma's wisdom and manner always made him feel at ease. It was not what she said but the way she said it that made him feel that things were not as bad as he thought they were.

He figured out that she had spoken to Gurudeva when the next day he asked to meet Ajita alone.

'I heard my words made you angry, Ajita. I was pained to hear that,' he said. 'It is irrelevant whether I was right or wrong, it does not matter if you agree or disagree with me but you should not let it stoke feelings of anger.'

'I did not stoke it, Gurudeva.'

'If you think about it, you will realise where you went wrong. It was when you let a small feeling of disagreement get bigger in you and take the shape of anger. Krodha, as you know well, is something we should avoid. A student like you journeying on the path of knowledge should surely not fall prey to it. Krodha is one of our worst enemies. It is our gullibility that makes us feel that it is an element of our essential nature. It is not.'

Ajita mulled over Gurudeva's words through the day but, despite thinking it over again and again, he felt it did not ring true, somehow.

'I have seen him get so angry—sometimes with us students, sometimes with the attendants. How do I believe him when he pretends to have mastered anger?' he thought to himself.

'Over the years, what I have found out about him is that he is not truthful. He does not do as he speaks.'

Ajita was restless all night and did not sleep soundly. He was up early and it was still quite dark when he set out for a dip in the stream. As he walked past a grove of trees on the way to the stream, he heard some sounds from the grove. Fearing that it was an animal, he stopped where he was and trained his ears to listen to the sounds. It took him no time to figure out that the sounds were human; not one but two humans were behind those trees and there was no mistaking what they were engaged in.

Ajita was stunned. 'Who are these people and how dare they do something like this in the Gurukula?' He hid himself behind a tree that offered him an unhindered view of the opening in the grove. A little later, he saw a woman peep out of the opening before she started running towards the Gurukula. When she was out in the open, he saw that it was Jana, the young woman who helped with the housework in the Gurukula. Ajita was already upset to see Jana but was just not prepared for what he saw next. It was the man Jana was with; when he was out and standing against the first rays of the morning sun, his tall frame, his broad shoulders and his flowing hair left Ajita with no doubt about who it was.

4. E

March 1983

Yusuf Chacha is busy at work today but Moksh has nothing much to do. Rummaging through a cupboard, Moksh finds a book, *M.N. Roy: Political Biography* by V.B. Karnik. Moksh turns it around and finds a black-ink inscription on its back: 'Sanjay Malhar, 22.01.1979, Bombay'. Yusuf Chacha looks up from his work and knows what Moksh is staring at and says to him, 'Sanjay was a good man.'

Chacha's first allusion to Sanjay in months has Moksh sit up. 'Did you know him, Chacha?'

'I did. Ours was an old association. I got to know him around 1954. I had just got my communist party affiliation. India was going through a lot of turmoil and, in particular, Bombay was in political chaos. Bombay was all of what is now Maharashtra and Gujarat—not just Bombay city. Linguistic division of India was put forward but it was a political plan of playing with linguistic jingoism. In Bombay, that was not all. Class dynamics was also coming into play—rich, trading and manufacturing-class Gujaratis against working-class Maharashtrians. Soon, it was not a conflict about Gujarat and Maharashtra but about Bombay city. Which part will Bombay city go to—Gujarat or Maharashtra?

'Was that in 1955?' Moksh asks.

'That's right. Our party got into this conflict too, but by taking a moral high ground, by focusing on class and not linguistic politics. Our party was an important part of a multi-party organisation—Samyukta Maharashtra Samiti.

'It was during this agitation that I got to know Sanjay. I found in him a thinking and upright individual and I hit it off with him right away. Sanjay was as fond of chai as I was so that was also a bond. I still think of our days fondly—sipping chai, smoking Charminars and discussing Marx.

'By January 1956 things took a drastic turn. Our plan was to ramp up our agitation, and Bombay's administration, in obvious panic, got in army jawans with shoot-at-sight instructions. It was bad! Soon our party high command was in jail and our only option was to go into hiding.

'Sanjay and I found asylum in a small hut in Bhandup. Staying in that hut for that many days in difficult conditions was tough but it also got us to form an unusual bond. Frankly, it is surprising that Sanjay and I got along. I was willing to concur with him on many things but not on God. I am a Marxist but I am also a Muslim. Islam taught us to think of us Muslims as custodians of this world and I think Marxist thought is a tool for a custodian to draw upon. But for Sanjay this was a totally wrong way of thinking about Marxism. I did not study Marxism from original books, not as much as Sanjay did anyway. I got to know of it through Indian books and, through my own churning, got a grasp of it. My approach was not scholarly as Sanjay's was.

'But also, my Marxism impacts my ways of looking at Islam. It is not just a faith or a philosophy. That I am living from birth in a Muslim locality brings in socio-cultural strands, part of which I am wary about. My discussions with Sanjay did go a long way in gaining my own insights into all this. That a rationalist should do this to my faith is a paradox, but that is how it is.

'His was a hard rationalism; I could not think of him in a mandir or praying. I told him, *"Kattar hum Musalman nahi, kattar tum rationalists ho."* Sanjay took it sportingly, though. I think all tags—Hindu, Muslim, Christian, Communist, Rationalist—work only up to a point. Humanity is what is important. Finally, I am not a Muslim or a Communist but a Humanist.

'And that was what bound us. Sanjay was human to a fault. So much so I would think of him as a saint, but a saint without faith—a rationalist saint. Rationalism for him was similar to what faith was for a man of God.

'Anyway, back to Bhandup. It was a full moon night. A party functionary was caught and got such a bad thrashing in custody that this man spat out all information, including our location. A group of army jawans got going to hunt us down in Bhandup. As soon as Sanjay and I got to know about it, our instinct told us to run. With four jawans on our trail, Sanjay and I ran frantically. At a point, our path split into two and Sanjay said I should go right. It was dark and I did not know that Sanjay's path was an uphill climb. A jawan, catching up fast, took aim at him and Sanjay was hit on his thigh. I saw him go down and was in a panic but could do nothing. That night what Sanjay did was truly magnanimous. I am profoundly thankful to him for it, always.

'Sanjay was in Arthur Road jail for four months or so and it was tough. On my visits to Arthur Road, I was sad to find out how sick Sanjay was. It took him many months to pull round but his spirit was strong all through. In my narrow thinking, such a strong spirit was a sign of faith. But through Sanjay I got to know that this is not so.

'Sanjay was also a sharp political analyst. Way back in 1961, Sanjay said how our party had not thought through fully what ramifications our participation in Samyukta Maharashtra Andolan would throw up. In trying to fight linguistic jingosim, our party's political stand would allow linguistic politics—schismatic politics was his word for it—to grow rapidly in this city. Sanjay was so right but his opinion did not find any sympathy within our party.

'Our city is changing so fast. It is scary to think what Bombay will transform into.'

January 1984

'I want to go to Zamzam to pick up mithais for tonight,' says Chacha, parking his car in an impossibly small gap. 'Do you know it? I am not talking of Kaaba's holy spring but of Mohammad Ali Road's famous mithai shop.'

'That Malpua is just fabulous and so is that Malai Khaja,' Chacha says. 'But I know what I want to buy. Shahi Aflatoon. Do you know what Aflatoon is? It is Arabic for Plato. And in Urdu it is a know-it-all, a man who shows off his wisdom. But in Bombay it is this sugary mithai. Isn't that fascinating? Though I always thought of a Sukrat Halwa and an Aristu Barfi,' Chacha says, smiling.

'Hmm, Plato in a mithai shop. Now that's unusual,' says Moksh with a laugh.

Chacha's is a big joint family living on Mohammad Ali Road in a flat which is not small but is bustling with activity, much in contrast to his own.

'This is my jaan, my child, Razia,' Chacha says. 'Razia is studying at Sophia's.'

'I am studying sociology. And you?' asks Razia, smiling.

'I just got into Wilson. I want to study philosophy,' says Moksh, awkwardly. It is difficult for him to talk to girls, and Razia's looks and aplomb disarm him. Moksh is happy that Chacha, pulling out a photo album of his family, starts a long introduction to his family history.

In 1837, Hussain Attarwala, a young Bohra Muslim, lands up in Bombay from a small town in Gujarat and, following his family's tradition, starts a small attar shop.

'I thought of you only as Muslim and not as a Gujarati,' says Moksh, slightly aghast. 'But, Chacha, you fought against Gujaratis during Samyukta Maharashtra Andolan, no?'

'Most of us don't think of Muslims as a part of any linguistic group,' says Chacha, laughing. 'But about Samuyktha Maharashtra … that's a good point. And as I said, for us Marxists it was all about class. Our fight was not against Gujaratis but against captialists.'

'And your family's roots in Bombay go back to 1837? That's long!'

'So long ago that our family has no photograph of Hussain Attarwala or his son, Sadiq.'

Sadiq Attarwala is born in 1841 and Hussain is comfortably moving up in his work, so finding accommodation for his family on Mohammad Ali Road is not difficult.

'Wow! So your roots in Mohammad Ali Road go all that way back?'

'That's right. And I thought our family would always stay on Mohammad Ali Road. But, for as big a family as ours, this flat is small. I bought a bungalow in Thana and a part of our family now stays in it.'

By and by, Sadiq runs Hussain's attar shop but is not as good at it as Hussain was. Sadiq is a family man and his focus is, in particular, on his son, Fazal, who is born in 1861. Owing to Sadiq's lack of absorption in his work and his frail physical condition, his attar shop is doing badly.

Yusuf Chacha's flat, at this point, was drowning in a strong aroma of biryani. But a lilting song sung by Lata and Rafi finds its way indoors through a window.

Fazal Attarwala is an innovator and a visionary who, without much formal schooling, has insights into transformations that Bombay is going through and works out how to go past his family's traditional occupation of trading in attar. As a young man, with his attar shop almost closing down, Fazal looks for a job and as soon as a vacancy in Bombay's Royal Turf Club shows up, Fazal opts for it. During his Turf Club stint, Fazal finds that sports is a growing passion with Bombay's population. Thanks to his charming disposition, Fazal finds rich patrons to support him and starts trading in sports goods. This work picks up rapidly and Fazal soon owns a sports goods shop in Dhobi Talao.

'So, this was around 1885?'

'That's right. Fazal got into sports goods around 1884 and his shop was built in 1887.'

Fazal has two sons, Rashid and Hamid, but Hamid, still a boy, succumbs to typhoid. It is around 1900 that Rashid starts assisting Fazal in his work. Politically, Bombay is in turmoil and Bombay's trading community is on its guard. Rashid's focus is on consolidating his position within Bombay's changing financial situation. Rashid's cautious approach pays off and by 1905, which marks his son Salman's birth, Rashid has a flourishing shop.

'Not a man in our family got past school till my Abba. Abba was a scholar and history was his passion which Abba took up for his graduation.'

Salman Attarwala, BA in History, fights with his family to go on to do an MA but, abandoning this, joins Khilafat.

'Khilafat is thought of only as an agitation to support a Sunni Muslim Ottoman Caliph but it was also a rallying point for all Muslims. In India, in particular, Shias such as our Bohra community took part in this agitation. Critics of Khilafat don't grasp this point.'

By 1924, building on Ottoman ruins, Mustafa Kamal Ataturk founds a Turkish nation which also signals Khilafat's conclusion. By now, Salman is gravitating towards Gandhi and his call for Satyagraha. That Rashid is still handling his sports goods shop is what allows Salman to follow his political activism.

'Abba was against his sons following him, so Tariq and I could go our own ways. Tariq was happy to work in our shop and I got into politics just as my Abba did.'

'My God!' says Razia walking in at this point. 'Abba, will you stop? This poor chap must find all this boring but you will not allow him to say so.'

'Moksh is fond of my story! And our family history is not boring in any way.'

'Family history? What you put out as family history is a history of our patriarchy. How is it that no woman finds a way into your history—not my grandmas, nor any part of Ammi's family?'

'I was talking of *our* growth as a family, of us Attarwalas. But it is also about Bohras in this city.'

'And in that story of growth, no woman counts? Abba, I find it disappointing. But I think you Marxists focus so much on class that you cannot wrap your minds around patriarchy!'

Chacha has nothing to say to Razia but Moksh, in total admiration, blurts out, 'I didn't think of that, but what you say is right.'

Razia walks up to Chacha and hugs him. 'Oh, no! Abba is sulking now. Grow up! Don't act childish.' Chacha cannot hold his sulk for too long and is soon laughing with Razia and Moksh.

That night, back in his room, Moksh's mind is buzzing with thoughts, mostly about Razia.

It is not just an act of fortuity that within a month Razia runs into Moksh. On his days off from work, Moksh walks around Sophia's, hoping to catch sight of Razia. In his mind, Moksh has a plan, a script—if Razia shows up, Moksh would watch from afar and Razia would not spot him. But now Razia is standing right in front of him and Moksh is at a loss. Razia, though, is nonchalant. A walk, a kala khatta and an hour at Haji Ali puts Moksh in a happy mood but his joy knows no bounds on finding out that Razia wants to catch up with him again.

Four months go by and, in actuality, only on a handful of occasions is Moksh with Razia. But his mind cannot fully focus on study or work. In his solitary nights in his room thoughts of Razia drown him. His aunt's gloomy air only adds to his agony. Moksh cannot talk to Chacha about this and his only option now is to talk to Razia.

'No, Moksh, no! Just stop,' says Razia. 'You will say things I don't want to know. I talk to you, I am fond of you. And I also know how difficult living on your own is. I thought by talking to you, I was doing my bit for you. That's not much, I know. But that is all, I am afraid. This may hurt you now but you will know soon that what I am saying is right.'

Imagination is hard labour. Months and months of planning and building go into making your world. Bits of it do not fit in, parts of this world do not hold up standards of rigour. You go back and plan and build again till it is all right, till it is living, inhaling air and singing. But imagination is duplicitous; it may hit you with a brutal unconscionability. So much work is put in to build a world but it can vanish in just a blink.

For days now, Moksh is totally withdrawn and distant. Chacha works hard on trying to draw him out.

'I am going to Thana for a fortnight tomorrow with my family. For our vacation. Do you want to join us for a day or two?'

'No, I can't.'

'If you want to think about it and call us in a day or two, that is okay too.'

'No, I don't.'

Six days go by without Chacha and by now, Moksh is missing him awfully. 'Why was I so curt and abrupt with him? I should call him and say sorry. What Razia did has nothing to do with him. I cannot do this to him. And Razia was right. It was wrong that I thought of us in that way. I am too young for all this.'

Moksh's mind is buzzing with such thoughts in a bus on his way to work and is oblivious to an air of agitation around him.

Finally, a man sitting by him, touching his hand lightly, says, 'Son, don't stay out now. It is not looking good.'

'Why, what's going on?'

'Did you not know? Bhiwandi has had riots for two days now. But today it is not just in Bhiwandi but in many parts of our city. You should rush back.'

Moksh has not known any man look so afraid. 'Okay, I will.'

Moksh is going towards Mohammad Ali Road with Mr Lotvala in his car. With its pollution and its milling crowds, Bombay is always a hazy blur, but it is totally out of focus now to Moksh who cannot stop crying. An air of gloom hangs all around which will always taint this day, though Bombay will limp back to normalcy.

It is almost half an hour now that Razia is sitting with Moksh and Mr Lotvala in Yusuf Chacha's drawing room but has not said a word. Finally, Razia starts talking.

'Our Thana bungalow was full of my chachas, chachis and cousins. For two days, it was a lot of fun. So much so that what was going on in Bhiwandi was not known to any of us. Abba got a call that morning about riots, but our family was still unmindful. It was not until Abba got to know about killings of Muslims in Thana that panic struck us. Our bungalow is in a posh part of Thana with many civic officials living in that part of town. So my chachas thought it was out of harm's way. Abba did not think so and was trying to work out how to transport us back to Mohammad Ali Road but …

'Abba was continuously trying to call and find anybody who could sort us out with a van or a minibus but didn't find anything. By that night, Abba was in a panic of a sort that I didn't think I would find him in. Locking us all in, Abba was pacing up and down all night in our balcony with a pistol in hand. I found out that Abba had got an authorisation for a pistol long ago.'

'I know,' says Lotvala. 'I thought Yusuf was at risk so I got him that authorisation through my contacts.'

'I did not know that and was in shock. His panic, that pistol—all of it was so scary. I saw that Abba had lost his sanity that night and I was afraid. My chachas did try to call him in but Abba just didn't want to.'

Razia stops, at this point, and says, 'Abba lost all faith that night, not finding anybody to turn to. I know, Lotvala Kaka, that Abba was trying to call you.'

'I was not in India, Razia.'

'I know and so did Abba. But his mind was blank that night. I think it was around four. Abba got a call and I saw him go into our living room. Abba was talking softly, and I did not catch his words but soon I saw him go out. Rahmat Chacha also saw him go and was afraid that this was not a good thing to do. It took half an hour to unlock our door and Rahmat Chacha, with my cousin Salim, ran out to find him.'

Razia starts sobbing at this point.

'I know nothing. What call was that? Who was it and why did Abbba go? I know nothing. All I know is that I lost my Abba. Who would kill him … such a loving man, who would kill him?' Razia bursts into sobs.

As Moksh and Mr Lotvala walk out, Razia calls out.

'Moksh, I want you to know that I am going away soon. I am marrying a distant cousin and will go with him to Sharjah. My Abba was so fond of you and had faith that you will do brilliantly. You will stay in my thoughts too.'

Moksh cannot think of going back to his flat and finds his way to Haji Ali. An hour of crying drains him out totally. His mind is hazy and in that blur it fills with visions of striking clarity. Of Yusuf Chacha and Sanjay in Bhandup running with army jawans in hot pursuit, of Chacha's family, of attar, of sports goods, of Razia with him in Haji Ali, and of Chacha pacing up and down in his balcony in Thana with a pistol in his hand. His mind stays with that last vision. What was Chacha going through? Razia said, 'Abba lost all faith that night.' But

Moksh thinks Chacha lost his sanity as his world did. Moksh now has a vision of Yusuf Chacha in his chair at work, a cup of hot chai in his hand, saying, 'Moksh, this was not a riot. Bhiwandi riots, my foot! It was an attack on a community by a political party. Sanjay was so right in saying that linguistic and communal politics, schismatic politics, is going to hold sway in our country. I am sad that this is our parting gift to you young Indians.'

5. F

Monsoon – 514

Another year went by and soon it was Ajita's last month in the Gurukula. He was now standing in Gurudeva's personal quarters, where he had been summoned.

'You should not leave in Shravan. That is not the month to leave the Gurukula. I will consult the almanac and select a date in early Bhadrapada when you can leave. We will organise a yagna to mark the occasion. I have sent a message to Govinda to come here by then so that he can be present during the yajna. We are also planning a grand meal at the time and you will have to assist in preparing some special dishes.'

'Yes, Gurudeva,' said Ajita.

'I wanted to bring up something with you. I have noticed that in the last year you have not been very interested in your studies or in anything that is happening in the Gurukula. Your eyes, which used to be radiant with enthusiasm earlier, seem to have lost their lustre in the last year. Your manner with me has also been distant. What is bothering you? I want to know now, because I am going to be very busy during this month and may not have time to discuss this with you later. The last year notwithstanding, I still think you are my best student, my best shishya. I wanted to recommend you to the great acharyas in Vaishali. An apprenticeship with these men will give you a good career ahead which will ensure your prosperity as well as your spiritual growth. These are the two wheels on which our existence's cart progresses and it is essential that you handle both these aspects well.'

'I appreciate your goodwill but I will go back home and give this some thought. I do not want to start with anyone right away.'

'Nobody will wait, Ajita, till you have made up your mind. I am happy to recommend your name to these acharyas now but in a year's time even I may not be so enthusiastic. You cannot miss out on such golden opportunities.'

'I am not sure they appear so golden to me.'

'You know, Ajita, I give up. Once you leave this place you are on your own. I am not going to try to help you when you are clear that you neither need the help nor do you respect the sentiment with which it is being given.'

Saying this, Gurudeva got up abruptly and stormed out.

Guruma had heard the exchange between her husband and Ajita. Later that morning, Ajita had to help in the kitchen. Guruma was already present in the kitchen when he went. When the girl who was working with her there went to the garden to get vegetables, she got Ajita to sit by her and talked to him.

'What is the matter, son? I am worried that you are looking so uninterested. Have all these years in the Gurukula not amounted to anything? Do you think all this time has been wasted?'

'It is not that,' said Ajita.

'Then what is it? You have learnt a lot here and learnt well. It is not just about doing yajnas; it is about knowledge and, more importantly, it is about thinking. You have learnt how to think and analyse and this is not something everyone picks up. When you disagree with your Gurudeva, don't let it just be an emotional response to him. Ask questions. Tell him why you are disagreeing. Ask what is your alternative. That is what will take you ahead.'

'Guruma, I have been thinking hard over the last one year. I am very muddled but, in all that, one thing is clear. That I want to be a thinker and not accept anything as given, just because someone says so or that it is attributed to some great Veda. I want to debate, discuss and argue. That is what I want to do most.'

'Then do it. Don't worry about making people unhappy with your arguments. But, at the same time, be honest. When someone's argument betters yours, accept it. That is a sure way to go ahead.'

'Thanks. I will remember this always.'

The month went by quickly and the ceremonies that were planned to mark Ajita's departure were much more subdued than they normally would have been. Gurudeva was making it very clear that he had lost all interest in Ajita and went through the rituals in an uninterested manner. Govinda, who had arrived in time to witness the yajna, noticed this; he was perturbed. When he sought out his old classmate to talk about it, the man was abrupt.

'There is not much that can be done. I don't know what has got into your son. He does not seem to be interested in taking my advice. I am happy to leave it there.'

'He is but a young boy. He does not completely understand all this. It is your guidance that will help him. Please don't be angry with him.'

'Govinda, I have tried talking to him not only because he is my student but also because I have known you this long. But he is not willing to listen. I think he does not respect me or what he has learnt in my Gurukula. So let's not discuss this anymore.'

A perplexed Govinda tried talking to his son on their long journey back home, but Ajita was silent all the time.

It was a sunny but cool morning and the sun streamed down on the two strapping young men standing out on the open ground. Ajita was the taller one but Ratna was more muscular. Ratna had started working in the tannery as a young boy and the years he spent there had hardened him.

Ajita watched as Ratna dipped the hides in lime water. He was struck by the care with which Ratna was doing his work.

'How long will you do this?' asked Ajita.

'Oh, this takes time and it is done to remove the hair on the hide. Some hair still remains, so I have to use a blade to get the remaining ones out. Then I wash it, get the lime out and soak it in salt water. This will take all day,' Ratna replied with smile.

'Can I try doing it?' Ajita asked.

Ratna looked a bit surprised. 'Yes, sure.' he said. 'But most people cannot stand the stink. I am surprised you are even managing to stand here.'

'It hit me initially. But one gets used to it,' said Ajita.

As he helped Ratna with the soaking, Ajita asked, 'So where do you get these hides?'

'I skin the animals at the place where my uncle works.'

That stopped Ajita in his tracks. 'What! You do it? With your bare hands!'

'Yes, but, no, we use some tools to do it.'

'It is strange. I have seen animals that have been slaughtered but never imagined someone actually slaughtering them. That would be done elsewhere and then brought to us and I had never really given it a thought.'

'We work with all the dead animal's parts that can be put to use—their hooves, horns, bones, muscles ... almost everything.'

'Actually, our bodies and animal bodies are so alike. I have been thinking about this. We pretend we are somehow superior to them but we are just the same.'

Ratna thought it was strange that Ajita should say this. He replied, 'But we are not quite the same, are we? We can think and we have a soul.'

'Animals can think too. I have watched them long enough to know that they think as well as we do. Even tiny ants.'

Ratna laughed. 'Ah, there you go. Ants! They are your pets.'

'Yes, it just makes me wonder,' said Ajita. 'Why do we think we are so special?'

'Our bodies are similar, but we have a soul. That sets us apart,' said Ratna, more tentatively this time.

'Who says so?'

'Well, learned people. All the people you studied with.'

'Don't believe anyone, Ratna. That is the only thing I have learnt. Don't believe anyone unless you can also see truth in what they claim. I have yet to see anyone show me what a soul is, though these "learned" people love to talk about it.'

Later that evening Govinda told Ajita that he wished to speak to him about something.

'Yes, Tath?'

Govinda's anxiety was etched on his visage as he spoke. 'It has been six months since you returned home. But you have not started doing anything. I have to understand what your plans are.'

'Why? What do you want me to do?' asked Ajita.

'I want you to do something. Anything. What is it that you think you would like to do?'

'I am spending time thinking about that, Tath. I don't want you or Maye to worry about me. But I want to be sure I like what I am doing.'

'And what will that be?'

'I don't know that yet. But I would like to get into understanding things. Deeply. I want to be what people call a philosopher. I want to discuss, debate and argue with other thinkers but also spend time developing my own ideas about the world and understand what ideas others have come up with.'

'And how do you propose to do that?'

'I am thinking. I go and attend discourses. I listen to thinkers engaged in debate. I came back only six months ago but I have already been to Vaishali several times to listen to these thinkers. I enjoy going there because it is in a big city like Vaishali or Magadh that you can get to listen to such people.'

'But I hear that you are spending your time with Ratna. I don't think you should be doing that.'

'Why not? I am very close to Ratna—you know that. And you know that I have known him since I was a child,' said Ajita, the irritation in his voice becoming somewhat more obvious.

'You know why. Don't be so naive, Ajita. Ratna works in a tannery and that is not a place you should be associated with.'

'But, Tath—'

'People are beginning to talk about this amongst themselves, Ajita. Two people whom I know well have already told me that I should stop you spending time with him. We have many people in this village who wish us well but it will not take them long to change their attitudes to us. Don't take this lightly, we could get ostracised.'

'Ratna is my childhood companion and he will always stand by me. The whole village can turn against us and he wouldn't care.'

'That is immaterial. We need people like us to support us. He is not one among us,' said Govinda, clearly wanting to say no more.

Ajita's voice was quavering as he said, 'I cannot believe you are saying this. I am shocked that this village's narrowmindedness has crept into your heart. Tath, I have always held you in the greatest regard. I never cared that people do not think you are a worthy scholar. To my mind, you are among the most humane people I have seen. To me you were a much bigger person than my Gurudeva. That is why I am shocked at hearing you say this about Ratna. Someone like Gurudeva saying this would not have surprised me in the least, but you . . .'

Govinda was silent.

Early next morning, Ajita resumed the conversation he had not completed the previous evening. This time Dhvani was also around.

'Maye, Tath,' said Ajita. 'I hope you won't be too disappointed but the path you want me to take is not one I desire to go down. I realise that this village is too small a place and I will not be able to live here the way I want to. I will be watched all the time. It is in the city that I see my growth. I have decided to move to Vaishali.'

'But what will you do there?' asked Dhvani. 'How will you survive?'

'I will manage, Maye. I have my learning to help me earn my living. I already know people in Vaishali, some important people. People in the cities are willing to pay money to learn literature and poetry. That is what I plan to do. It is not what you wanted but—'

Govinda interrupted him, saying, 'You mean, you will not be doing the duties your dharma tells you to do? That you will throw all that away and live like a jungle-dweller?'

'Tath, I spent many years studying things related to my dharma but I am now convinced that it mostly does not make sense. I want to leave that behind to explore what lies ahead. I want to see what I arrive at when I have given up all that was taught to me. I have to go.'

'You are our only child,' said Govinda, the words choking in his throat.

'Yes, Tath, and I will always be that. I will be there whenever you need me. But don't stop me now. Please.'

Later in the day, Dhvani came to talk to Ajita again. Govinda was with her but remained silent.

Dhvani spoke with the clarity that she always displayed. 'I thought over what you told us in the morning, Ajita. I think you are right. This village is probably too small and too constricting. You should go to Vaishali. But I want you to listen attentively to what I have to say and then decide. While you are saying that you will teach literature and poetry to the rich merchants' sons in Vaishali, I am not sure that alone will work in the long run. You need to have something stable to be able to live in a big city. I am not insisting, like your Tath, that you do your duties as prescribed by your dharma. Instead, I think that you should go and live with Aiyya in the mountains.

Spend two years with him and learn all that he has to teach you about medicines and remedies. And then you can live in the city. The knowledge you acquire about medicines will stand you in good stead there. Also, Aiyya is getting old now. He is sad that he has not been able to teach my brother much. My brother is not interested and lacks the discipline to be a student, but you will learn quickly, I'm sure. Aiyya will be so happy to teach you.'

Ajita was quiet.

'Son, I know you are eager to go to Vaishali soon. But think about what I am saying. You will see it makes sense,' said Dhvani.

The next morning, Ajita sat in the garden thinking about his mother's advice, when he saw her walk up towards him.

'This tree has grown so big,' she said, as she sat by him. 'It was still a sapling when you went to the Gurukula, do you remember?'

'Yes. I planted it . . . I remember very well.'

'It is quite a miracle how a tiny sapling like that grows into this massive tree, its branches spread out. Very much like you. You were a baby when you went to the Gurukula and now you are a young man who has branched out and wants to determine which direction he would like to grow in.'

Ajita did not reply.

Dhvani continued, 'In all these years that you were away, Ratna would come regularly to water the tree, prune the dead branches and enrich the soil around it. He would come about twice a week to look at it and give it what it needed. It is thanks to him that the tree has grown so well and yields such good mangoes. When Ratna came, he would also look at the other plants in the garden and make sure they were doing well.'

'Yes, he told me, but I did not realise that he was here regularly,' said Ajita.

'Very regularly. He would make sure to come at a time when Tath was not around. Except there were some days when Tath would still be at home. He didn't say anything to Ratna but made it clear that he did not like his presence around. But Ratna and I would always talk when he came here. He would want to know whether we had any news about you. His eyes would light up when he spoke about you. He really likes you a lot.'

'I like him too. I want to take him to the city when I settle down there. But he is not interested. He thinks the city won't change things in his world. That he will continue to be in the city what he is here in the village. He does not think the city as liberating as I do. Though I don't agree.'

'So, what are your plans now? Do you want to do what I suggested to you?'

'Yes, Maye. I think there is sense in what you are saying. I remember the last time I met Aiyya on my way to the Gurukula. I really loved the time I spent talking to him. I think there is much I will learn being with him and you are right in saying that it will equip me to make a living in the city. I am ready to go and live in the mountains with Aiyya.'

One thing about the Gurukula that Ajita genuinely missed was the abundant natural beauty around it. The trees, the creepers, the plants, the rugged hillocks around and, more than anything else, the river. Ajita had spent many days by the river and it was mother, companion, teacher and God all together to him. Almost as soon as he arrived at his Aiyya's home, Ajita saw that he would have some very dear companions in the woods close by—the trees spoke to him as their branches swayed gently in the breeze. It helped Ajita settle down in his new home quickly and he was able to start his education with his Aiyya, which he discovered soon was in two parts: one was to commit to memory textual and scriptural material and the other was to understand practically the herbs, plants and animal products alongside their uses and proportions in preparing compounds and potions. Aiyya was both pleased and surprised at the ease with which Ajita learnt the textual sources. He had a great memory and had honed his learning and retaining skills at the Gurukula. It was not without reason that he was Gurudeva's pet student. Aiyya was delighted that he was able to teach a student who, unlike his own son, excelled in learning the texts. Ajita was new to the apothecary's practices but he was excited about the things he was getting to learn.

'How are you liking it here?' his Aiyya asked him some months later.

'I am enjoying all that I am getting to learn.'

'Is it like your Gurukula?'

'My Gurukula trained me to learn and to learn well,' said Ajita. 'But that was mainly the knowledge that existed in texts. There was not much we learnt as practice—there were some practical skills that were taught to us but that was all. What I am learning with you is just not the same. When we prepare the potions and medicines I actually get to understand what each ingredient is doing and why we use the proportions we do or what ingredient will not be used with what and why that is so. Also, because nature has so much to give, we can discover new medicines and remedies and not just stick to what is given in the text. What we may discover could be new or it could correct what exists in the texts. That is quite unlike whatever I learnt in the Gurukula.'

'I know. But what you learnt there was not about the everyday world but about what lies beyond. About the soul and gods. It is knowledge that transcends the everyday world,' Aiyya said.

'But what is that world which transcends what we are in? Who has seen it or experienced it? What is this thing called soul? And what guarantee do we have that all that we are told by the texts about these things are true? Is there a way we can discover it ourselves?'

'You have many questions, Ajita, and I am no expert in these matters. But I think it is not possible to discover everything on our own. We need to believe learned people on many matters. What exists in the texts is what has been discovered earlier and passed on so that we may build on that knowledge. We vaids devote our lives to studying human health but health is not only about the body. Our own texts teach us that a healthy person is one whose body, mind and soul are in proper equilibrium. We cannot say there is no soul.'

'I am not sure I agree.'

'To learn you need to accept. Accept what exists. When you do not accept something you have to replace it with some knowledge that is equally valuable. Simply disagreeing with existing ideas is not the way a wise person proceeds.'

'Aiyya, what you say is true. I need to think a lot more about all this, which is what I am doing and want to continue doing. But let me share this with you. When I went to the Gurukula I was impressed that my Gurudeva knew so many things. Even on the day I joined the Gurukula, he amazed me with details about ants that I did not know. I was surprised because I had spent so much time with ants and he knew things about them that I did not, and who knows whether I would have ever discovered. Then he said he knew all that because he relied on books, on texts to get his knowledge. His words convinced me to take his path to knowledge. But in my last two years in the Gurukula, I realised that textual knowledge has limited validity. We have to subject that knowledge to our own experience to know whether it is true or not.'

Ajita's two-year stint with Aiyya came to an end.

Aiyya was very happy with all that Ajita had learnt in this period and was convinced that Ajita could set up his practice in the city and do well. Even though he wanted very much to go and settle down in Vaishali, Ajita was sad to leave Aiyya's home. He had become accustomed to the gentleness he knew in his mountain home and the calming silence that he experienced in the woods that surrounded it. It was an uncomplicated existence and he knew that was not how it would be in Vaishali. But when he thought about how exciting living in Vaishali would be, the people he would meet and engage with, the libraries he would go to, the big assemblies he could attend where he could listen and learn, develop and debate—when his mind imagined all the other charms that Vaishali held in its store—he was quite sure he was ready to leave.

When he set out to leave, Aiyaa walked with him some distance. They said little to each other and they both realised that, given Aiyya's age, this may be their last time together. Ajita stood and watched when the older man turned to go back home, knowing that he was going to miss Aiyya deeply.

6. G

June 1985

It is exactly a year after Yusuf Chacha's death. The office just does not feel the same so Moksh limits the amount of time he spends here. He spends more time in his BA classes and uses his spare time to explore the vast collection of philosophy titles in the library. His study of philosophy opens up new worlds for him and that makes the work he does in the office seem even more mechanical.

Nilesh Borkar is the person who now takes care of the journal production and publication. Nilesh Uncle, as Moksh calls him, is a pleasant person quietly committed to his communist activism.

'I just sent out posters for Professor Rane's talk,' says Nilesh, pleased with what he has accomplished. 'You will be there, I hope.'

'It is about the Bhiwandi riots so I can't miss it,' says Moksh. 'I will definitely be there.'

Professor Rane teaches History at Bombay University but is also a communist party worker and is one of the people the party approaches when an academic presentation is needed. His talk, 'Bombay after the Bhiwandi Riots', is a Marxist analysis of the political situation after the riots with the history of post-Independence Bombay as its backdrop. Professor Rane's mastery of his subject is impressive and he has the audience spellbound for well over an hour.

It is not until the talk is thrown open for questions, however, that the action starts. The first couple of questions are quite standard and do not elicit any serious response from the speaker. Moksh notices that there is a woman to his left who has her hand raised but the chairperson pays no attention to her. After a few more minutes, the woman stands up and the chairperson cannot not take notice now.

'Okay, you may ask your question but please keep it brief,' he says.

'Actually, mine is not a question but a comment and I will not keep it brief because what I have to say is very important,' she says.

Moksh is impressed with her already.

'Professor Rane, you said that these riots in Bhiwandi mark a point of transition in Bombay's history. That they are unprecedented and that they will make this city's future communal and that it will also be a way to divert people's attention from class issues. I have heard this said by other Marxist analysts too. But I think it is a Marxist version of the history of this city that completely obliviates other perspectives to the history of this city. I do not deny that Bhiwandi has shown how fascism has flexed its muscle in the city to quell Muslims but what about Dalits? It has been ten years now since the riots in Worli happened and the same fascist forces unleashed violence there. But I never find any communists talk about Worli. Why are the Worli riots not as important in Bombay's history as the Bhiwandi—'

The chairperson cuts in. 'Sorry, you have made your point. But we don't have any time left. So I will have to stop you here.'

'No! You will not stop me!' the woman shouts back. 'The time when you could do that has passed. You'd better listen now. Many of us Dalits have tried to find allies in the communists and, in fact, think that a Marxist framework which is suitably adapted to address Dalit questions and issues is what we would like to move towards. But we are always turned away, disappointed. That is because you do not want to address the issue of caste.'

'I am afraid we cannot allow you any more time. We will close here,' the chairperson says, and then he and Professor Rane leave the rostrum. But Moksh can see that Professor Rane is visibly shaken.

When he comes out of the auditorium, Moksh sees the woman in an animated conversation with Nilesh. He joins them and listens quietly to her.

'Nilesh sir, you are one of the few people I can talk to here. The others are useless. They will just not listen,' she says.

'They will slowly come around, Maya. You have to persist with it, all the same,' says Nilesh. 'By the way, this is Moksh. He works with me in our office. Moksh, this is Maya Jadhav. Dr Maya Jadhav, sorry. She has done her PhD in Education. She now runs a school in Worli.'

'It is a small school for children who have no recourse to education,' Maya turns to Moksh and says.

'I would like to hear more about it.'

'Join us for dinner. Maya will also be there. That way you two can speak freely, with no restriction on time.'

At the restaurant Moksh finds a comfortable corner seat just opposite Maya.

'I must tell you that I had not heard of the Worli riots till you mentioned them today,' he says.

'No surprises there. To understand what really happened, you need to know more about the context of Dalit movements, especially in this city, and, in particular, you must know about the Dalit Panthers.'

'I have only heard of them.'

'It was around the late 1960s that a radical faction of Dalit youth felt disenchanted with Dalit political parties, which they felt were too centrist and would never be able to deliver Babasaheb's dream of caste annihilation. In fact, they went even beyond Babasaheb Ambedkar's vision, which they felt focused on the cultural and did not pay attention to economic disparities. So they turned to the Marxists but they had paid no attention to caste. The Dalit Panthers believed that caste annihilation required a major upheaval of class structures: that caste and class should be tackled simultaneously. So it was really a call for an attack on the institutions that upheld caste and class.

'Did you actually interact with any of them?' Moksh asks.

'Yes! When I first met them, I was only seventeen. I was completely taken up with the intellectuals in the Dalit Panther movement—people who had read and absorbed so much and believed that would be the key to their transformation.'

'Which year was this?' Moksh wants to know.

'It was 1973. My cousin Narayan Kamble, who was a few years older than I, was already a part of the Panthers. It is because of him that I came into close contact with their key members. It was a heady period—we talked and talked till those ideas became us. We could see very clearly a vision of a different world.

'In January 1974, there was a by-election announced for the Central Bombay Parliamentary seat and that is when the Dalit Panthers decided to launch an all-out offensive. They decided that the elections should be boycotted and that they would take it upon themselves to convince the electorate not to vote. I remember clearly the day when a massive rally was called on Ambedkar Maidan—Namdeo Dhasal, J.V. Pawar, Raja Dhale were all there. What an atmosphere that was! If someone had just lit a match that day the whole place would have burned down. That was the kind of tension in the air. I think this city was not prepared for the kind of speeches that were made that day. It shook them, it scared them but it also exposed them. It was clear to us that they would retaliate.

'You mean, the fascists?' Nilesh asks.

'Yes. And their political machinery. They came down on us with the state and the police on their side. It was brutal. The elections happened, the Panthers' appeal to the electorate was successful and the constituency saw the lowest turnout ever. But the fascist, communal forces were out to destroy us. The attacks on us in the chawls went on for two months. People were brutally beaten up, some were killed, many injured for life and even children were not spared. My own cousin, Meena-tai, was stripped naked by the police and taken in a procession around the area. I remember how she was thrashed. She was due soon but did that stop them? The women pleaded with the attackers to spare her. But they didn't listen. One of them kicked her stomach. She lost the baby and the way she bled we felt we would lose her too.'

Maya pauses, and Moksh notices her shiver. He waits a bit and then quietly says, 'So they were not riots. It was a planned attack on Dalits. A retaliation?'

'Yes, absolutely. But everyone refers to it as the Worli riots.'

'Like the Bhiwandi riots.'

'Yes, that too. I raised this issue in the talk today because I feel that a new character of Bombay came forth in 1974. Till then we believed that this was a cosmopolitan city and we believed that its politics was pro-workers and to an extent these were true perceptions of an older Bombay. But 1974 shattered all that and what has come out of it is a city that is parochial, communal and anti-poor. This communalisation of Bombay has not started with Bhiwandi, as these Marxists say. It had already started with Worli. I also raised this issue because at least the Leftists, whom we Dalits think of as allies, should show support to our cause. But, no, the whole history of the Panther movement is wiped out.'

'What became of the movement eventually?' asks Moksh.

'Well, the movement was put down but I believe that it transformed Dalit lives forever. I don't think you can ever crush such revolutionary movements. For the moment, we have to put aside the radical politics that they stood for and work within the community. But the Dalit Panthers' time will come—sometime in the future maybe, but it will.'

'And, in the meantime, you decided to run a school?'

'It is a school of sorts—to make sure these kids can read, write and count. And learn a few useful skills. We also do some work with adult education and have vocational courses for women, who can then work from home. I used to think of this kind of work as "soft" but it is only now I realise that education has immense revolutionary potential.'

'I would love to come and see your school sometime.'

'Yes, please come. In fact, if you can come and spend time with the students, maybe teach them, that will mean a lot.'

'Really?'

'Yes. See if you can find time for that. Even if you come once a week it should be fine.'

'And what should I teach them?'

'Any subject that you know well. But first visit us and see if you would like to teach. Then you can decide the rest.'

'I will.'

November 1988

It is three years and a half now since Moksh first started work at Maya's school. He is also busy with his Master's in Philosophy but still tries to spend as much time as he can in Worli. He realises very early on that it is not easy to teach children. Much of that difficulty, he feels, is to do with the expectations he has of the classes and the outcomes that he thinks he should achieve. The class he teaches has seven-year-olds side by side with fourteen-year-olds. Much of what he tells them in the class is unimportant, he learns soon. What he transmits to them in informal conversations outside the class is valuable. He is less a teacher, more a mentor and a friend. He also learns to listen to his students—their stories, their jokes, even the lewd and bawdy ones, the tales of their dreams and aspirations, the accounts of their loves and crushes but, most importantly, their reports of broken homes, of alcoholic, abusive fathers and of poverty, deprivation and humiliation.

This is also a time when there is much tumult in the city, in fact, in Worli and in the nearby Lower Parel areas more than anywhere else. The textile mills of the city have been the mainstay of Bombay's industry for a hundred years and mainly located in Central Bombay of which Worli is a part. This industry has been virtually demolished after a two-year strike.

The industry's two lakh workers are the worst hit. The mill owners are only too happy to close down what, by now, are sick units and sell the land to build new, swanky commercial premises. The process, however, is not easy to execute and while the workers still make attempts to resist the closure of the mills, the politicians, the builders and the underworld—and, at this point in Bombay's history, these three lobbies are constituted of the same people—have also come to demand their share of the pie. The fact that the workers' homes in Worli and Parel are so close to the mill lands makes this an even more complicated proposition. Part of the deal offered by the politician–builder–underworld nexus is to violently put down the workers' resistance. Consequently, if one sees a day without any skirmish in the chawls in Worli, one is worried that there would be a riot the next day.

And it happens one afternoon when Moksh is in his class with his students. He hears some commotion from down below and before he knows it there is someone at the door of his classroom whose voice is shrill with panic as he asks the students to run home. Moksh makes sure to escort them to their homes and when he is sure of their safety he decides to leave. When he steps out, he walks into what looks like a scene of a battle. The hoodlums are armed with metal rods, chains and sticks and the residents counter them with stones, soda bottles and whatever else they can lay their hands on. People are pulled out of their homes and beaten. As two men thrash another mercilessly with rods, Moksh notices a small boy run towards them. He realises it is one of his students and it is probably his father on the floor, bruised and bloodied. Moksh is worried for the boy and his instinct is to run towards him and shepherd him to safety. But as he reaches him he hears someone yell from behind, a rod makes contact with his head and he is knocked unconscious.

It is three hours before he recovers consciousness and he finds himself on a hospital bed with Maya by his side. There is a man next to her and it takes him a moment to remember that he is Mr Lotvala's driver, Mohan.

'How does it feel … your head?' asks Maya, a smile across her face.

'I'm fine. How did I land up here?'

'You were badly hurt and we had to take you to a hospital. I called up Mr Lotvala and he sent Mohan with the car.'

'You know Mr Lotvala?'

'Yes, of course. We have known each other for many years.'

'Till when will they keep me here?'

'The doctor said he will keep you under observation for a day after you have recovered consciousness. He thinks you are fine but he may do some X-rays to be sure.' Maya pauses for a moment and says, 'You know you were very brave to have jumped in there to help my student.'

'He is mine too.'

'Yes, but still. Brave. But somewhat rash. You could have been hurt much worse.'

'I didn't have time to think of all that. I just saw that boy there and ran in.'

Maya takes Moksh's hand and pats it. 'Thanks,' she says.

'How are you now, Moksh?' Lotvala asks him.

'I am fine. The doctor is also satisfied with my recovery.'

'That's a relief. I was worried for you when Maya called. But I am happy it was not more serious.'

'I did not realise Maya knew you too. Everyone seems to know you,' says Moksh.

Lotvala smiles. 'Well, I am an old-timer,' he says. 'I helped Maya set up her school. She needed the funds for it.'

'It really puzzles me why you are so committed to these leftist causes when you are . . .'

'Are what? On the other side? A capitalist? Yes, I have been asked that often and even called a capitalist spy or an infiltrator of sorts. People have said all this to my face sometimes. But I don't pay any attention to that. I look at myself as someone who can use this money to further these causes.'

'But why would you do that? Why would you, for example, not invest that money to make more?'

'I don't know if you know about my ancestor—my father's uncle, Ranchoddas Lotvala. He was a scholar and a visionary. He made a lot of money very early in life because of some clever investments he made but his scholarship had led him to explore philosophy, politics and history. He was, like so many others at that time, involved with India's independence movement but he was more a thinker than a doer. He published a journal and established a society and became more inclined to the Left. His stint in London made him come under the spell of Fabian Socialism but when he was back in India he shifted his political orientation several times. He became a Marxist first, a Trotskiyist later and even ended up as an anarchist. Anyway, our family respects him and they support a library that he built. When, at seventeen, I first read about him and his work, I felt I was blessed to be born as a descendant of someone who, even if he was a maverick of sorts, was an inspirational scholar and a thinker. I felt more needed to be done than simply fund the library. I also realised very soon that I was not capable of his kind of scholarship and I still find it difficult to understand these abstract discussions that Marxists have. I felt that I needed to keep alive the tradition of Mr Ranchoddas Lotvala somehow and that is how I ended up as a supporter of the Left.'

'That is quite a story. I had no idea!'

'Anyway, I called you here to discuss another matter. I have seen and been told by others how exceptional a mind you are. People are already impressed by the depth of your scholarship. I believe you have less than a year to complete your MA. I think you should plan to do your PhD abroad. Maybe in the UK, but that is your choice. I am sure you will be awarded a scholarship but I am happy to fund all other expenses. Even the full amount if, for any reason, the scholarship does not work out.'

'A PhD in the UK?' Moksh is stunned.

'Yes. I think you don't need to be in our office any more or in Maya's school. They will do fine without you. Other than the time you need for your MA studies, I think you should find out about universities and what the admission process involves. You have only a few months left for the application deadlines.'

7. H

Winter – 511

'I belong to a city now, not to a village! Look! You see mansions and palaces, beautifully decorated market streets alive and buzzing, gardens adorned by fountains and flower beds, well-dressed men and beautiful women,' said Ajita, staggering a bit.

'You must go to bed now, Ajita. You are very drunk,' said Ratna.

'I am but not on wine. I am intoxicated by my new life.'

'But we must start work early tomorrow. I don't need to tell you.'

''Yes, yes ... But let me be awake for some more time. Let me be awake to my city, to its visions, sounds and smells.'

'Fine, but don't be late or else we will never complete our pending work tomorrow.'

Ratna was up early next morning and ensured Ajita was awake too. It turned out to be as busy a day as expected. Several orders for medicines and potions were to be taken care of and new patients to be met. Ajita and Ratna worked till late. After dinner Ajita lay down to relax and Ratna decided it was a good time to talk to Ajita.

'You know, it is almost a year since we left our village,' Ratna began.

'I do.'

'Of course, your work as a vaid is going very well and beyond your expectations. You are very popular and celebrated by a large circle of friends and admirers.'

'So?'

"Ajita, I am saying it is good you are doing so well, but your social life is a distraction for you. Your aim was not just to be a medicine man. You wanted to be an intellectual, debate in big assemblies, develop a new understanding of our world, of life, of soul and God and stuff I don't even know, frankly. I do know you are not doing any of it. You are too busy playing games and drinking and are surrounded by 'friends' not possessing your abilities or your intellect,' said Ratna.

'It is my turn today to tell you to go to sleep because you need to get up early tomorrow and go to my Aiyya to bring our stocks,' said Ajita, dismissively.

'Ajita, you know I am already prepared for my long journey. But you are simply trying to avoid talking to me about your social distractions.'

'You are being unfair,' replied Ajita. 'I am reading and absorbing ideas. I am working quietly.'

'You know you are not being true to yourself.'

'You don't like my friends?'

'It is not for me to like or dislike your friends. I just want to alert you to your own distractions. Time will fly, Ajita, and you will regret it later.'

Ajita remained silent. As Ratna got ready to leave next morning, Ajita did not speak.

'I am leaving, Ajita. See you in four days.'

Later, Ajita mulled over Ratna's words very carefully.

'Ratna's assessment is correct. I need to seriously reconsider my life and put it back on track. My prosperity gives me access to comforts and pleasures. I believe enjoyment of pleasures is not contrary to an intellectual life. I do not believe in becoming an ascetic, I do not believe abstinence is a necessary condition for knowledge. I gave in to a life of pleasure because it was new to me and I wanted to experience it, but I must be careful not to overindulge. I need to balance it or else, like Ratna says, I will regret it.

'I can ask myself if a life committed to knowledge brings any greater satisfaction or is of any greater value. For a person like me it is of greater value. My process of asking questions started a long time ago. And so, my mind is bound to question mere sensual indulgence. Ratna's questions are only bringing out similar issues troubling me for some time now. I could see boredom and ennui peeping from under moments of pleasure and I would be doing myself grave injustice if I did not act upon it.'

Ratna returned after four days, carrying stocks of leaves, twigs and brambles, all carefully selected by Aiyya.

'I wouldn't be able to manage if you were not assisting me, Ratna,' said Ajita. 'Only because you go up and down to get stocks can we do our work. I will not be able to repay you.'

'I am your friend, Ajita. And you don't need to repay me in any way.'

'You are a very special friend. Anyway, you will be glad to know, I pondered over your parting words and realised you were absolutely correct in your understanding of my social life and its many distractions. My mind is made up. I will make all necessary alterations to my daily routine needed to give me time for my reading and for attending assemblies. I am starting on it immediately.'

'My joy knows no bounds, Ajita! I was worried about you forgetting your true mission.'

Ajita smiled. 'To mark my resolve, I will be letting my tresses grow. My long curls will serve to remind me of my commitment to an intellectual life. I know you are going to be amused by my decision—I see you smiling already! But I want to do it.'

'You are mad, Ajita,' said Ratna, guffawing.

'My mind is made up!' said Ajita, smiling. 'I need to give myself some time every day to take care of my curly locks.'

'I will prepare some fragrant oil for you to use,' said Ratna, still cackling.

'Bikrama! It is a surprise to meet you. I didn't know you come to attend talks or are interested in learned discussions.'

Bikrama was a nobleman, more likely to be seen in pleasure gardens and not at talks.

'I pursue my interests quietly, Ajita. Also in our group of friends, we never find time to talk about more serious matters, do we?' said Bikrama. 'In fact, I am surprised we did not meet earlier. I come quite often to listen to talks.'

'Well, I started only a few weeks ago. I will be coming regularly now. But I fear, I am a bit disappointed. Nobody seems to want a different point of view to be expressed,' said Ajita.

Bikrama smiled. 'You did not expect to talk in assemblies, did you? It is impossible because some groups exercise control over every single word uttered. So no divergent views are allowed.'

'And yet you come, in spite of not being able to express your view?' asked Ajita.

'I only come to listen and observe.'

'But we need to debate to arrive at conclusions and not accept prejudices about people. It is not fair.'

'It is unfair. In fact, out of a need to carve out a different space, some of us formed a group and meet regularly. We are like-minded people but we talk and allow different viewpoints to be put forward. If you are interested in coming, you are most welcome,' said Bikrama.

'It sounds interesting. Let me know about your next meeting.'

'I will be certain to invite you.'

It was not long before Ajita got to meet Bikrama's group. It seemed to be a meeting of a mix of people of varied backgrounds, different professions and diverse age groups. But it was clearly a space attempting to create a new way of being.

An older man, Maitreya, spoke first: 'Four new friends are in our midst today and, as I welcome all to be a part of our group, I want to talk about some of our activities. We are, I believe, living in an age of transition. Old orders, customs and ways of living are being questioned and disputed, and new ones will be put in place. Life in big cities is very different from its rural counterpart: our cities magnify disparities between groups of people but also generate new ideas to confront inequalities. As a consequence, large-scale transformations are likely to take place and are, in fact, already underway. But our old systems will resist any revision or reorganisation and are backed by power and money of kings and states. Our group came into being because we felt a need to invigorate and energise forces of transformation. To be successful, we need to act but we also need to develop a conceptual framework:

a framework to understand our world and make sense of it. We are limited in intellectual resources so far but some of our new members will add to our existing talent. I am particularly referring to Ajita, sitting to my left. If you don't already know, Ajita is a well-known vaid. But you may not know of Ajita's background. Ajita studied in a gurukula known across our land for producing brilliant students and so Ajita knows and understands our adversaries very well. We are truly lucky Ajita is going to be one of us. Ajita, it will be good if you can tell us briefly about your position. But please serve yourself some wine before you start.'

Ajita's manner did not betray any nervousness but deep inside a little tremor asserted its existence. It was a long time now since Ajita was called up to speak to a crowd.

'I completed my religious education,' began Ajita. 'But I felt dissatisfied so I decided to learn medicine. I now work as a vaid but I want to commit myself to a life of ideas and eventually develop a new world view. I start by taking a few principles to be true. I firmly believe, only by observing our world will we be able to gain knowledge of it. If we use reason we must use it to talk about observable facts. If we come to some conclusion using reason we must be able to verify it in some way or else it is useless and must be discarded. My principles will, for me, serve as a base to build up a structure and every stone, every brick in it must be true to my doctrine.'

Before people could respond, Maitreya spoke up. 'Well said, Ajita. You are succinct and precise. Your brief statement of your beliefs is a condensation of several days of rigorous reasoning, I am sure. Now, would anyone else want to respond?'

'Yes,' said a young man. 'By observable, do you mean only objects we can see?'

'No, not at all,' said Ajita. 'Of course, we know of objects we cannot see but feel. Like air. But take, for example, my glass of wine, a nicely fermented glass of juice. People believe fermentation is caused by microorganisms—small creatures we cannot see or feel. I do make fermented medicines myself and I believe microorganisms exist and cause fermentation. But as someone committed to reason and to understanding knowledge, and not just as a vaid, I don't believe microorganisms exist. We need to figure out ways to confirm it or else for me it remains an interesting, even compelling, conjecture or an explanatory framework but not more.'

After a pause, Ajita said, 'I remember an experience from my Gurukula. A rivulet close to it started flooding one day. Some of us worked all day long, placing rocks and boulders to make a dam. We managed to avert any flooding and, in fact, I returned proud of our work. But I was appalled to listen to my Gurudeva attribute it to a yajna. It was a turning point in my life. Can mere utterance of mantras transform objects and create new events? It is absurd to believe so. I vowed to myself to not to accept unreason of any kind.'

An older man spoke up: 'One objection to your propositions could come from making a distinction between apara vidya—ordinary, quotidian knowledge—and para vidya, esoteric knowledge. It is not an objection I would raise but I imagine someone, especially someone coming from a traditional position, raising it. You, as a vaid, are extrapolating your knowledge of observable reality to an esoteric, transcendental reality. I would be interested in knowing your response.'

'If I allow a transcendent reality to exist, I guess I will accept your objection as irrefutable. But I am totally denying any possibility of a reality beyond observation. And again, it is not being imposed by me as a fiat. I want to keep focusing on observables and leave no place for esoteric reality.'

'So, do your principles imply you will not take any Vedic scripture as a source of knowledge?' asked Maitreya.

'I am not one to say an absolute no to scriptures. As a vaid, I study and use scriptural texts for my work. My medical texts give me a good deal of useful, but contingent, knowledge. I regard Vedic scriptures similarly. It may contain some useful knowledge, valid even. But I am not going to accept "as said in Vedic scriptures" as a way of settling an argument in a debate. Vedic knowledge needs to be disputed and questioned too.'

'It is an interesting position. I would request you to consider presenting lectures in our next two meetings so you can tell us in greater detail about your position,' replied Maitreya.

'Sure,' said Ajita. 'I will be glad to do so.'

In a span of a weeks, Ajita presented two lectures and after Ajita's second lecture, Maitreya went up to Ajita. 'I wanted to talk to you, Ajita. I am very glad you are a part of our group. We needed someone of your erudition and clarity amongst us. But our task is not easy. Our work is not just intellectual but also deeply political.'

'Political?' Ajita looked puzzled.

'Yes, if we take on religions and scriptures we will be upsetting many people, not just religious leaders but kings and ministers. We will need to tread very carefully.'

'You did mention it in your introductory talk on my first day in our group. But I did not fully understand it,' said Ajita.

'Well, you know,' Maitreya continued, 'in present times, old religious orders are being confronted by Ajivikas, Jains and, also more recently, by Gautama's followers. Traditionalists are naturally wary and resisting more strongly. State support is also slowly moving away from traditional religion to newer ones. It is a climate of great risk for a group like ours because we will be attacked from all sides. And by attack, I mean violent ones sometimes.'

Seeing Ajita's worried look, Maitreya said, 'Don't worry, we stand united. We will work out our strategies. We already started going to assemblies as a group but so far we could, by and large, only be disruptive. A couple of new entrants like you will embolden us to coerce assembly presidents to let some of us debate. If we can do so, it will go a long way in giving our group a more solid foundation.'

Maitreya was correct in predicting it would take a long time of sustained effort before Ajita could even get an opportunity to be part of a debate. It arrived after almost a year, as an unexpected vacant slot in an assembly. Convincing an assembly president was not going to be an easy task; Maitreya was well aware of it. So Ajita's Gurukula was foregrounded. Gurudeva being a well-known person in learned circles turned out to useful after all. Maitreya's strategy worked and Ajita was pitted against an unwitting Mimamsaka. Ajita's opponent, totally ignorant of Ajita's position, decided to talk about spiritual attainment and performance of rituals and made it worse by making a weak argument in its favour. Ajita literally tore into it, using every device available: argument, dialectic, logic and even sarcasm. Ajita's opponent knew it was a no-contest and quickly made an exit. But even a brief spell of Ajita's eloquence was sufficient to make a big impression on people.

After a few more successful outings, Ajita came up in an assembly against a well-reputed nyayayika called Somadutta, known for a deep understanding of logic. Maitreya was worried if Ajita would be able to stand up to as formidable an opponent as Somadutta but Ajita was confident.

'Maitreya, I feel you are looking at it all wrong, if you excuse my saying so,' said Ajita. 'I am not worrying about Somadutta at all nor am I worrying about nyaya. I am focusing on today's subject of debate and trying to see my own position on it. I don't want to better Somadutta in argument, I want to arrive at an argument I believe in.'

Maitreya could only look at Ajita in admiration. Somadutta started in a way only a master debater could. 'It is not going to be easy,' Ajita felt.

As Somadutta started going deep into vyapti or universal concomittance, Ajita, in an unusual gesture, asked Somadutta to stop and explain some difficult terminology being used. It made Somadutta stop and go back and gave Ajita valuable time to start formulating a rebuttal. Ajita also decided to fall back on clarity to combat Somadutta's dense arguments. 'Inference is a valuable tool for us to use to conduct our everyday activities but, in logic, can we grant it universality, like you want to?' Ajita asked, arguing persuasively.

'Inference is limited in its validity; it may be used as a tentative way of knowing but cannot be made a sound basis of knowledge. I don't doubt at all its utility as a means of knowledge but I will not grant it universal validity,' Ajita went on to add.

To counter Ajita, Somadutta talked about inference as a relation drawn from universal categories but Ajita, insisting on a rigorous empiricism, argued against universal categories and was declared winner.

Ajita's win over Somadutta became a talking point amongst intellectuals and many felt Ajita was a new voice, maybe unconventional but original and stimulating.

'We are doing very well, Ajita,' said Maitreya, in a conversation a day later. 'People are talking about you and about us as a group. Not just our admirers but also our opponents. Of course, our opponents are saying derogatory stuff about us. Our group is pejoratively called Cārvākas—sweet-tongued—but we don't mean to please anyone, do we?'

Ajita smiled, 'I feel sorry for our opponents' lack of creativity. I can suggest very many derogatory terms, a lot more interesting, for sure.'

'But, for you, our opponents found a more creative name—Kesakamblin. Apparently, your long tresses are being discussed a lot and being likened to a kamblin, a blanket.'

'I cannot imagine intellectuals sinking so low as to make attacks on my personal appearance,' said Ajita, disgusted.

'Don't let it irritate you, Ajita. Ignore it. A lot needs to be done and we cannot afford to get distracted. In fact, a cause for real worry is tackling our opponents' systematic but dubious ways of cataloguing and recording of current events. Especially debates, confrontations and disputes get recorded but always from a perspective favouring specific interest groups and particular doctrinal orientations. For example, Somadutta is a nyayayika so a Vedic cataloguer recording your debate will present it as a victory for Somadutta blatantly lying about yesterday's debate results. Over a period of time, your victory may not be remembered but a cataloguer's efforts will be.'

'I cannot believe it! Won't reality eventually win over fabricated documentation?'

'Only if it is remembered. We need to make efforts to create our own narratives. If we don't we will be wiped out, erased.'

'I agree, Maitreya. But I feel we first need to spend a lot of time developing a system, an ideology, and only worry about documenting it later. Of course, a lot needs to be done as you said but, in my opinion, efforts need to be directed towards developing new ideas,' said Ajita.

'New ideas?'

'Yes, as of now, our system is barely a skeleton. In fact, it is no system to speak of and it is fine if we want to continue as we did earlier, to disrupt and break existing systems. But I feel we must work towards a bigger goal, not simply a negative role of being disruptors as we played earlier but a positive one, as system builders. In fact, we need to begin by giving a clearer definition of our starting principles and use it to address a range of primary issues. I can already see we need to fundamentally understand life and, relatedly, questions of body, mind and self-identity; basis of our intellect, emotions and feelings; matter and its origins; questions of logic and modes of knowledge; about living and functioning as moral creatures; questions of value. I could go on ...'

'I agree, Ajita. It is a long road to our destination and we need to begin our journey.'

8. I

December 1988

Maya has just returned from Surat where she has been for the last two weeks to attend a conference.

'Moksh! You were supposed to have stopped your classes,' she says. 'But you seem to have come here regularly over the last ten days.'

'Came to teach my students, Maya. How was Surat?' Moksh asks.

'Surat was okay. But, no, Moksh, Mr Lotvala told me you were not to teach here any longer.'

'He told me that too, but my heart tells me to go on.'

'You shouldn't do that, Moksh. Mr Lotvala may get upset.'

'Maya, Mr Lotvala was very generous to offer to help me do a PhD. But there are other aspects to worry about before my plans get made.'

'What other aspects?'

'You know, after my father's death four years ago, only Yusuf Chacha and you have been there for me. There's my college, of course, but very few of my college mates are close to me, so college for me means lectures and books and not much more. After Yusuf Chacha's death, the journal work also could not engage me much. As a consequence, your school has become my home. Your school has taught me a lot more than what your students have learnt from me. You don't learn so much about class struggles through books and lectures as you do when you see your young student attend your lecture on an empty stomach. For many years, one heard about poverty as an abstract concept but understood what struggles the poor go through only here. Poverty as an abstract state makes no sense when no reference gets made to people who are poor. Just as hunger does not make sense when no reference gets made to an empty stomach. So to stay back and work here seems a good path for me. On the other hand, the thought of the PhD and that too from the UK appeals to me a lot. But my heart seems to be here, for now at least.'

'For now, maybe. But forever?' asks Maya. 'Moksh, to be able to do that forever may not be very easy.'

'But why not? You have done that. So why not me?'

Maya laughed. 'Oh, come on. My journey has not been the same as yours. My roots are here. My students' parents are known to me closely. We grew up together. My PhD was my way to come back to my people and work for them. The abstract conceptual framework of left scholars seems to you as a movement away from the real struggles of people. But these struggles also get erased when lofty calls for a war towards a casteless world get made. That classless, casteless world turns out to be as abstract as any of the concepts you talk about. My need to get back to the everyday world of my people began to grow and took the form of a school. Of course, the urge to start the school there and then was great but, after careful thought, a PhD seemed to be the correct way to start. The PhD really helped me get a better grasp of pedagogy.' She pauses and then says, 'Moksh, don't let the chance go. Go to the UK and get a great degree. You can come back to Bombay and choose what you want to do after that.'

Moksh does not reply but even Maya knows that he has hardly budged from where he was.

The next day, Moksh gets a call from Maya's husband, Prashant. He can sense the alarm that Prashant's tone betrays. 'Maya has a severe headache and fever. We are at a health centre near Byculla.'

When Moksh gets there a couple of hours later, he learns that Maya's fever has worsened.

'What do the doctors say?' he asks Prashant.

'They have tested her blood but the report takes a day to come.'

'Don't worry. Maya should get better by then,' says Moksh, fully aware that he has no way to know that to be true. Actually, her state worsens the next day. Mr Lotvala comes to see her and manages to persuade Prashant to move her to Breach Candy where, he feels, she would get better treatment and care. Maya moves to Breach Candy after her test results show that she has dengue.

'Never heard of dengue before. Have you?' Moksh asks Mr Lotvala, when they come out of Maya's ward.

'Not much. The doctor told me that Surat has had an outbreak so we know where she got hers from. Apparently, they need to check her blood platelet count and make sure that stays good.'

Over the next two days, Maya's platelet count goes down to dangerous levels and the worry shows on the doctor's face as he speaks to them. 'We need to transfuse platelets to make sure we can get her count back to reasonable levels,' he says.

Moksh gets back home late but cannot get sleep.

'Why does the same pattern always recur? Why do my closest people get cruelly snatched away from me? Mamma went to cancer, then Pappa got murdered, then Yusuf Chacha too. And now Maya? To dengue? No, that can't happen! The cycle has to be broken somehow.

'Maybe what Maya told me that day was a sort of portent. She wanted me to go away from her school and from her because she probably sensed that my presence was not good for her. Maybe the UK makes sense, after all.

'Hell! No! Me and all the garbage about portents! No way! My response to the present problem cannot be unreasonable and absurd. Why on earth would Maya's recovery be related to my presence around her? That's just absurd!

'But, on the other hand, death has taken away each and every one of my closest people. After my parents' death, what were the chances that Yusuf Chacha would follow them? But that happened. And now Maya. Maya cannot succumb to the same pattern. My plans to go to the UK, far away from Maya, and do a PhD are made. No power can alter my resolve.'

When he reaches Breach Candy the next afternoon, he meets Prashant near the entrance.

'Moksh, good you are here. Can you get me some food from the canteen? There has not been a moment all day to even grab some food.'

'What news of Maya?'

'Too early to say but her platelet count has gone up. The count was so low around 2 a.m. that the doctors had to be called. We were all very scared then and even the head nurse told us that we should be prepared for the worst. But the count became stable by about 4 a.m. after they transfused a good amount of platelets. The doctors feel that by tomorrow she should be completely out of danger.'

'That's a remarkable turnaround. That's just so good!' says Moksh, exultantly. He feels reassured that the plan he made to move away from Maya has helped her recovery. Moksh starts to look at places to apply to for a PhD.

August 1990

'We met last year,' says Geet. 'A year goes by so soon.'

'Though one feels we have known each other forever. Depends on how you measure the year, probably,' says Moksh.

'Maybe that also means we are bored of each other.'

'Why do you say that?'

'Just a joke. But, really, what do you feel? Are we ready to take ourselves to the next level?'

'And what does that mean?'

'Oh, oh! That worry on your face! You are so funny. Just felt that we should work out a future together for ourselves. But whenever we talked, you steered clear of the whole subject. You seem to have some deep-rooted fears. Tell me, do you want us to be together?' Geet says.

'You don't have to ask me that! Don't you know already?'

'Then?'

'You know my fears surface when we talk about our future together. You also know about the people who were just taken away from me—my mother, my father, Yusuf Chacha. We have talked about Maya and how she almost went too.'

'Yes. And you feel that you saved Maya when you came to London. That's about as vacuous as anyone can get. On every other matter you project youself to be the Prophet of

Reason. So where does your reason go now? And to now persuade yourself that we should not be together because you have concluded that some great tragedy may occur were that to happen. That's just nonsense!' She paused only to go on, 'Maya had dengue. Her platelet count went down. They transfused platelets and she recovered. You feel you and your goddamm PhD plans somehow pulled her out of her dengue? Bullcrap!'

Moksh has no defence to offer. But very soon Geet feels she has spoken too much and too harshly. She puts her arm around Moksh as she can sense he may be about to cry.

'Sorry. Please don't be upset, Moksh. Most of us cannot even start to comprehend what you have gone through at such a young age. One can understand that you fear more losses. But you have to know that you are not to blame for the deaths of your parents or Yusuf Chacha. Don't be so hard on yourself.'

Moksh can no longer hold back the tears. Geet holds Moksh close to her as the floodgates open and he weeps uncontrollably. When he speaks at last, he says, 'The journey through all these years has been very tough. Just so hard to handle these many losses. But forget that—do you know of the French author Georges Perec?'

Geet makes no attempt to conceal her awe. 'That's so you! At your core, you are sorted. You have suffered more than most people but you don't allow yourself to get totally hopeless. Just love that about you. One moment you were all tears and now you talk about some Georges Perec! No, but you've got me there! Haven't a clue about Mr Perec.'

'Perec lost everyone he had to the World War. Then, he went from Poland to France and wrote a novel—a remarkable novel—that had no "e".'

'The whole novel had no "e"?'

'Yes, and the absence of the letter became a way to denote the absence of Perec's closest people. An absence that suggested a presence. But often fate hands you a worse set of cards—or a worse set of characters, to keep the metaphor coherent. One becomes an author granted only a stated set of letters at any stage. You learn to get over the absence of an "e", however hard that may be, and to do that you need to maybe get closer to "g". And then "g" just evanesces one day and you have to now learn to handle the absence. And before you can do that you have lost the "m" you were now fond of. Worlds emerge out of words, they say, but when you don't have the full set of letters you lose out on words and your world never becomes complete. Except that you are not Perec. You had not chosen to play Perec's game—fate chose that for you. Nor do you possess Perec's talent—you are not adept at the game he has mastered. So you use what characters you have and work on your book. But then you learn that your book auto-generates, works out another plan, moves all over the place and makes a mess of the story you thought you had control over. And then fate hands out to you what Perec never thought of—a twenty-seventh letter not part of the alphabet. You encounter a Maya, for example, who exposes you to a world that has never been a part of yours, that you have never been a part of and that leaves you completely at a loss. The encounter made me feel totally unlettered. The twenty-seventh letter does not come alone. There are new sounds now, a new vocabulary and a whole new thesaurus. But you slowly learn the new words and learn to pronounce the new sounds. You learn to be a part of that world, you absorb whatever gets thrown at you and slowly the world of the twenty-seventh letter becomes very much a part of your story.' Moksh pauses to look at Geet and says, 'You should stop me or my babble could go on forever.'

'No, go on,' say Geet.

'Well, thankfully, that's all.'

'Your talk was great though somewhat heavy to follow. A lot to ponder over. But you, more than your talk, are the greater challenge for me even though one has known you so closely for so long. You can talk about yourself, about me, about us only very abstractly. We become some letters that may or may not be part of a book that resembles, through a convoluted analogy, the book Perec wrote. You talk of letters that form words and words that form worlds, but our world just does not feature here. Our world—you and me and our future—as us,' says Geet. Then she holds Moksh's hand and says, 'So to go back to where we started: does all that you just spoke of mean that we are ready to move to the next level of togetherness?'

'Yes, we are, aren't we?' says Moksh, as he moves closer to Geet.

'And your Perec analogy has one more problem,' says Geet. 'For you and Perec, people whom you encounter, become close to and then eventually lose are characters, and your ego makes you the sole author. That's not the case. Because these "letters" are empowered and autonomous and are authors themselves. So there are many other books and they get created and they auto-create and whatever happens to your book happens to all the others. And then when two people come together they take the books they have created thus far and merge them. And so on and so forth.'

'Well, you have taken my analogy to another place altogether,' says Moksh.

'Yes, probably to a place that has more hope and cheer than yours, and less male ego!'

July 1993

The last phase of a PhD always comes too soon. Much happens at the start of a PhD programme and then, before you know, you learn that you have to run the last lap. All that happens between the start and the end just evaporates. Geet and Moksh both enter that phase together and the hard work that they have done over the last several months allows them to feel somewhat relaxed. Relaxed enough to want to take a long Saturday afternoon walk.

Geet stops by a bench at Regent's Park and turns around. 'Moksh, do you remember we were here three years ago when you told me some crap about how you thought of me as a letter of the alphabet from a book that you were the author of?'

'You have teased me so often about that analogy.'

'And you thought that people you get close to leave and go away. That's so funny.'

'How can you say that about my deepest fears?'

'Your deepest fears, eh?'

'Yes, of course. You know that. Of course, these three years of our togetherness has set those fears to rest. But there's always the chance that they may come back to haunt me.'

'Don't say that! You know that when you have me around, no harm can come to you.'

'Yes, that's true. But my fears crawl back when they get the smallest chance.'

'Moksh, you have come a long way over these past three years and have found enough strength through our togetherness to want to marry me. That's a huge step.'

'You make me nervous when you say that.'

'Just to say that from where you were three years ago, you have really moved ahead.'

'But you know that the ceremony and all that makes me nervous.'

'My parents have been told and there won't be any ceremony except for the half hour at the court.'

'But the party?'

'Oh! That's just a fun event and only some very close people are expected.'

'A couple of hundred close people?'

'No, maybe just a hundred.'

'That's a lot of people!'

'No! You don't know about the effort to get the number down to a hundred. Left to my parents, there would have had a thousand people. But don't worry. My closest people have offered to take care of you. The party should be fun.'

'Hope so!'

'Also, even though she recovered from the stroke, mummy's health has been weak and she has been told not to take on any stress. So, to some extent, my dad was actually happy to keep the party smaller than what they had planned. But the number would be close to a hundred, no matter what. There was no way we could pare that down further. And we'll be back to London soon, though my parents wanted us to stay back longer. To make them understand that we are so close to the end of our PhDs and that we need to be here was not easy.'

'Yes, we must get back to London as soon as we can. But the thought of a longer stay tempted me too. At least you went back home once a year. For me, the gap away from Bombay has been four and a half years. Also, would love to show you Bombay—my Bombay! But so much has happened over these years. . . . The clashes and upheavals Bombay went through after the Ayodhya mosque was razed, and the bomb blasts soon after must have changed or even erased my Bombay.'

'Much of our country has changed, Moksh, not just Bombay. Chaos has taken over our country and the new economy has not done much to stem the rot. On the contrary, our people are probably not able to comprehend the vast changes they are a part of now as they become partakers of a global economy and a new world order.'

'Partakers or puppets?'

'Puppets, maybe, but puppets who feel empowered by the apparent upward turn that the economy takes and by the fact that they don't have to smuggle clothes and food from abroad.'

'Anyway, next week we'll be back and get to see how our homes have changed.'

'Yes, maybe, but that would be the backdrop to the major reason we are there for. Don't forget that we are to enter a state of wedlock next week!'

'Wow! That sounds formal. Wedlock—who'd ever use such words!'

'My guess was that the more commonly used terms may scare you even more. But, Moksh Malhar, when we are done and we return to London, back to your Hegel and Adorno, you won't feel scared at all. We shall return to where we are now except together as a couple.'

9. K

Winter, Early – 508

Maitreya was convinced that Ajita's success in the debate against Somadutta was a big achievement, one that the group needed to capitalise on. It would help them reach out to a larger number of people with their ideas. He felt it was important to expose the excesses of ritual practice and carry the message of the importance of reason over authority to the people.

'I am planning a congregation where we can present our ideas to the people,' he told Ajita. 'I will place it in the context of the present political and social climate. After me, Priyasi can address the crowd; he is a fiery orator. We need to whip up some emotion around the slaughter of animals in these sacrifices and he can do the job. The general public feels strongly about this and we need to galvanise it into becoming a movement. Also, the Jains, the followers of Gautama and of Goshala are all very much against the mindless sacrifice of animals. It would be good if we could also count on the support of these groups. Following Priyasi, you should present our new emerging philosophy in an accessible way to the crowd. Focus less on technical issues such as inference, for example, but more on how we see human beings and their place in the world, of life and death and of the beyond.'

Ajita realised that he was more comfortable debating or lecturing to smaller niche audiences and did not share Maitreya's enthusiasm for large-scale action, but he had to admit that it did have the potential to cement their group as important in the existing philosophical traditions.

It was not until they approached the day of the planned congregation that Ajita realised what a master organiser Maitreya was. He had managed to confer with and get Mahavir, Gautama and Goshala to pledge their support. Not just that, he had also convinced them that it was in their interests to put up a united front against the traditional systems so they would mutually agree to continue to support one another. Once the support was in place, Maitreya, with his group, made sure that there would be good attendance for the event.

The numbers far exceeded their expectations. Ajita had never seen such a sea of humanity in his life. When he climbed on to the podium with the others, he felt himself trembling. Maitreya and Priyasi were trained orators, experts in the art of projecting their voices to reach a large audience. Ajita had no such experience and he was not sure how he would even be heard. He needn't have worried. Maitreya had planned the order of the orators with Ajita's inexperience in mind. Maitreya's booming voice could reach the crowds and he conveyed his thoughts with such force that the congregation quietened. It was quite a magical experience.

Maitreya, in his speech, brought out the fact that with the new urban cultures that had developed recently, both the social and political orders were going through massive transformations. Cities such as Vaishali were already being ruled along democratic lines and the shift in administering patterns was from models of authority to those of participation. It was religion, Maitreya persuasively argued, that still moved in outdated ways, tying down common people to false values and superstition. It now needed, he said, to be replaced with new systems of thought.

Priyasi, following Maitreya, made an equally powerful speech on an issue that had an even greater impact on the audience. He focused on the excesses of religious rituals, the amount of grains and other food wasted. He also argued against the cruel and indiscriminate slaughter of animals in the rituals. It was evident that the crowd was already sympathetic to these ideas and the cogent set of arguments that Priyasi presented was very readily accepted.

Ajita had a much bigger challenge ahead of him. He was not an orator of the sort the other two were and he had to discuss matters of philosophy in a manner that the larger public would find accessible. He had to strain his vocal cords as he began his speech but as he got into the main part of his presentation, he got more comfortable. Using a combination of argumentation, rhetoric and irony, he examined and demolished the metaphysical pillars of traditional religion: soul, God, the cycle of births and deaths, and salvation. The effect it had on the crowd was dramatic—they were left spellbound.

Maitreya, seeing what a massive success the congregation was, did not lose time in organising a series of events where lectures and discourses for smaller groups were set up to reach a larger fraction of the populace of Vaishali and the neighbouring cities. Also, Maitreya made sure that with every meeting, the critique of the ritual practices grew much more trenchant. 'There is no purpose in performing these yajnas. It benefits no one except the priests who perform them.' Maitreya also set in motion acts of interventions and disruptions of mahayajnas, specifically not allowing them to carry out slaughter of animals. Anticipating the negative reaction his group would garner, he had instructed them to withdraw to safety if things got too violent. But he managed, through these events, to draw attention and importance to his group and before long they were respected and regarded as highly as the other schools.

It was a couple of months later that Maitreya called Ajita over.

'Ajita, you will be glad to learn that I have now employed two scribes who will be recording and archiving details of all that we are doing as a group—our activities, interactions with other philosophers and also the various programmes we have conducted. But it is my wish that one very important part of this archive should be a systematic and comprehensive account of the philosophical position that we are developing and beginning to occupy. Once that is done it will cement our place in the history of philosophical thought. Nothing we do now will be quite as valuable as that,' said Maitreya.

'That is a great idea. I had been hoping to discuss this with you at some point but you are always a step ahead of me at planning things. Have you made arrangements for the money to pay the salaries of these scribes?'

'Yes, I have. I have raised a substantial amount so we won't have to worry about it for a long time. It has been a very educative experience to interact with the business community, both in Vaishali and Rajgriha. They are willing to come forward with large sums as donations, which is a definite indication that they are ready to change their world views and belief systems.'

'I am so glad to hear that.'

'Yes, so, Ajita, I want you to give as much time as you can to sitting with the scribes and recording a systematic exposition of your ideas. I do not want you to get involved with any of the activism or the fight in the streets we are engaged in. Your time is precious and we would rather have you spend time here at our centre helping to develop the archives,' said Maitreya.

'I am happy to do that.'

Winter – 507

Ajita settled down on a low seat, feeling somewhat tired.

'The last few days have been so busy, Ratna,' he said. 'I haven't been sleeping for more than five hours a night for over a fortnight now. I really need to catch up with my sleep and rest now.'

'Yes,' said Ratna. 'And the travelling must be exhausting too.'

'It is. Also, I don't feel rested until I sleep in my own bed. I need you to tell me about all that has been happening with our practice when I was away.'

'It was much the same. Most of the people were old patients who had come to collect fresh batches of medicine. There were a couple of new patients who visited but I told them that you were away and would be returning soon. I also visited your grandfather's home to get more provisions.'

'You call it my grandfather's home even though it has been three years since he died. But I am happy my uncle has been able to handle the collection of plants and herbs.'

'He is doing that quite well. He follows the instructions your grandfather left behind to the last word and does not use any of his own judgement but that is a good thing. He is well aware of his limitations.'

'I can't imagine what I would have done without you, Ratna. I am able to spend more time being a philosopher than a vaid only because I have you with me.'

Ratna laughed. 'Well, some people believe I am a vaid too and want to find out where I got my training in medicine. I just avoid saying too much to anyone.'

Ajita turned sharply towards Ratna. 'Just ignore such people. You are not obliged to offer any explanation to anyone.'

'Often it is just friendly curiosity, Ajita. I don't get affected by any of that, don't worry.'

'If you are sure . . . I should get ready for the day now,' Ajita said and headed upstairs. Before he could come down, Ratna came up. 'Ajita, there is a woman waiting downstairs. Her mistress, who lives in one of the big houses by the river, is very ill. She wants you to accompany her to their house.'

The woman seemed worried enough for Ajita to set out immediately. Just one glance at the house was enough to tell Ajita that he was entering the home of a very rich family. However, he was surprised to see the mistress of the house. He had expected to see someone much older but the woman lying in front of him, moaning with fever, was young. She could not open her eyes or say a word. After an examination, Ajita left some medicines for her and a few instructions for her diet.

'Give her these medicines for three days, once in the morning and once before she retires for the night, and I am sure she will recover. I will come after three days to see how she is feeling.' Saying so, he left.

On the fourth morning, Ajita went to see how his patient was doing. She had completely recovered and the colour had returned to her face. As she sat in the courtyard of her home, the glow of health surrounding her, Ajita realised how beautiful she was. She told him her name was Japa.

'I have seen you often at Ananda's home when he would host those poetry sessions. His wife and I are good friends so I used to come often. I did not get a chance to meet you there though,' she said.

'I thought you seemed familiar too, but, sorry, I did not remember where I had seen you earlier. Anyway, how're you feeling now?'

'Much better, though I feel I tire easily post my illness. But I expect I will be fine in a couple of days?'

'Yes, you will.'

'I heard that you are more than a vaid now. You are a famous philosopher.'

'I am not famous but, yes, I am interested in issues that matter to all of us. And if that is what philosophy is about then I am a philosopher.'

'I am having a small celebration and dinner for the festival of Paush with my friends. I will be very happy if you can come too. We would benefit tremendously from your erudite company.'

It was not usual for Ajita to accept invitations to dinners from his patients but Japa had made an impression on him and another opportunity to meet her was something he was interested in.

It turned out to be a good evening. Ananda was the only friend around but the others were cordial and also excited about meeting the budding philosopher. For the first time, Ajita realised that he was beginning to get something of a reputation as a philosopher. He felt a strange sense of satisfaction.

The evening, however, only deepened his curiosity about Japa. He did not get to spend too much time with her because she was busy with the arrangements for the dinner. But he was intrigued by the fact that she seemed to be hosting by herself.

'She is probably married but there seems to be no sign of her husband, or anyone else from her family for that matter. Does she live alone? Who is she and what does she do?' he thought.

Piecing together all that he could find from Ananda and a couple of other friends, he made up a story about Japa for himself.

Japa's parents had been married several years but had no children. They moved from Rajgriha to Vaishali just a year before Japa was born. Her birth made them very happy and they doted on their little girl. Japa's father, Gangadhara, was an official in the royal granary in Vaishali and the family was comfortably off. But Japa was nothing less than a princess in her home. Her parents showered her with everything they could, even if it meant they had to ignore their own needs sometimes. For Gangadhara, it was important that Japa grow up learning and imbibing the best that Vaishali could offer. So from a young age, she was exposed to music, dance, literature and poetry. Gangadhara himself maintained the accounts for the granary and, to his delight, he found that Japa was naturally gifted with numbers. So he taught her all the mathematics he had access to. It was in this idyllic world of music and poetry and numbers that Japa grew up.

Japa's mother, Bhagirathi, often worried about her daughter's marriage but Gangadhara would hear nothing of it. He didn't want Japa to get married too young. But when Japa was about fifteen, her father fell seriously ill and was bedridden for months. He grew anxious about how he would provide for his family and became very worried for Japa and Bhagirathi. When he finally recovered and was ready to resume his duties at the granary, he discovered that he had lost his position to someone younger. A friend in the granary suggested that he approach Nateswara, a young and enterprising businessman who was the biggest supplier to the royal granary, for help.

Nateswara had the sharp eye of a businessman and could immediately ascertain that Gangadhara was still not well enough to assist him in his business. Gangadhara had to admit that Nateswara was right but pleaded with him for help. Nateswara agreed to help him with money but he proposed that he marry Japa. Nateswara's wife had died a few months earlier and he had plans of a second marriage. Gangadhara had no choice.

So Japa, not yet sixteen, was married off to Nateswara who was almost twice her age. She moved into a life of comfort in the big house by the river. Nateswara's mother and brother lived in a house not too far from their own. His brother had been afflicted by a mysterious condition years ago and would stay at home all day, doing nothing and saying nothing. He had attempted suicide a couple of times so Nateswara and his mother felt it was best to leave him alone and not try to get him to do anything.

Japa would go down to meet her mother-in-law every day as she was expected to. But there was not much else to fill her time. Nateswara was busy all day in his shop and what little time they got together in the mornings and evenings were undemanding, He was a man of few words but he was gentle with her. It was only at night that Nateswara transformed into a beast. There was no tenderness in the way he made love to her, in fact it was a brutal act of lust. Initially, Japa cried out because of the pain she felt but soon she grew numb to the physical assault. She still cried at times, but only because she missed the love she had never experienced. The mornings that followed would restore the normalcy of quotidian living. Nateswara would go about his day as though nothing had happened because for him, in fact, nothing had happened.

Japa reasoned that Nateswara's nocturnal behaviour had much to do with the stressful days he spent at his shop and so she tried to relieve his mind with conversations and music, hoping these would help foster a loving bond between them. Alas, not much else other than his business interested Nateswara. He had neither an ear for nor an interest in music. Left with no choice, Japa started discussing Nateswara's business with him and very soon Nateswara realised that his wife had a sharp mind and a great facility with numbers. This discovery on Nateswara's part did change things for Japa: not by night but, in fact, by day. Nateswara understood that Japa was smarter than the people he had employed and her presence in the shop would really help him run the business. He had other plans too. For generations his family had been trading in food grains but the margins in grains were diminishing and Nateswara had been planning to diversify his business interests. He had thought about getting into spice trading but since much of it was not produced in the region, it would mean that he would have to travel to places to source the spices. He needed someone else to handle the existing food grains business when he was travelling but he was not sure any of his employees could be trusted to handle it when he was away. Now with Japa's assistance he felt that he would be able to start travelling once she had familiarised herself with all aspects of the business.

Japa was excited about her new responsibilities; she had nothing much to do at home and this new job engaged her in a meaningful way. She relished the challenges, mostly unexpected, that came up at the shop and put her mind to coming up with solutions to them. Nateswara was pleased with the order and high standards she brought to the running of the shop. It also brought the couple closer, especially because he started viewing her with more respect. It did not change their nights dramatically but she did feel that Nateswara mellowed down somewhat and was less aggressive with her.

Confident that he could leave Japa to run the business, Nateswara started planning his travels. Initially, he went on short trips of ten to fifteen days each but soon he started staying away for longer than a month. In his absence, Japa got time to organise the business even more efficiently. The employees, tired of Nateswara's overbearing and domineering manner, felt good in her presence and that helped in building an environment which was friendlier and more productive. Even when he was in Vaishali, Nateswara spent more time in the new business with spices and left the old family enterprise to Japa. In the next few years, through their joint efforts, Nateswara and Japa were running two very successful businesses. It is indeed true that the unexpected happens when things are cruising along smoothly—that is why it is called the unexpected in the first place. But what disrupted the rhythm of the years—of seven years, to be precise—did not happen all at once. It did not announce itself on Japa's doorstep one fine morning. Rather, it was over a period of days extending to a month or more. Nateswara had gone off on one of his longer trips to a place in the north-west and he had planned to return in about a month and a half. But, at the end of that period, he did not return. This did not alarm Japa because these long travels were fraught with many uncertainties and Nateswara had returned later than anticipated from earlier trips too. For the first ten days or so, Japa was not worried. But days passed and there was still no news of her husband. She was in touch with the regular travellers along these routes, so she sent out messages with them to find out about Nateswara but none of them returned with any information. Japa's days went by in the shop and in caring for Nateswara's mother and brother so much so that she had little time in the day to worry about him. It was during the nights that she thought of him. She missed him in spite of all that she had come to associate with the nights that she spent with him. She was bewildered by her own mind, puzzled by the fact that it was capable of playing these games, of actually convincing her that she was missing a person who had inflicted pain on her. But just as she had grown numb to the pain, she grew numb to the feeling of missing him, and soon six years passed. He did not return nor was there any news about him.

Monsoon – 508

As they set out on their journey, Ajita said to Maitreya, 'I wonder why you are so eager that I meet Goshala. It is not something you do often.'

'You may be right, but when you meet Goshala you will understand. He is an exceptional person. When I was young I spent some time with him. So did Vardhamana and Gautama. Eventually we all left him and went our own ways. But that experience of being with him was an important one and did change me in a significant way. When I heard he is coming to Vaishali I felt you must meet him,' said Maitreya.

'That is more than you have ever said about anyone. Now I am really curious to see what this man is all about.'

When they reached the house where Goshala was staying, they were told that he was close to completing his period of silence and that they should wait. Goshala appeared older than Ajita had imagined. He was quite a sight with his long, unruly, matted hair and beard. Ajita's own hair was probably as long as Goshala's but it was well groomed—washed, fragrant, combed and tied. Goshala clearly did not adhere to any rules of grooming.

When it was noon and the sun was exactly overhead, Goshala came out of his self-imposed silence.

He greeted Maitreya warmly. 'Maitreya, I am so happy to see you. Who is this you bring along with you?'

Ajita was surprised and happy to find out that when Maitreya mentioned his name to Goshala, he recognised it immediately.

'I have been hearing a lot about you, Ajita,' he said. 'Rumour is that you debated and won against Somadutta. That's commendable. There are many people saying really good things about you. It is wonderful. These old systems need to be challenged and brought down. And I am an ally of anyone who is heading towards this goal. But tell me about your own position. I hear you commit yourself to materialism?'

Ajita summarised his philosophical postion, his materialism and his adherence to a philosophy which is grounded in the observable, external world.

'Then I guess you are an atomist. I have accepted the reality of atoms. Everything we have around us is made of these indivisible units and I find that fascinating. Atoms are governed by their own cosmic laws—how they move, how they come together to create the composite world that we see, including our own selves, how they interact and cohere. We believe that we are able to exert our will and act freely but in that substratum there are processes happening that are beyond our control. As individuals, our freedom to act only has small, local consequences. On a cosmic scale, none of this matters because that is completely determined by the laws that govern the atoms. Of course, most people don't understand this or don't want to and instead caricature me as a fatalist,' said Goshala, smiling.

'I find the idea of atoms an attractive possibility but I am uncomfortable with the fact that they are not observable. I can accept the fact that everything is made of elements because these elements in themselves are observable . . . '

'You seem to be too worried about observables!'

'Yes, I am. Because I feel if we give that up then anything goes. We need to be grounded in the reality of the world we live in.'

'What is the world we live in? We? You or I? Do we live in the same world?'

'Of course, we do!' says Ajita, a bit agitated.

'Your world does not account for my dreams, my fears, my anxieties or even something as real as my toothache.'

'But that is your subjective experience. We all agree on a world, an external objective world, don't we?'

'Pay attention to dreams. To the worlds that spread out in your dreams.

You don't practise any austerities, do you?'

'No, I don't see any point in doing them.'

'You have to learn to be a sramana. I tell you this, stay without food or water for ten days and ten nights at a stretch and you will see your world changing. Extend that the next time to twenty days and twenty nights and you will see another world altogether.'

'What are you saying? That is not even sensible.'

'I am saying you live the comfortable life of a city-dweller. Have the courage to give that up. I tell you that when I have stayed without food or water for forty days, I have seen beings and creatures you can't even imagine.'

'Those are called hallucinations.'

'And because you don't have a name for them, they don't exist? I have seen them and why should anyone tell me that my experience is not true.'

'I have heard stories about you, Goshala, fasting for forty days at a stretch and having nothing more than a dry stone to rub on your tongue. I am sure your mind starts playing games when you push yourself to that extreme. But it proves nothing. Meanwhile, you and I can both see that tree right now, and that is a given. There is no disputing it.'

'We have only agreed that my sensory experience and yours actually coincide and it is just one tree. How are we ever going to verify that that is true? Also, if I were to go off to sleep now then my tree would disappear. What about yours? You are going by only the experience of the conscious world. But there is a world that is beyond the conscious, there are other states of existence. There are meditative states where one can experience the dance of the atoms. The world of experience is the world of *your* experience, and if you do not account for your experience then that is simply an abstraction. Don't get miseld by gross materiality. There is the bamboo of the veena and its strings but beyond that there is the sound. What is the sound of the veena? It is not the vibrations of the string, nor the vibrations of the air that the sound passes through. It is not even the vibrations of the inner ear that receives the sound.

It is none of these gross material entities. I still believe it is material but not in the way you conceive it. And then dwell on the fact that you can dream of a veena, you can even feel its wood in a dream but you can also hear its music in a dream. There are worlds and worlds.'

'I don't understand what you are saying.'

'Don't try to. Just hear the veena's sound, just remember your dreams.'

'So one is supposed to believe that these dreams and hallucinations are real and one should indulge in crazy practices of fasting? How is any of this reasonable?'

'See, what you are calling real is a world that shares its borders with what you have dubbed unreal. These dreams and hallucinations, these illusions and mirages are what give your real world its sense of being clear and constructed. The real world, the dream world and the vast unconscious go hand in hand. Fasting and feasting do too. You don't need to fast; fasting does not have any value in itself. What you experience with fasting does. I do exactly the opposite often. I feast on food and wine for days at a stretch and I dance and I can feel the same throb of existence.'

'You really do live in the extremes, don't you? There is a lot of merit in moderation. And it certainly helps one's health to practise it.'

'There is only one thing I practise in moderation and that is moderation itself.' Goshala laughed.

Ajita saw that the conversation was not moving in any clear direction and decided to remain silent. In a little while, Maitreya and he got ready to leave. Goshala called out to Ajita and said, 'I am happy to have met you. I appreciate the fact that you are trying to come up with a whole new philosophical position and that is not easy. I have been around for a long time and met many people so I will share two things with you which you may ignore if you want.

'Firstly, we both agree on materialism but differ in the details. But there is one thing about materialism that is a conundrum, at least to me. If everything is just matter, how did everything non-material come out of it? What about life, what about consciousness, or thoughts—where did they all come from? How are they related to matter or are we forced to admit that matter does not account for everything and that there is something about life which cannot be reduced to matter? The second thing I want to tell you is that, in spite of respecting your intentions in creating a system of thought the way you have, it is important to realise that a system that does not promise soteriological goals will never be attractive to us. Human beings want an end to their suffering, they want salvation, and if your philosophy denies them that you will not find any followers. You may have decided that you don't want followers or disciples; that is a different matter. But this is a piece of advice from an old man and you may want to consider it seriously.'

Ajita nodded and that gesture indicated his respect for the older man. 'I have been bothered by some of these questions too. But I must admit that I never stated them as clearly as you have done. But I am sure I will find answers to these some day.'

'I wish you well and I am confident that we will meet again soon,' said Goshala.

10. J

April 1994

Nine months have passed since their wedding, and Geet and Moksh are on a flight back to London after a three-week stay in Bombay and Delhi.

'It's already been two weeks since your interview at SNDT University. I think we should hear from them very soon,' says Moksh.

'Yes, possibly another week of waiting. Oh God! How I hate this. It's like waiting to hear about exam results. You had it so much easier. You learnt that you had got the position at the University the morning after your interview,' Geet says, pulling her blanket more tightly around herself.

'Are you feeling cold? Should I reduce the blast from the vent?'

'No, I am fine. You will start sweating if you do that. This blanket is keeping me warm enough.'

Moksh smiled and pressed her hand softly.

'Well, I was lucky because Professor Parikh was on the committee,' he continued. 'He knows me well. And it was nice of him to call and let me know.'

'Precisely my point. You are from Bombay, you have studied there, you are a known face in the academic community there.

I know no one in Bombay, except you. Why will they give me the position at SNDT? That is why I felt we should go to Delhi. I would certainly have found myself a teaching position there and, with a little luck, even a full-time research position. And given that Delhi has so many more opportunities in the humanities and social sciences than your city does, I am sure you would have found yourself a position easily too.'

'But why do you think you will not make it to SNDT? I am sure you will.'

'I don't think I fared well in the interview. The expert was a professor of Ancient Indian History and was one of those old-fashioned historians. She didn't look too happy with me. At least, that is what I felt.'

'Let's wait to hear from them and then we can decide. If SNDT does not work out, we can stay another year or so in London. We will manage to get some research grants, I am sure. In the meantime, we can both apply to places in Delhi. But let's wait to hear what SNDT says.'

'Frankly, somewhere deep inside I almost don't want SNDT to work out. Then we can simply go to Delhi. That'll be so much better for me.'

'I thought you liked Bombay this time around!' says Moksh.

'I did, I really did. I liked seeing the city with you. I liked its energy, its zest for life. But Delhi means something else to me. It is about my friends, my familiarity with the nooks and corners of the city, its gallis famous for specific types of food, the smells of Delhi winters—I can go on and on. But it's not only that. It is, more than anything else, my parents. They are getting older, my mother is not in good health and it will be better if I am there to help them. That is also something I worry about.'

Geet stops at that point and looks at Moksh. She knows that the last thing she said may have hurt him and reminded him of being an orphan. She takes his hand in hers and says, 'I'm sorry, Moksh. You are right. Let's wait till we hear from SNDT and then see what we have to do.' She is relieved to see him smile.

Ten days later, Moksh returns home late in the morning with some shopping and walks into the entrance hall of William Goodenough House where they have their tiny flat. He checks his letter box to find a letter from SNDT University addressed to Geet. He opens it, reads it in a hurry and runs up to his flat. Geet has already left for work so he calls her office.

'Guess what! You got the offer letter from SNDT!' He realises he is yelling as he says this.

'Wow! I don't believe this. I really didn't think that I would get it.'

'Are you happy?' he asks, breathless.

'Yes, bloody hell I am! It is a faculty position, dammit! I am really, really happy.'

'And happy that it's in Bombay? It means we move there.'

'Yes, Moksh. Believe me, I am.'

Moksh grins happily. 'We have to celebrate this evening. I will try to come back early. I am off to work now,' he says and hangs up.

When he gets back, Geet is already waiting for him. 'Yay! I am Professor Geet Sabarwal now! I can't believe it,' she says as she hugs Moksh. Moksh holds her in an embrace and says, 'I thought we were going to Bombay this morning after I saw your offer letter. But now I am confused.'

'Confused? What do you mean?'

'I had a chat with Bryan this afternoon. He had been wanting to talk to me after my viva but he was busy and then we left for India. So, finally, we sat together this afternoon for a discussion. You remember Professor Holt from Oxford? He was my thesis examiner. He is at Pembroke and has a research grant that pays for a postdoctoral fellow. He was looking for someone who has worked on Hegel and has looked closely at the British idealists and that, as you know, is my area of interest. He has been asking Bryan to convince me to take up this fellowship even though Bryan told him that I was looking for a position in India. I told Bryan today that we both have offers from India now but he wants me to give the Oxford position some serious thought. It was also nice of Bryan to say that he thinks I am among his best students and that is why he feels I should go on to work with someone like Professor Holt. So, there, I am not sure what we should do now.'

'But that's fantastic! A postdoc in Oxford!' Geet exclaimed, putting her arms around Moksh and holding him tight.

'Is it? It muddles things. We both have positions back in Bombay but if I accept the Oxford fellowship you will have to start looking for something in Oxford. Unless we can both get something there, I don't think it is worth pursuing.'

'Moksh, you have a brilliant offer. Take some time to sit back and feel good about it. We can worry about what we need to do eventually later. For now, as the Brits say, I have got the thirst. So tell me which pub we are going to. SNDT and Oxford! Calls for a big celebration!'

The next evening, when Geet returns from work, Moksh is waiting to talk to her.

'I had a long chat with Mr Lotvala today,' says Moksh.

'What did he say?'

'He was very happy that I had got the postdoc at Oxford but, at the same time, he was also happy that we had both got offers from universities in Bombay. He said that if I take up the postdoc offer then we both lose the offers from Bombay. Neither of the universities will wait for us for two years. But, he felt that if we accept the offers from Bombay we could go for postdoctoral assignments later. He said that we could plan and apply together so we could get postdocs in the same city.'

'That makes sense to me.'

'But what was more interesting was what he had to say after this. He has, in the past, funded the higher education of a few students like he had mine. But now he wants to do it in a more systematic way. He is thinking of starting a trust in the memory of his grand uncle that will run a philosophical society. There are plans to organise seminars and talks and bring out a periodical devoted to social sciences and humanities. He would like us both to be involved with this trust in a big way.'

'My God! There's so much happening it is becoming difficult to process all this! But this is all so exciting.'

'It is. So, if we were to return to Bombay, he will have us involved in the trust work right from the beginning. He also said that he would compensate us by providing us a flat to live in. He owns several flats across Bombay but I think he was talking of one in Gamdevi which he has in mind for us.'

'I think this more or less settles the matter in favour of going to Bombay, right?'

'I think so, yes.'

Moksh is sitting in the balcony of his Laburnum Road flat in Bombay, sipping tea. The street, despite its central location, has a tranquil atmosphere, especially in the mornings. The laburnum trees, planted during the colonial days, are gone but other flowering trees have taken their place.

Geet settles down in the chair beside him.

'What time are you going to the university today?' she asks.

'I am not going to Kalina today,' says Moksh. 'I have some work in the Fort campus and then a meeting in the afternoon at the trust. The trust's tenth anniversary is coming up and Mr Lotvala wants us to organise some events to mark it.'

'Ten years already? Time has gone by in a flash.'

'True, it has been eleven years since we returned to Bombay. Eleven years and three months, to be precise.'

'Doesn't feel that long, really. I am still discovering new things in this city. Though, in a sense, it does feel like home now to me. That reminds me, I am meeting Ananya in Kala Ghoda this evening. We plan to do some shopping.'

'Ono! How is she doing? I haven't seen her in a while.'

'She is well. I can't believe you still call her Ono. You are the only one who does that.'

Moksh laughed. 'I like to pull her leg but she's a real sport. She is one of your many friends I really like. I wonder why she didn't ever become an academic. She seems to be cut out for the profession.'

'She did toy with the idea of doing a PhD after her MA in Calcutta before she took up a position as a trainee sub-editor with *The Telegraph*. I think her love for the life of the mind started here in Bombay with two friends whom she talks of fondly. I remember one of her friends was called Laila—I love that name. In any case, I will be having dinner with her and come back late. But you can ask Vimla to make something for you.'

'No, you know how it is with these meetings. They go on and on. I'll grab a bite somewhere too.'

Later that afternoon, Moksh is in the trust office when the secretary comes in to say that there is a call for him from home.

'Geet, I am in the middle of a meeting. What is it?' Moksh speaks into the receiver.

'It's raining like crazy here. I am in Bhakti's car.'

'Whose car?'

'My colleague, Bhakti.'

Moksh vaguely remembers meeting Bhakti once at a programme organised by SNDT University. 'She offered me a ride to Santacruz station because I could not find a rickshaw,' Geet says.

'Geet, I am busy here. What did you want to tell me?'

'Moksh, it is looking very bad. There is water everywhere. Our car has been stuck in one place for the last forty-five minutes.'

'Where are you now?'

'At the first signal after the SNDT main gate. We haven't been able to budge from here.'

'That's very close to Santacruz station. Leave the car and walk. It will take you ten minutes.'

'Moksh, you have no idea what you are talking about. Water is coming in from the sea with such force. Our car is more than half submerged. We will have to wait in the car till the rain stops. I wanted to let you know so that you don't worry. I will call you when I am able to get out of here.' And she disconnects her phone.

When Moksh enters the meeting room again he sees the other trust members talking amongst themselves, looking anxious. 'Moksh, we have to call off this meeting. We've been getting calls about the rain. Things are very bad in the suburbs.'

The others leave in a rush but Moksh is in two minds—should he go home or should he wait at the trust office, in case Geet calls there?

Almost as if in answer to his question, the phone rings. This time the panic in Geet's voice is very evident.

'Moksh! The driver managed to take a right turn at the signal but things are worse on this road. The water levels are rising. The car does not feel safe. It can get carried away in the floods. Moksh, I will be okay, na?'

'Yes, love. You will be fine. I am going to set out right now to bring you back.'

'No, don't be crazy. There is no way you can come here.'

'But … '

'Moksh, listen to me. Don't step out. I'll be fine. I will … ' And the phone goes off.

As Moksh puts down the receiver, he realises that it may be a much more serious situation than he had first imagined.

The phone rings again. He hurriedly answers it. 'Moksh,' says the voice at the other end. It is not Geet. 'Ana here. I called to check on you both. Glad I found you. Where is Geet? Is she is safe?'

'Ana … I thought it was Geet … She had called a little while ago. She was caught in the rain. She'll call again, I'm sure.'

'But where was Geet when she spoke to you?' Ana asked. 'Our correspondents say the situation is very bad in most parts beyond Bandra.'

Moksh stares blankly at the receiver in his hand. It is only now that he fully realises the extent of the danger. A cold dread sweeps over him.

When he find his voice again, he says, 'She was near her university, headed towards Santacruz. But then she took a right turn at the first signal. That's all I know.'

'That area is very badly affected. Give me your mobile number. I will call you if I have any updates.'

'I don't have a mobile phone. But you can call me at home later in the evening.'

'All right, you take care.'

After pacing the room in some agitation, Moksh suddenly decides he will set out for Santacruz to look for Geet. Luckily, he finds a cab outside his office and the driver agrees to take him.

As the cab struggles in the rain, the driver says, 'I hear that the suburbs are flooded, so I don't know how far we can go. If things look bad, I will turn back.'

They do not even get as far as Babulnath before realising that they will not be able to go further because of a massive traffic build-up.

'Sir, the situation is too terrible. I don't think we'll be able to move,' the cabbie says.

Moksh gets off the taxi and walks home. He tries to convince himself that he is worrying unnecessarily. Geet must be fine. She has to be. Perhaps her phone is damaged and that is why she hasn't called yet. He decides he'll reach home and call Bhakti.

Moksh finds Bhakti's mobile number in the little diary Geet keeps by the phone. He tries repeatedly but the number is unreachable.

'Must be the network,' he tells himself.

He finds her landline number in the diary and tries it. After repeated tries, someone answers and he hears a man's voice on the other side. It turns out to be Bhakti's husband who takes quite some time to understand who Moksh is and why he is calling.

'Bhakti called me around 4 p.m. She said she was with a colleague and was stuck near her university. But there has been no news from her since and I have not been able to reach her or my driver,' he says.

'Oh! Even the driver's phone is unreachable? The last I heard from Geet was that they were going to try and get out of the car and walk to a place where they could be safe.'

'I am very worried.' Moksh hears the man sniffle.

'Maybe their phones are all defunct or out of charge. But they would have found some shelter, I am sure,' Moksh says, hopefully.

'I don't know. I hope you are right. My children are very anxious. They refuse to eat or drink anything.'

'Don't worry. I am sure we will hear from them. Please make a note of my number. If you hear anything, let me know and I'll do the same,' says Moksh.

After disconnecting the call, Moksh moves to the balcony and sits on the large swing that hangs from the door frame. It is Geet's favourite spot in the house where she spends every morning with her cup of tea, listening to the birds chirping in the trees. It is that time of the evening now when the day is giving way to darkness and, in that crepuscular haze of twilight, as Moksh lies back suspended in mid-air, he realises that he is simultaneously occupying three boundaries: between the day and the night, between the earth and the sky and between the inside and the outside—on the threshold, the limen: the domain of liminality. It is the failing light that often reveals the invisible and it now becomes apparent to Moksh that there is also a fourth boundary that is staring him in the face: the one between life and death. This is the boundary that brings out most sharply the slippery character of Hermes—the messenger of Zeus, who is the god of the liminal, the lord of all boundaries, including the one between life and death. It is a boundary that is replete with deceit and illusion, but then Hermes is also the guide to the wayfarer, bidding him to take a turn—a hermeneutic turn—so as to be able to delve deeper into domains that are liminal.

He is still on the swing, lost in thought, when Maya and Prashant come over. 'Mr Lotvala told us. I did not want you to be alone at this time,' Maya says, putting her arm around Moksh. It is then that Moksh allows himself to cry.

The night passes excrutiatingly slowly. Time moves like a thick drop of honey, dripping down the side of a table. The morning, when it finally arrives, is a dull, dreary grey. The news has it that the floodwaters have receded a good deal. Moksh leaves for Santacruz to look for Geet. Ana accompanies him, insisting that it will be a good idea to have a media person like her by his side.

Ana's presence is, indeed, a help. Moksh is able to access even the areas cordoned off by the police. They walk knee-deep in filthy water for more than two hours but it turns out to be a futile exercise. Then comes the gut-wrenching task of visiting the nearby hospitals and looking at the rows of unidentified corpses in the morgues. And then the soul-draining exercise of filling out a missing person's report at the police station. When they get back home late in the evening, exhausted, the telephone rings.

'Hello, is that Mr Moksh Malhar?' asks the voice at the other end. It is Bhakti's husband, Vipul Mehra.

'Yes! Do you have any news?' asks Moksh expectantly.

'Nothing about the three of them but the police found my car in a ruined state. It was found a little way from the signal near SNDT. Bhakti did tell me they would abandon the car and try walking, but we have no idea where they went or what happened to them. I thought I will let you know.'

Moksh is disappointed. 'Okay, please call me if you learn anything more,' he says.

And then, the wait begins. Every sound of the doorbell, every ring on the phone seems to hold the possibility of bringing Geet back. He waits to hear the familiar click of the key turning in the lock and seeing Geet enter the house, carrying her favourite Bombay sandwich in one hand and strings of her favourite mogra buds in the other. The silence of the home underlines how much he aches to hear her voice.

By the end of the second day, the floodwaters in the suburbs have completely receded.

'She should come now, shouldn't she? There is no flood to hold her back. Or is she lying wounded somewhere? Why is there no news of Bhakti either? Or the driver?'

Vipul Mehra calls early next morning. 'Mr Malhar, can you come to the Santacruz police station?'

'Yes, what happened? Did you find out anything?'

'Please come to the police station by 11 and I will tell you,' says Vipul and hangs up.

He is already waiting outside the police station when Moksh arrives.

'Mr Malhar,' Vipul says after a brief greeting, 'I think we have to accept that Bhakti and your wife, Geet, are no more. But we have found no bodies.'

Moksh is shocked at how casually he seems to be talking of his wife's death.

But Vipul continues in quite the same vein: 'The police would have made you file a missing persons' form. But let me tell you, that will go into a file and nothing more will happen.

I spoke to my lawyer friend about it. If a person goes missing, we have to wait for seven years before we can say that person is dead. You know what kind of complications that can cause—property matters, insurance and all that? And don't forget, I also have two young children who will need a mother to take care of them. It does not make sense to leave this matter in the missing persons' file.'

By now, Moksh is shaking with anger.

'Are you in your senses?', he yells. 'You are talking so cruelly about your wife. You are planning your life ahead when we are not even sure she is dead.'

'Mr Malhar, you may think I am cruel, but I am a practical person. My wife was dear to me but I am not going to fool myself by thinking she may be alive. I need to move ahead because I have to think of my children.'

Moksh's anger muffles the words that seem to be struggling somewhere in his throat.

'I struck a deal with the inspector here,' says Vipul, 'and he is willing to let me identify one of the unclaimed bodies as Bhakti's. He wanted two lakh rupees for this but I made him settle for one and a half. If you also want to do this, we can bargain with him and make it an even better deal for the two of us.'

Moksh feels the bile rising in his throat.

'How dare you! How dare you include me in your … your despicable scheme!' he shouts.

Vipul looks at him coldly for a second. 'Mr Malhar, really, I was doing this only to help you. If you don't want it, let it go. There's no need to get nasty.'

Moksh will never forget this conversation or this moment. But whenever he remembers it, he recalls not remembering what happened after it. He only knows he was at home that evening, but what happened after he left the police station seems to have vanished from his mind.

When he is back home it is twilight hour again, the moment of Hermes. Hermes, the messenger, is also a psychopomp who delivers the souls of the departed to the abode of afterlife. The moment of death is when the soul has escaped and the body is left behind, lifeless and breathless. But when there is no body left, there is nothing to even pin the death on. Hermes realises that his effort at delivering the soul to the afterlife is futile because that is not death. It is rather the formal recognition of the absence of the soul in the body. Without the body then, there is no death.

11. L

Winter – 507

In a few weeks, Ajita and Japa progressed from being acquaintances to friends and then to an association more intimate. Ajita had tried to piece together Japa's story after their second meeting when he was invited to dinner at her home. But, for obvious reasons, there were parts of her story that remained hidden from him. He knew about Nateswara having disappeared but he had no idea about the private aspects of Japa's marriage and the pain and trauma she had experienced in being with Nateswara. Over these years of being on her own after her husband's disappearance, Japa had consigned her body's needs to a corner that she never visited. The reason she sought Ajita out was because of her need to connect with his mind and, somewhere deep down, she was convinced that if she succeeded in doing that then the bodies may not enter the equation. As she grew nearer to Ajita she found that there was a certain comfort she experienced in his presence—in the presence of his body, to be precise—and she found that when he sat next to her she did not experience the repugnancy that proximity to Nateswara brought to her. But Japa did not want to move beyond this point.

As it became more obvious to her that Ajita desired her, she worried about hurting him by her passivity. Japa decided to share with him the story of her pain and trauma.

The two of them went down to the river. The setting sun, the serene river and the breeze conspired to work their magic on Ajita and his entire being brimmed with desire for Japa. But, when he heard her speak, describing her experiences and her fears, Ajita was saddened. It became apparent to him that it were her fears that needed to be addressed first. As the evening kept obscuring more of her face, he saw both her beauty and her pain and understood how broken she was. There was one thing that the growing darkness brought to the fore; he needed to stay by Japa.

'You know what I dread,' she said, teary-eyed, when she had narrated her story, 'is that one day Nateswara may show up. I don't know what to do if that happens. Though it has been six years and there is no news of him.'

'There is not much chance of that. Nateswara has gone but your fears have stayed with you. You need to get rid of them.'

'It is not that I am not trying, but I am fighting these fears on my own with no support from anyone. It has been scary.'

'I am with you now, Japa.'

'I know you are, but when I am on my own at night, I can't take it. The fears consume me.'

'I can be by your side forever, Japa. Perhaps we can get married?'

Japa was taken aback for a moment. She turned to Ajita and said, 'That cannot happen. I can meet you, be with you, spend time with you. Who knows, in some time I may even find comfort in being intimate with you. But I cannot marry you.'

'Why do you say that?'

'Ajita, you must understand. I am a woman who is running her home and her business. As if that is not enough, I take care of Nateswara's mother and brother too. I am riding a tiger and, for now, I have the reins in my hand. I am perched on the tiger's back, but one wrong move and I am done for. I need to keep my business and home running the way it is because that is my protection.' She paused and then continued, 'Of course, our meetings are not hidden. My workers, subordinates, companions and servants know that we meet. They may be gossiping about us and I won't be surprised if even Nateswara's mother knows by now. If she doesn't it's just a matter of time. But no one can dare say a thing to me—not even her—if I am in charge. But a marriage changes everything. Now I am the mistress of Nateswara's house but if I marry you I forfeit that status. It is strange, but the way things are, a marriage is an act of transgression and no one is going to accept it. And I am surprised that you are the one discussing marriage. I thought you are proud of your anarchist image!' Ajita did not miss out the ironic tone in her voice.

'Anarchist! Maybe I am an anarchist in the sense that I take on the existing order. But that is more in matters of metaphysics.'

'But I thought you have issues with questions of right and wrong and how the system is prescriptive about it.'

'That is true.'

'And you propose marriage to me when you don't have faith in that institution? Is that not strange?'

'Japa, it's true that I am not in favour of marriage as an institution. But marrying you is quite another thing. It is about being with you and about making that commitment to be with you.'

Japa's eyes teared up as she took Ajita's hands in her own.

'It is enough for me to hear you say this. We are together, Ajita, even without being married.'

Spring – 506

Maitreya had just returned after spending three months in Rajgriha and Kashi and Ajita invited him over for dinner.

Maitreya embraced Ajita with a warmth that showed how much he had missed the young man in the time that he was away.

'How are you, my friend?' he asked.

'Our meetings have been going on just fine but the good thing is that we have a few new members who have joined us and two of them are rich merchants. I have spoken to them and they are quite happy to aid our cause with money. But I am more interested in hearing from you about your time in Kashi.'

'It was good to go to these cities to see what is happening there,' said Maitreya. 'I met my friends and made some new acquaintances too. I was very happy to find out that even in faraway Kashi, our group is known. We are referred to as the Cārvākas but this has just become our identity now, so I did not react to it in a negative manner. On the contrary, there were many whom I met who had good things to say about our work. I got the sense that there is expectation of much more from us.'

'That is good to know,' said Ajita. 'I am happy our work is being discussed. As I have said so often before, these are the first steps we are taking on the path towards a system. So I am sure they are right in expecting much more from us.'

'I met quite a few Ajivikas. You know I have many friends amongst them. Some of them are worried. They are facing resistance from many other sects but some of it is beginning to get scary.'

Ajita was surprised. 'Scary?'

'Yes,' said Maitreya. 'I have been saying this for some time now that things are not going to be easy—neither for us nor for the Ajivikas. We are seen as heretics and when the orthodoxy cannot defeat us with words, they may use force to put us down. Some of the Ajivikas I met have been threatened but a few have even been beaten up.'

'I know you have been predicting this reaction but I don't know how thinking human beings can stoop to such savagery. It is good that our city is not yet succumbing to this madness.'

'You are right, Ajita,' said Maitreya. 'But I don't know whether that state of affairs is going to continue. Many of my friends are concerned with the growing power of Magadha. The weaker states around Magadha are in danger of being overpowered by it.'

'But our kings are great friends with Emperor Bimbisara,' Ajita interjected.

'They are more than friends,' said Maitreya. 'The queen of Magadha is a sister of our kings. But what I am getting to hear now is worrying. Emperor Bimbisara is getting on in years and the young prince Ajatashatru is preparing to succeed him. Ajatashatru is a great warrior but he is too ambitious. He is no Bimbisara and may stop at nothing to ascend the throne and to expand his empire. Bimbisara has accepted the path of Gautama, or the Buddha as everyone refers to him these days. We may not see eye to eye with the Buddha on many matters but his effect on Bimbisara is, we must accept, positive. I don't know who can exert a sobering effect on Ajatashatru's impetuousness and aggression.'

'Don't you think we are a bit confused about this issue? On the one hand, we as a group do not want to seek patronage from kings or emperors but, on the other, we know for sure that we can have wider impact if we work with them. We can ensure that the code of conduct of the kings benefits their state and subjects. But we have positioned our group as one of anarchists and that makes us ineffective in the sphere of the government. I have no idea what the way out of this conundrum is.'

'Anyway,' said Maitreya, somewhat weary of the serious direction the conversation had headed in, 'I think when I go to Kashi next I want to take you with me. It is a great city. Its streets, its markets, on the one hand, and its music, theatre and highbrow debates and discussions on the other—it makes one energised. There is no city that has the magic Kashi has.'

'I want to go there too,' said Ajita, excited at the prospect.

That night many thoughts buzzed through Ajita's head but not about Magadha or Bimbisara. He was, in fact, thinking about what Maitreya had said about Kashi. When he went to meet Japa the next day, the conversation with Maitreya was fresh in his mind.

'He was so ecstatic about Kashi, Japa,' said Ajita. 'He wants me to go with him some time.'

'I have heard so much about Kashi too,' said Japa. 'My dance teacher was from Kashi.'

'I was wondering,' said Ajita, 'what makes a city what it is? Why do we think Kashi has the magic no other city has?'

'I think because it just does,' Japa said.

'I suppose what I mean is, how does a city acquire its character? How does that character become synonymous with that of the city? So much so that it starts determining the character of its citizens even? I find that fascinating.'

'It sounds pretty obvious to me. It's not the citizens who acquire the character of the city but the other way around.'

'No, I am quite confident it is not so,' Ajita insisted. 'What interests me is that if you take a modest group of homes together, it does not seem to have any distinctive character. You may have a street where a few houses of musicians stand and that is going to be just that—a street where a few musicians reside. But when we speak of a big city, it is as one entity that acquires a certain make-up not seen in any of the tiny parts of the city.'

'But that is because cities, for economic reasons, attract different kinds of habitants. Are you saying something more than that?'

'I understand there are reasons, economic or otherwise, that migrants make their home in a city. But that is not what I am interested in. What interests me is the question of how the character of the city rubs off on them as time passes. Or a more intriguing way of posing this question is to ask how the city shows a character, a disposition, a temperament,' said Ajita.

'I can see you are trying to take this track of reasoning somewhere but I can't see where,' said Japa, bemused.

'You know when I was young, I was fascinated by ants and how they work together,' said Ajita, moving to his favourite topic. 'I wondered how they organised their groups. Even then it was obvious to me that it was akin to how cities are organised. I don't think the organisation is put into a city in each and every specific way we want it. That is never how it happens. There are some basic ideas that go into it, some guiding codes and canons maybe, but what makes a city work is its size and the fact that it is not one homogeneous, big entity but that it is composite. A big, composite organisation begins breathing on its own and starts doing things none of its parts can. I don't know but maybe this idea even works for how a big business, of the kind you run, works. If you start with the idea of a tiny shop where the owner does everything and then try to extend that to the shop getting bigger and becoming as big a business as yours, then you may agree with what I am saying. For there are features in the way the business runs that don't exist in the tiny shop.'

Japa nodded and Ajita went on: 'A few weeks ago I had a meeting with a famous Ajivika. I had a discussion with him and we did not agree on many issues but as I was about to go, he stopped me and asked me to think about the connection between the organic and the inorganic, the animate and the inanimate.'

Japa gave him a confused stare and said, 'Sorry, you must give me the context, otherwise I don't understand.'

'See,' said Ajita, 'I have been arguing for some time now that there is nothing except matter and every being, human or otherwise, is just made up of inanimate matter. But this Ajivika asked me to think my argument through, not because he disagreed with my position but because, in a very obvious way, the inanimate and the animate domains do not share many features. Animate creatures can breathe, eat, move, reproduce and do so many things that a stone or a piece of wood cannot. They show consciousness, have a sense of identity, can think, can show emotions and do many things. So what is the connection between these two domains, or do consciousness and identity have independent origins? That becomes the primary question.'

'Wait,' said Japa, interrupting him. 'When you say animate creatures can reproduce, what about those that cannot? There are creatures that are …'

'Yes, I know. I need to say that in a different way. I mean if the creature is part of a species and if some of the members of that species can reproduce that is a good enough condition. But, yes, that was a good question.'

Without as much as a pause, Ajita continued: 'The Ajivika was right in asking me to think of atoms—these tiny bits of matter. I was somewhat wary about accepting the idea of atoms because we cannot observe them, but if I were to take it as a tentative idea that every form of matter is made up of atoms then there is an interesting way forward. These atoms cannot be seen so they need to be very tiny. To make up a chunk of ordinary matter we need to have a huge number of atoms. I am beginning to think that it is this huge number that does the magic—when that kind of a number get organised in a spontaneous manner, I think new properties emerge that were not present in the atoms to begin with. Does that make sense?'

'Can you repeat that?' asked Japa. 'It is not a concept that is easy to grasp.'

'Think of it this way. Take a bit of jaggery. It is brown and sweet and, as with any other piece of matter, it is made up of atoms. But the atoms of jaggery are neither brown nor sweet. The brownness and the sweetness of jaggery emerges as a property when a great number of atoms come together,' said Ajita.

'I think I understand better now but it is something I need to think about.'

'I've been thinking about this, Japa, but it is the very first time that I am putting my thoughts together in this fashion. I am happy because I see it is taking a cogent form.'

'It is an interesting thought and I can see what you are working out but it is somehow not easy for me to accept that we are nothing but inanimate matter,' Japa said. 'It takes me back to the conversation I was having today with Nateswara's mother.'

'And what was the conversation about?' asked Ajita.

'She was remembering Nateswara and weeping for him, saying how much she missed him. Then she said it was not just Nateswara who had gone missing but Nageswara, her other son, too. I was confused for a moment but she meant that he just sat in his room day and night, not responding to anything or anyone. She said it was as if he were a body with no consciousness. So, when you said this about us being just matter, I wondered what personhood meant to you. What is it that makes one a person?'

'I think that personhood or identity emerges when matter gets organised in spontaneous ways.'

'What is the spontaneous organisation of matter that gives rise to identity?' asked Japa with the characteristic narrowing of her eyes. 'Is it how one searches for patterns of stars in the night sky? When someone is showing you a pattern it emerges from the dark, but when you turn away and gaze at the sky again you find it has disappeared. I think I see the connections you make but then they disappear when I try to return to them.'

'I fear my own ideas are very rudimentary and need sharpening. Perhaps that is why you are not convinced about them,' said Ajita. 'In any case, how is Nateswara's mother doing? Has she been taking the medicines I sent her?'

'She is better now,' said Japa. 'But she is trying to cope with a very bad situation. And, in spite of the immense strength she shows at most times, sometimes she just gives up. Today she spoke for hours to me. Over these years, she has become very fond of me and she appreciates the fact that I take care of her and Nageswara. She even admitted that it was wrong to get someone as young as me married to Nateswara. Though it appears that she did not have much say in the matter. It was Nateswara who wanted the marriage and she did not have the courage to stop him. It seemed to me that it weighed on her. But, foremost on her mind was Nageswara, and the sense of her own imminent death. In fact, she wanted me to promise something to her.'

Ajita was curious. 'What?'

'She wanted me to promise his care—which I agreed to. I think that gave her peace of mind and she, in fact, said something that I was not prepared for. She said that it was time I found a companion even if marriage remained a distant dream. In that one conversation she managed to make sure that she tied me down to my duties even as she set me free!'

'But does that mean she knows about us?'

'I think she does,' said Japa. 'This conversation was her way of making sure I don't marry you and abandon them. She encouraged me to take a companion but on the condition that I continue to take care of them. I never imagined otherwise. But at the same time it is true that this conversation has begun to free me up deep inside.'

As she finished speaking, Japa moved across from where she was, sat by Ajita and put her arm around him. As Ajita took her in his arms, a shudder ran down her spine but that was for a moment and it passed. Japa dropped her defences and hugged Ajita tighter.

12. A

September 2005

Moksh is mid-lecture when he suddenly goes out of the room. His students sit, bewildered, wondering if he will return; there is still some time for the bell, but Moksh is outside the lecture complex by now, sitting by the tree, looking listlessly into the void.

Moksh's ninety-minute lectures often continue for two hours. He is not one to finish before time. But his students still enjoy them. While he knows his subject, he peppers his lectures with humour to keep things from turning stodgy. But, in the recent months, the humour is nowhere to be found.

'He isn't quite who he used to be,' the students whisper between themselves. It is impossible to ignore how different Moksh is post the incident with his wife.

Indifferent to everything else, Moksh sits on the bench, seemingly lost. It is not yet dusk but it is cloudy. It is in this subdued light, he finds, one sees things in the right perspective. The bright light of the sun obscures things by presenting well-defined objects with pronounced edges. In the fogginess of this softer light, they seem less like objects, more like the breeze which is blowing gently.

Much like the breeze he feels Geet touch him gently. Though there is nothing of her left behind, he feels her presence in the moment. It is not just her memory, it is Geet. The life they built together: their home, their work, their thoughts, their words—they themselves—every bit of them. But, in the eight weeks since the incident, there were times when he did not feel her presence. When he missed her, he would feel the biggest void inside him whose immensity would consume him. Moksh could not, then, seek refuge in books or friends, they proved ineffective. So he turned to the city streets. The mindless crowds of the city set his own loneliness in striking relief. Moksh felt perversely heroic, for even in his moments of utter helplessness he could not stop being the performer. Though, of course, the crowds took no notice of him.'

'Hello! You seem to be lost to the world. Is everything fine?

He looks up to see Michelle, one of his few friends from the university.

'Come, I need to get some coffee,' Michelle tells him cheerfully.

'I don't feel like it,' Moksh replies but she ignores him, pulling him up from the bench.

Over coffee, Michelle tries to lift Moksh's spirits.

'I did some Buddhist philosophy with my students this week. It's just not my scene. I never studied this stuff, so I struggle with it. How're you doing with your students? I guess you know everything so there is no problem.' She smiles.

Moksh does not reply.

'You're on Hegel, right? Isn't it your home turf? You could lecture on Hegel with your eyes closed.'

'Yes, I'm lecturing on Hegel. It is going well but I think I no longer see Hegel like I used to.'

'Why so? How do you see him now?'

'For so long, I've discussed Hegel's vision of history with the students: the power of its method to expose the logic hidden in the unfolding of events in time. I find myself doubting this vision now. I need to find something beyond this objective description. But where would I find it—in those interstices in Hegel's edifice where objectivity finds it difficult to get into?'

'I just love listening to you. You sound so much the philosopher. No one uses such big words over coffee. But, Moksh, sometimes you need to tone down, I think.'

Moksh smiles.

'I know I must sound pretentious sometimes,' he replies. 'I should go now. I'm meeting Ono over dinner.'

'Ono? I remember meeting her once. How's she doing?'

'She's fine. She's coming over to discuss my book.'

'Oh God! Just thinking of your book gives me the shudders. The kind of things you do, Moksh! Come, let's go. I need to be home in time for my son to return from his tuitions.'

When he is home, Moksh gets busy with putting the living room in order. Something of Geet's punctiliousness did rub off on him. He remembers how when Geet would return home from work she would fluff the cushions, dust the flower pots, sometimes even move the furniture till the room seemed right to her. Their long-time help, Mohini, could never figure out Geet's precise requirements so, in spite of her trying to put everything where it ought to be, she knew Geet would still fiddle with everything when she returned home. Moksh used to find the whole exercise funny but little did he know he would imbibe some of her eccentricities in due course.

The doorbell rings, Moksh lets Ono in.

They settle down on the couch with their drinks. 'So, tell me, how you've been?' questions Ono.

'Fine. It gets very lonely sometimes but I try to cope.'

'I wish I could come to meet you more often but you know how my work is.'

'Don't worry, friends visit me some evenings but this loneliness ... doesn't go even when I'm with them.'

Ono nods. 'So, you were telling me you would like to discuss the book,' she tells him, trying to move on to something else.

'I do, Ono. I did discuss the book with you before, you remember?'

'Yes, of course I remember. The book on some philosopher from the fifth century BC, right? It sounded like high philosophy to me when you described it then.'

'Right, but I now feel it should be fiction.'

'Fiction?'

'Yes, I thought I should check with you before I plunge into it. In your editing work, do you do fiction too?'

'Not in my current work, but I did become involved in one fiction project once.'

'You wrote something or ...?'

'Something much messier. I got into something with two of my closest friends, which I ended up regretting. We got to know this writer deluded enough to think he could rewrite our lives. I see even you're shocked by this! So he wrote some fiction which he thought would be our futures. One of my friends got too involved with him but I didn't like it so I ended it. I lost touch with these friends for quite some time but then, more recently, we reconnected ... they're together now, blissfully wedded.'

Moksh's interest is piqued. 'Did the novel predict they would come together in the end?'

'Well ... it did end with them coming together,' she replies. 'But, come on! You don't believe this rubbish, do you? My friends went through much trouble before things worked out for them, but the writer did not rewrite their lives, for sure. Don't know why I thought of it right now … I think it is this blurring of the fiction–non-fiction dichotomy. He thought fiction is truth but you think truth is fiction. But forget this. I'm surprised you think your book should be fiction. Tell me more.'

'I've been struggling with this question throughout: how much of my book is history with roots in something like evidence? I've put in quite some effort coming to grips with my subject but, in the end, I don't feel convinced.'

'But you would know your sources—the texts—so well, I'm sure. They would give you the evidence you look for.'

'The texts only tell me so much. I piece together the story from the bits I find in the text. The story is reconstructed, but is it history or is it fiction?'

'But your book isn't fiction in the form it is now, is it?'

'No, but I will rewrite it.'

'The whole thing!'

'It is only sixty per cent done. It will require time but I'm not short of it. There is no hurry.'

He continues, 'You know, somewhere in presenting this objective description of events, history loses sight of the person. These events in history somehow reflect the sum of every person's life—the prime figures, if not everyone—so one needs to shift the focus to the lived experiences of these people. One needs to revisit their lives, their homes, their work, their loves.'

Ono's phone rings, interrupting him.

While she is on the phone, Moksh keeps muttering to himself, not willing to let go of his thoughts. When she puts her phone down, he picks up from where he left off.

'I've found myself getting more interested in the question: why did this person do this when he or she did? To get to the bottom of this, I need to comprehend the person's inner life. How did he feel when someone hurt him, or when she felt love for the first time or when her mother died? These tiny rivulets flow into the river we term history.'

'But I thought you were writing philosophy not history.'

'Well, this is one more schism. Philosophy is positioned with respect to history, like history is with respect to fiction. Philosophy gives up on the person while moving further from history. Even the river dries up. In my writing, I return to philosophy energised by history.'

'So, from here, you move to fiction, then?'

'I think fiction will give me the freedom to go beyond the text, to move from the text, then return to it but to be unfettered in between where one listens to the soft music of lived experiences, of joys, of sorrows, of even boredom. History will dub these contingent—its quest is for necessity. But, in fiction, contingency does not get excluded but gets blurred with necessity. Necessity seems much less forbidding in fiction.'

'It sounds like you know very well where this book is going. If I know you well, I know you will do it once your mind is set on it. So my verdict is: do it!'

'I needed you to tell me just this.'

Ono looks up to see the clock. 'Gosh! I must go now, Moksh. I hope you will be in touch.' Moksh nods. She continues, 'To be honest, I wondered why you were inviting me over to your home to discuss your book. It's been only two months since you lost Geet so I felt you needed to process your loss, your grief. I couldn't, for the life of me, see the point of discussing some book in this period. But I think I see it now.'

Moksh smiles. 'You're right.'

She gets up then, hugs him comfortingly before she steps out.

Moksh gets into bed but sleep eludes him. He shuts his eyes but his mind is restless. It is still fully occupied with thoughts of the book, of how successfully he will write fiction, of how the issues of philosophy, which he needs to bring forth, will work in this mode of writing. Soon he finds himself thinking of his lectures, his students, Hegel, philosophy. He tries to push these thoughts out, he tries to silence his mind. He succeeds but not quite. When his mind is quiet, he finds himself thinking of Geet.

'Why do I miss Geet?' Moksh wonders. 'How is it possible to miss someone? I don't miss Pirondutriyen for I don't know him or her. Moreover, there is no Pirondutriyen: it is just some nonsense word I invented. One only misses someone who existed, someone they knew. But does this person just stop existing suddenly to become one fissure in the continuum of existence? The experience of someone dying or simply not being present lives on in the experience of someone else missing them—times gone by returning in the present continuous. To remember is to simply run the film once over; to miss is to respond deeply to the film. In the very moment of deep response, the film becomes something else, something more.

'This is how I miss Geet,' he thinks. 'Implied presence' is the term he uses: this is the presence of someone who is not there. Like the colour which is shining through even though it is not present in the spectrum.

But Moksh wonders who he misses when he misses Geet. Geet, the person with whom he spent his life is gone. So is it only her memory—not her but some reflection of her? But then who did he spend his life with? If she did not exist in his mind, where did she exist?

Moksh remembers now the time they first met. October 1989. He finds himself huddled in one corner of the room where the students' union meeting is going on. It is only his third week in London, which is evident in the form his whole existence is expressing itself, even if it is doing so very quietly. Sensing his discomfort, Geet comes up to him. Interestingly, when he recollects this scene now, he sees himself in the pin-striped blue shirt which Geet remembered. Geet's incredible memory stored these tiny specifics: it is her memory he is recollecting now. You don't know whose memory it is when you live together long enough.

Moksh is struck by Geet's confidence. He does not know then but she is not new to London like he is. He tells her he is in London to study Philosophy but there is not much else he remembers telling her. With Geet, he simply needs to listen. She did not put people off with her long monologues like he did. When people spoke to her they felt included, even welcomed to contribute their own perspectives. Geet's voice would become the voice of everyone present. Moksh listens quietly while she guides him through her commitment to history, the PhD she is working on, her home in Delhi, her friends, college life in Delhi, the best beers in London, Nietzsche, feminism, her music interests—Pink Floyd, Bhimsen Joshi—her love for poetry, lines of Prufrock. Moksh feels befuddled by the end of it. He is still overwhelmed by her when he is in bed trying to sleep. He thinks he will get over her, but he will discover he is wrong.

He invites her to his room one evening for dinner. He is too shy to be with her on her own, so George, his friend from college, is there too. He cooks the best dinner possible working in the tiny common kitchen down the corridor on his floor, while his own room is tidied up for the guests. He is nervous when they come: there is only one thing such nervousness does to the bottle of red wine one holds. The bottle decides to plunge down to the ground, blowing to smithereens. The floor, which is now covered in red, needs to be wiped but Moksh simply freezes. Mortified, he sees Geet on her knees wiping the floor with the closest mop she finds. It is in this moment Geet suddenly seems very different. She is no longer the person he is out to impress, no longer the girl who gets him tongue-tied but someone he could be friends with, someone who could be his friend.

It is one of those cold mornings where the greyness enveloping the city is trying to voice some gloomy foreboding. It's been five months since he commenced work on his PhD. Moksh remembers the scene vividly. He is sitting in between the bookshelves, poring over the newly published Wittgenstein book, *Zettel*, the complex discussions of which he is trying to work through. When he looks up, he sees Geet. She is quiet but her bloodshot eyes tell him everything. He knows something is very wrong. Her mother, she tells him presently, she is very ill.

The right side of Geet's mother's body is left immobilised post the ischemic stroke she suffers. It will be months before she recovers. Geet wishes very much to go home to see her mother but the ticket to Delhi is expensive. Moreover, there exist burgeoning work commitments. In the end, she decides not to go but Moksh senses how upset she is.

In the weeks to come, he is there for her whenever she needs him. He knows he needs to sit by her, listening to her pour out her emotions. Sometimes she tells him engrossing stories of her childhood but in other moments she is content to just sit by him, weeping silently. He is not sure how to conduct himself when she bursts out crying. He is not the kind of person who knows instinctively how to comfort others. Geet senses the effort Moksh is putting in to help her through these difficult times. But she finds out the point beyond which he won't budge. Even for Geet, Moksh will not bend some principles.

One morning when her mood is quite low, she lies in bed trying to think of something which would help her get through this gloom. She is not very religious but this is the kind of morning she feels the need to go to the only temple in London she knows—the one in Wimbledon she once went to with some friends. She thinks Moksh would be willing to go with her but is surprised not just by his refusing to do so but by the vehemence with which he expresses it. She is hurt by his response, which she thinks is unkind. It is only when she reflects on it does she see how he cherished his unbelief. This comprehension of something so intrinsic to his person brings her closer to him.

The intensity of these few weeks does not just open up new routes for them but they suddenly find themselves journeying these routes together.

13. M

Winter – 504

'Ajita, I need to speak to you,' said Ratna.

'Of course. Is everything alright?' asked Ajita.

'Everything is fine. I wanted to talk to you about Tuli.'

'Tuli? Yes, I have seen her here often, but I haven't spoken to her at all, so I can't say I know her well.'

'But I do,' said Ratna. 'In fact, she has been helping around here with the work.'

'I did notice that too.'

'You know, I have got to know her rather well ...,' said Ratna.

'Ratna, are you saying what I think you are? Are you in love?'

'And so is she! We are thinking, in fact, of tying the knot,' Ratna gushed.

'I cannot believe this. This is big news and I get to know now! At the very end!' Ajita laughed. 'But this news is worthy of celebration. When do you plan to have the wedding?'

'In a few weeks, hopefully. I was thinking of first finding a place to live in.'

'What? You have a place to stay. Why would you want to leave?'

'Well, after the wedding, I thought that would be the sensible thing to do.'

'I don't see it as sensible at all. That is ridiculous. Why would you want to go? And what would I do? Live alone in this house?' Saying so, Ajita walked away in a huff and did not return till very late that evening. Ratna was waiting for Ajita, a worried look on his face. 'Ajita, it's a relief that you are back. I did not want to upset you at all,' he said. 'We have lived together for years now. But this had to happen one day. I cannot live here forever.'

'Ratna, I seek your forgiveness. I know I should not have got upset with you, it was wrong. But, look, this is your house. This is where you live and will live forever. The fact that I also live in this house does not change that. We will continue to live together and Tuli will live here too. We have enough space for all of us.'

'But, Ajita it would be—'

'Ratna, I won't be able to live alone. Please don't go,' Ajita said, pleadingly.

Ajita opened his eyes with the first light of the sun pouring in through a gap in the window. As he lay in bed, his first thoughts were about his parents. It was two years now since he had visited his village; between his practice as a doctor and his work as a philosopher he had been too busy. He felt a sharp pang of guilt because it took just about a day's travel to reach his village. He also knew his busy life in the city was not the real reason he had avoided visiting the place of his childhood. The truth was he had grown used to life in a city and had begun to find the ways of the village provincial and narrow. But while the village held no particular attraction for Ajita, he still loved his parents a lot. He decided he would plan a visit soon and spend a few days with Govinda and Dhvani.

However, later in the day he found a visitor waiting at his door. Ajita did not know who he was but he was apparently a business acquaintance of Govinda's friend. Over the last week, the visitor said, Govinda had taken ill and Dhvani had been desperately trying to send word to Ajita.

As soon as he heard these words, Ajita wanted to leave for his parents' house. But Ratna felt it would be sensible to do so the next day at the crack of dawn.

'If you go now, Ajita, you will reach very late in the night. There is a stretch of forest on the way and it is not safe after sunset. We also need to figure out what potions and herbs you want to carry for your father.'

'I do not know what his illness is, but you are right. I need to carry whatever I can. If I need anything else I will send word to you. Perhaps it is best if I spend today evening with Japa. I don't know how long I will have to stay there. It could be a while since I don't want to return till he is fine.'

'Don't worry, Ajita. Your father will be well soon, especially when he has you by his side,' said Ratna in a reassuring tone.

The next day, it was late in the afternoon when Ajita reached his village. He noticed that in the seven years he had been gone, hardly anything had changed. When he reached his house, he could scarcely recognise the structure; it was so run-down.

If he was disappointed by the state of his house, he was shaken to the core when he saw his father. Govinda was a shadow of his old self—a bent, shrunk figure lying in bed, suffering his pain silently.

Ajita saw Dhvani and held her in a tight hug because he could see she was on the verge of tears.

'He will be fine,' he said softly, barely believing his own words.

Later, when they were alone, Dhvani told Ajita in detail about Govinda's illness. For over a week, Ajita's father's body had lain hot with fever. He had terrible pain in his gut and was throwing up often.

'I will try to see if his fever can be brought down,' said Ajita. 'I have to prepare a decoction of herbs that I have brought. I also have a potion which will help relieve his pain.'

'Is he going to get better?' asked Dhvani, worried.

'Yes, he will get better. He is going to need a lot of care but I will not leave till he is fine. You stay strong and cheerful. That will also help his recovery.'

Dhvani's face still betrayed a lot of anxiety. 'You have to be sure to get a lot of sleep and rest too. You look very tired. Now I can take over Tath's care in the night,' Ajita said.

Dhvani's relief showed on her face. Not only was her son taking on the responsibility of his father's care, but he was also a qualified vaid, one of the best in fact. She had always had great faith in her father's abilities as a vaid, and now felt that Ajita was his rightful successor.

With Ajita's constant care and attention, Govinda's fever did abate for a while, but his pain and agony continued even as Ajita tried to figure what would give his father a little relief.

The nights were difficult. Ajita stayed awake tending to Govinda as the patient's agony increased at night. After his father had slept with the help of sedatives that Ajita would concoct, he would be too exhausted to sleep right away. He thought often of Japa and, with no one around to share his fears, his thoughts started taking the shape of long conversations with her.

I have been thinking a lot about you, Japa. You know, when I got here I found Tath very ill—a lot worse than I had thought he would be. He is a little better now but I think this is going to be a long struggle. I don't want to return to Vaishali till he has fully recovered. But then I also want to be with you, spend evenings with you, go for walks by the river, talk about everything that can possibly be talked about.

When I lie down at night, you are all I can think about. But then I hear Tath groaning in pain. I felt guilty initially—guilty for feeling desire when Tath was suffering. But then I reasoned carefully and realised that the guilt was not necessary. It was possibly to do with growing up in the Gurukula. I was taught to be suspicious of all desire—sexual desire, especially. It is through a process of unlearning that I have been able to get over that but it is still difficult to get over the fears and guilts that one has internalised as a young person. But the feelings that I have for you are as natural as the light of the sun and they exist and persist through all kinds of situations.

As days went by, Ajita tried all that he could to take care of Govinda. He concocted a new blend of herbs to relieve his father of his pain. He sent word to Ratna to help replenish his stocks. But despite his efforts Govinda's body stayed feverish and the pain did not ease at all. Towards the end of the second week Ajita discovered blood in his father's stools and was worried.

Japa, Tath's condition is worsening in spite of everything I have tried. I don't know what else I can do.

I have realised that in spite of being a vaid and working to help the diseased and the ill, as a philosopher I have not been able to think about the body in disrepair. I need to think about this properly. I have a positive conception of the body but I also need to develop an understanding of the diseased, abject body. Since the conception of life that I have is essentially corporeal I need to figure out why one living being is healthy and the other diseased given identical physical conditions in both. One way to think of it is to see diseases as being caused by invisible living entities. When these attack a body, signs of disease appear. The act of trying to cure a diseased person is like waging a war on these invisible entities with whatever potions or herbs we use. But the big question is, what about a body that shows no consciousness, like in the case of Nageswara. That day when we were discussing all this, your question was about Nageswara and why a body like his shows no consciousness. I did not know the answer then and I don't think I have an answer now either, except for a few vague ideas ...

By the third week, Govinda's condition had worsened considerably. His bleeding increased and he grew delirious in his febrile state. He would lie inert with his eyes closed and hardly show any sign of being conscious. But then he would wake up, his body stiffening as he would grab the bed or extend his hand to clutch at non-existent objects in the air. It also appeared that he was trying to speak but what he said was barely audible. Ajita tried everything he could but he knew he was fighting a losing battle. He knew that his father's end was near.

Tath is dead. He is gone. We are going to wait till dawn for the funeral. As I sit here next to Tath, I feel a pain that I have never felt before. I was saying earlier that I need to understand disease but the bigger question is that of death. I have thought about life and of our bodies in a particular way, I have insisted that there is no soul, no higher being, no cycle of births and deaths, and I have disagreed and even ridiculed those who have believed otherwise. But tonight, in this darkness, I can see one thing clearly, that the sadness I feel now is what a philosopher who I disagree with will also feel when he loses his father. Whether you believe in a soul or not, whether you believe in an afterlife or not, this sorrow and desolation will be no different.

Our intellectual constructions can be what they are but our deepest existence is very often in the world of instincts and feelings. This is the truth.

I can already see a conflict with others brewing in a few hours. I do want a funeral for Tath but none of the rituals that go with it. However, in decisions of this kind it is others—uncles, aunts, cousins, neighbours and friends—who will have their say. I will have to get all the strength possible to hold on to what I believe.

Dhvani entered and said quite abruptly, 'Ajita, we need to conduct the funeral soon after the sun rises. I do not want Tath to wait and suffer. He has suffered a lot already. When the pyre cools down, we need to collect his bones and the ashes and let it all go in the river. That is all I want you to do. I do not want any rituals to be done because I know how you feel. No, it is not just a strong feeling—it is your philosophy, your belief. I do not want you to do anything that goes against your own philosophical ideas. It is hard to say what Tath would've wanted. He believed in rituals, you know that. But, in the last few years, I know that he was very proud of you and all the good work you were doing. It gave your Tath great joy and pride to know that his son was now a scholar and philosopher of repute. If I know your Tath, I think he will be happier if you stay true to your own principles and do not get involved with rituals. As for dealing with others, don't worry about that. I will let everyone know of our decision.'

Ajita was too stunned to say anything in reply. He held her as his eyes welled up with tears.

The next day when he lit the pyre and the fire leapt skywards, he thought of the days he went with his father to Vaishali, holding his hand and knowing that this was where he was safe. With that recollection, Ajita broke down and wept like a child.

After spending another two weeks in the village, Ajita felt he needed to head back to Vaishali. He wanted to take Dhvani along but she refused.

'No, Aju, what will I do in a big city? You have your work and your life there, and I have no place in that. For a while now, I have been longing to go to Aiyya's house in the hills. I will ask your uncle to build a tiny shack near his house and I will live there. The hills and the forest are what I look forward to and I know I will find peace there.'

The next afternoon, Ajita was all set to leave for Vaishali. Dhvani would be leaving a couple of days later. With her setting off for a new life in the hills, the house that had been Ajita's all through his childhood would now be uninhabited and abandoned. As if to touch and feel what little the present had to offer, Ajita went and sat in the garden—under the tree that he had planted as a child. In the present, neither he nor the tree were what they had been when he was a child and the tree only a seed. The tree had now grown to a great height but its shadow changed length as the sun traversed the sky through the course of the day. It is the varying length of the shadow, however transient and fleeting, that keeps track of births and deaths, growth and decay. And because it is the shadow that is the scale we are fated to use, the shadow of transitoriness is cast on our lives. Death is darkness and in the darkness there is no shadow.

On his long journey back to Vaishali, Ajita thought of his father's suffering in the weeks leading up to his death. He also recollected the gathering that they had after the funeral where relatives and friends shared their thoughts and feelings about Govinda. It struck Ajita that there was not one but several Govindas. In his own experience, the father he knew as a child was a hero he looked up to. But after his years in the Gurukula he faced the fact of his father's ordinariness. However, he continued to respect and love his father, especially in contrast to his Gurudeva, a person he had grown to dislike. He found his parents' relationship unusual: they were a couple who loved each other but because Dhvani had a very different upbringing, their relationship was quite out of the ordinary. Even though she loved her husband, she never hesitated to differ in her opinions. The relatives talked of Govinda as a caring person always ready to help anyone in need. This was a description Govinda could relate to. There were others, friends of Govinda, who knew of his world view and how he valued the religious life. Then there were a few people, largely business folk, who knew Govinda through the services he provided for religious functions. They talked of his father in such reverential ways that Ajita was taken aback.

Back in Vaishali, Ajita tried to piece together the different versions of his father. He wanted to talk at length about his father's death to Ratna because he knew his friend would understand his grief. It is when Ajita asked Ratna later to share what he felt about Govinda that he was shocked. He realised that he should have expected it—it was just that he did not want to hear anything negative about his father.

'I respected your father but it was because he was your father,' said Ratna, with a good deal of candour.

'Not otherwise?' Ajita asked, the anxiety showing in his voice.

'No, not otherwise,' said Ratna.

Ratna was being frank because he thought Ajita wanted it. Ajita did want to know what Ratna truly felt but he was not prepared for it. Ratna was forthright about his feelings for Govinda, so Tuli was worried that he was crossing a boundary that he ought not to. It was only after her wedding that she had got to know how close her husband was to Ajita but even then she felt that Ratna's words could offend Ajita.

Ratna had no such worry and he continued: 'I was disappointed because I was not seen by your father as your friend. I was, for your father, tainted by the fact that I was not born into caste. I was a faceless entity and did not deserve your friendship.'

Ajita knew that Ratna was right about his father. He had confronted his father about the way he talked about Ratna very often. He felt that he was justified in being critical of his father but he could not accept another person, however close, doing it. It took Ajita a while to realise that this was another Govinda—another valid way to look at his father.

Several weeks had passed since his father's death and Ajita had slowly settled back into his routine. It was a pleasant evening, there was a cool breeze blowing and Ajita and Japa sat under a cluster of trees in her garden.

'So, I wanted to ask you,' Japa started by saying, 'do you really think there is nothing like a soul or a spirit?'

'Yes, that is true. I have asked those who believe in a soul to prove it but all they can point out to is always to do with the body.'

'But we can think of a dear one even after they are gone,' said Japa.

'Yes, but what does that prove?' asked Ajita. 'It is just a recollection of being with that person.'

'But what if there were spirits? What if you were to see the spirit of a person you know is dead?'

'If I have never seen the spirit before, how would I know who or what it is? The spirit would not look like the body, surely,' was Ajita's response.

'Well, who knows. It is possible it continues to look like the body it left till it finds another one to settle in.'

Ajita laughed. 'One can go on building such stories but it is only that—a story, a lie,' said Ajita.

'Oh! So, if you don't believe in spirits would you be able to spend a night in a funeral ground?'

'That is a strange question.'

'No, it is not. Since you don't believe in spirits why would you be scared to go there?' asked Japa.

'I don't know why I should be scared of spirits even if I did believe in their existence. If they are spirits of people I knew well before they died, why would I be afraid? It just doesn't add up.'

'The fear is the fear of the unknown, perhaps,' said Japa.

'But we don't fear spirits,' Ajita said. 'We decide as a people what we should fear and how we should react to things. These prejudices are deeply ingrained in us when we are children. We fear the dark and non-existent objects like spirits, ghosts and ghouls because we are taught that these have to be feared. So if I were to go to a funeral ground at night and if I were to react instinctively to sounds and sights there, I will be scared because I have been taught this as a child. But if I think about it with reason, I will know I have nothing to fear. Usually, though, our fears paralyse us and it is not easy to be reasonable.'

'You are so sure of your reason,' said Japa. 'But there is a lot we don't know, a lot we have no clue about.'

'That is for sure. We are largely ignorant of things, but that is not the point. The real issue is: if we have to journey in this darkness, what is going to lead us? I believe it should be reason and, especially, reason based on facts.'

'But if you are journeying in the darkness and chance upon a snake, I don't think reason is your best bet.'

'Oh, not at all! I would definitely fall back on instinct then. Reason is not our only path, all I say is that very often it is the best path.'

'Okay, let's go back a bit. When a person dies, there is definitely a soul or a spirit or whatever you call it that leaves the body. Because while we can see the body, we still say that the person is dead,' said Japa.

'Of course, the body is there even after death. But life or death are just different phases in which the body exists. It is only a body that can live or die.'

'The logic appears circular,' said Japa. 'If you say life and death are two phases of the body, what distinguishes those two phases? For a person who believes in a soul it is easy to answer this question; the two phases are distinguished by the fact that the soul is with the body in one phase and has left the body in the other.'

Ajita appeared to think deeply before he spoke. 'I think the soul is just a linguistic convenience,' he said finally. 'You bring it in to precisely do this—distinguish between life and death. But it is a piece of fiction.'

Japa disagreed. 'The soul is brought in not just to distinguish life and death. Isn't it also about selfhood?'

'Yes, but we went through that before,' said Ajita, a little exasperated. 'All that exists is the body and these are aspects that are brought forth when the body is organised as it is.'

'If that is so, when you say you love Japa what is it you love? Your desire for Japa—is that only a desire for Japa's body? Because there is no Japa except her body, according to you,' Japa said with a naughty look in her eyes.

'Oh! Stop the teasing!'

'I thought you liked being teased,' said Japa, even as she bent forward to kiss Ajita.

14. N

October 2005

Twelve weeks post the July floods, Moksh arrives at Mr Lotvala's office. He wishes to take a break from work as well as his regular life. He has come to his guide for advice.

'That may be a good idea. You have had a tough time . . .' says Mr Lotvala.

'As always, I have come to seek your help. I will have to apply for leave but it is the Registrar who decides. He likes me so he may approve the leave. But I felt it is better to be sure. Will you please talk to the Registrar? He will pay heed to what you say.'

'Well, yes, I helped him some time back so he owes me a favour. But is that required? As you say, he may just give you the leave.'

'I have to be sure.'

'So where do you propose to go? Have you thought of some place?' Mr Lotvala asks.

'I have a vague idea—it is a place close to Dharamshala. Maya told me she will get me a place to stay there. I am supposed to meet her later today to discuss the details.'

'Dharamshala?'

'Largely because it is quiet, a place where I will have my solitude but, at the same time, I may be able to discuss Buddhism with some people there.'

'Buddhism, eh?'

'Yes. There are several Buddhist scholars from Tibet there. I will be able to discuss their philosophy, also get access to Buddhist sources. These are crucial to deal with the materialists who are the focus of my research. I may also try to study Buddhist practices. I am curious about them.'

Lotvala laughed. 'It is difficult for me to associate a seriously committed Marxist like you with religious practice! But you did say you were dissatisfied with Marxism. After the fall of the Soviet, the left is decimated all over. It is the same for our city, especially after the riots of 1993. Though you are disaffected with Marxism at the level of theory, the political issues also matter. I am also weary of today's politics. I fully sympathise with your desire.'

'I am dissatisfied with Marxism at a political level. But after Geet it has become a deeply private quest to look at religious or spiritual practices. I must also admit that I have looked to adopt some religious or spiritual practice for a while. I suppressed it for several years but it has reasserted itself with full force. My mother was religious so maybe this is part of her legacy. Because of my father's diehard aetheism, I had always pushed it away. But, at this stage, I have decided to allow it to take me over.'

'I will talk to your Registrar tomorrow. Will you apply for a year's leave?'

'Two.'

Mr Lotvala looks up at Moksh.

'Two years? But I will have to figure out who will take care of your part of the work for our Society.'

'I have already had a chat with Raikar. He has worked closely with me over the years so it will be easiest for him to take over.'

'You will come back to this, I hope?'

'Let's see. Each day as it comes.'

It is quite late by the time Maya comes over to Moksh's place. Moksh is surprised to see that her thick hair has greyed a lot.

'My fiftieth birthday is a few weeks away, Moksh. I am old,' she says, almost as if she read his thoughts.

'Yes, of course. But you were always ageless. For me, I start over at forty,' he says, wryly.

'A fresh start is always good, Moksh. I have felt terrible as I have watched you suffer. Geet will be with you forever but you also have to move forward somehow. I hope this break will help you do that.'

'That's the idea.' Moksh tried to smile. 'Okay, you have to tell me what this place is.'

'It is a small village close to Dharamshala—about sixty kilometres away—called Bir that has become home to some Buddhists from Tibet. A Dalit scholar who I worked with lived there for three years. He had a cottage there to himself, which he had leased from a lady who lives close by.

'That should be ideal.'

'Here is the address. My colleague suggested you call up this lady to book the place. He had a lot of small tips that he felt may be helpful. I will mail those to you,' says Maya.

As she gets up to leave, she clasps his shoulders. 'It will be a while before we meet. Maybe years. Take care of yourself. Do write me mails so I am aware you are well.'

Moksh likes Dolma Tashi's cottage so much that he decides to go for a full two-year lease right away.

It was sometime after 1959 that Dolma's father had fled Tibet to come to Sikkim where he met her mother. After their marriage a year or so later, they moved to Bir. The day of Dolma's birth marked the first year of their stay there. So, right from the time of her birth, Bir was Dolma's home. The first house Dolma's family built was a small cottage but they slowly built a bigger house close by. Dolma's father died rather early so her mother decided it was a good idea to let out the cottage to visitors. After her mother's death, Dolma decided to make a part of her home a guesthouse.

Dolma Madam, as she is called by her staff, is amiable. She respects the fact that Moksh values his privacy. She makes sure that his food is delivered to him at exactly the time he likes it. Dolma's staff come over to take care of the basics but they try to keep out of Moksh's way. It is a couple of weeks before they are comfortable with him.

Moksh loves to walk through the village roads, especially to stop at the tea shops, so full of the old-world charm that Bombay has completely lost. The day he discovers a bookshop with a pretty impressive stock of titles he is sure he has a good two-year stay ahead of him. He is also eager to do exploratory treks of the high slopes that are visible from his cottage. Before the third week of his stay, he is already familiar with the area. He discovers a good place to rest at the top of a hill which affords him great views of the valley below. At times he reads a book there, other times he relishes the sights.

It is probably the fourth visit, that he spots paragliders as they float slowly through the air. So slowly that there is a surreal quality to the spectacle. He is captivated by the sight. They move so aimlessly that it feels like it is true freedom from all will: the state where some object becomes pure quiddity. 'That is where I have to go,' he tells himself, 'to that space where my body just floats mid-air, that space where I am free of every pull the earth may exert, but also every desire to reach the skies.'

Moksh discovers a tea shop called Lhasa, quite close to the market, that is just the type of place he loves. He usually carries a book with him to read or simply looks out to watch the locals go about their daily tasks. There are a few regulars like him at the tea shop but Moksh keeps to himself. Today, he looks up from his book to see a tall figure by his side. Moksh tries to act busy but Olivier Mercier, for that is what he is called, stays rooted to his spot. Moksh is forced to ask him to sit.

Olivier Mercier is a psychiatrist from Paris who has come to Bir to study Buddhism.

'So, what do you do?' he asks Moksh, as he sips his tea. 'I teach philosophy,' says Moksh.

'Oh, you're a philosopher!'

'Well, I prefer to call myself a teacher or researcher. Philosopher is too big a label. Plato or Hegel—they were philosophers,' Moksh says, with a smile.

'Or the Buddha.'

'Well, yes.'

'Hegel? Did you study him?'

'Yes, I studied a lot of his work for my PhD.'

'But why? You should study philosophers from here. I believe, this is the part of the world where philosophy is. Why would you go to Europe for that? To read about dead systems from old books? Philosophy has to be part of your life—or,

I believe, all of your life. This is why I came here to study Buddhism. As a bhikku, a seeker.'

'Philosophy has several shades to it. What I study or research is academic but I discovered that the philosophies of Europe have a lot to offer. That is why I persist with them,' Moksh says.

'Philosophy has to be about yourself. It should have the ability to reshape you, I believe.'

Moksh realises that this is the third time Olivier has said 'I believe'. He also realises that Olivier's idea of philosophy is very limited. He feels weary.

'So do you read Buddhism?' Olivier asks.

'Yes, I do. As I said, for several years, the philosophy of the West is what I pursued. But, of late, the materialist philosophies of the East have become the focus of my work. Most of the textual sources about them are from Buddhist literature. So, I have to read Buddhism.'

'But I believe you are a spiritual people. It is the West—our Europe—that is totally materialist,' Olivier says.

'I use the word "materialism" as philosophers do,' says Moksh, visibly irritated.

'Okay, maybe. I agree I may have a limited view of philosophy but I came to the subject because I felt totally uprooted after my lover's death. He was all I had. I felt I should give up. I thought I should die, kill myself. For years, I had tried to help people with the psychiatry I had mastered, with the hope that it was of some help to them. But as I suffered after my lover's death, I saw that it was useless for me. I realised that psychiatry puts forward a picture of the self that is diseased, traumatised, shattered. But what we seek at a troubled time is a positive idea of the self. I would have destroyed myself at that time but luckily I met a Buddhist master who spoke about the self with such positivity that it gave me the will to live. For me, that is philosophy—that which gives me a fresh perspective to live my life.' Olivier pauses.

Moksh is startled by this outburst from Olivier. He realises he was too quick to judge him. It is still difficult for Moksh to talk about Geet. The ease with which Olivier speaks about his grief surprises him.

The slight bit of formality that holds Olivier back so far drops. He talks about Michel, how they met years ago, how they grew close, how they lived together. The love he feels for Michel is crystal clear—his face lights up as he speaks about him.

Moksh realises that what Olivier feels for Michel is very similar to what he feels for Geet.

'We live the same lives everywhere. We love, we lose, we suffer,' Moksh whispers to himself.

Olivier wipes his eyes. 'I miss him very much,' he says. 'We were together for twelve years but I met him much earlier. We did our Master's together at Yale—Michel studied Chemistry. That is where we met. What brought us together was that we were both from Paris. He left after his Master's degree while I stayed back to do my MD. I lost touch with him over the years but met him, out of the blue, at a choir recital. That's how we got back. I miss him. Sometimes I cry but I try to have positive thoughts about him or remember our good times together.'

From that day, Moksh meets Olivier regularly over the weeks to follow either at the tea shop or for walks. Olivier's familiarity with the area, especially the hills, is a help but sometimes they just stick to the usual routes they are both familiar with. After such a climb, as they relax, legs stretched out, Olivier asks Moksh, 'So who are these materialist philosophers you told me about the other day?'

'My research is about the Cārvākas, also partly the Ajivikas. So I study philosophers like Ajita. Also Makkhali Goshala,' says Moksh.

'Sorry to appear clueless, but who were these people?'

'They were philosophers from the time of the Buddha. Makkhali Goshala was probably a little older. Ajita was a thorough materialist while Makkhali was, at least, partly committed to materialism.'

'Makkhali?'

'Yes. Makkhali Goshala, who is referred to as Makkhali as well as Goshala. At that time, the Ajivika was a major philosophical system, with Makkhali as its most famous expert. That system of philosophy disappeared a little after Ashoka.'

'Because of the growth of Buddhism?' asks Olivier.

'Partly. But more so because Buddhism offered a lot more to the people. Buddha spoke to people directly whereas Makkhali was a hard ascetic whose practices were difficult to follow. Whatever we have today as his philosophy seems quite obscure.'

'Hmm, most of Buddhism is quite practical. It is easy to follow. Except maybe their idea of rebirth. Do you believe we have just this life? Or there were previous lives? Future lives?'

'Of course, just this life. What we have is all that we have,' says Moksh.

'I have thought a lot about this. It works for me. I feel liberated by the possibility that there are other lives we go through. I feel there is so much more optimism there,' Olivier says.

'We could be deluded by such ideas, whatever comfort they may offer us.'

'You philosophers would say that we are deluded about this life too. If this life will persist, if there is hope, I believe that is good. Buddhism talks a lot about this—especially people from Tibet. They see this life as just a bead—part of a rosary of beads. It is very real for them. They shift the focus from the bead to the rosary. Much of our grief, our misery is because the bead is all we have.'

'Yes, I am aware of their beliefs. But it is too difficult for me to accept.' Moksh shook his head.

A few days later, perched at their favourite tea shop table, Olivier decides to revisit the issue he had brought up with Moksh.

'You remember I talked to you about the rosary of lives the other day? It was my way to try to talk to you about your grief. I have watched you closely over the last few weeks. I see how much you struggle to deal with your wife's death. I fear you will lose the fight with this grief if you let it overwhelm you. As a psychiatrist, but also because I am close to you, I would like you to deal with your grief. If you isolate yourself like this it could harm you,' he says.

'I am good,' says Moksh with a smile.

'I have to disagree with that. If you will take my advice, I would ask you to meditate. It helped me a lot. I am sure you will also be hugely helped by it. I see you are sceptical. But you should mull over this thought before you decide.'

'Olivier, I have decided right away. I have to reject what you propose. I am very familiar with the stuff you talk about. I have studied it but, for me, all of it is mumbo-jumbo. Let your thoughts flow freely, try to become thoughtless, feel bliss—it's all just claptrap. I have, from my early years, embraced Marxism. I did move away from Marxism somewhat because I realised it was limited. I could reach further with philosophy,

I could go deeper with politics, especially Dalit politics. But Marx left me with a critical apparatus that will always stay with me. For that, I am grateful to him. That apparatus protects me from this sort of religious rubbish. As for my grief, yes, I lost Geet. It is very difficult without her. But it is level-headed thought that will take me out of here. The rest is bullshit!'

'Sorry, I got you agitated. But I would still urge you to give some thought to what I said.' Olivier gets up to leave.

For a good part of the day, Moksh is restless. He tries to read a book but he is distracted. He has his supper early to be able to go to bed, but he lies awake—sleep completely deserts him. After what seems like hours, he is so exhausted that he falls asleep. But his sleep is plagued by scary images. He wakes up with a start, covered with sweat. He suspects that he is awake because he screamed while he was asleep. After what seems like forever, he sees the first light of the day. He is relieved but gets out of bed to discover how tired he is. He decides to stay home all day—just curl up with a book with a pot of tea beside him. The day goes by but as it gets dark, his head is filled with morbid fears. He lies wide awake—sleep has left him like a perfidious lover. He struggles for hours but his sleep is disturbed by dreams about Geet.

She is there but so are some others—it could be a party, yes it is. There is food, there is music. He sees people talk but they whisper too softly for him to hear. He holds Geet's arm tightly as she tries to talk to other people. The room becomes very hot, they are asked to leave. They step out to see a huge fire outside. Geet screams for help. She has moved away from him. People try to pour water to douse the fire but it just grows bigger. Moksh spots a tap, tries to get water out of it but it breaks. He is agitated to see the patio flood with water. As the water levels rise, so does Moksh's fear. He screams for Geet but she has left. The water levels rise so high that the whole house is submerged. He swims through it as he searches the area for Geet. People from the party float past him as the water drags them with it. Their eyes are closed but they smile at him as they go past.

'This is how the dead smile,' he says to himself.

The thought that they may be dead fills him with dread. 'Is Geet dead too? Where is she?'

He starts to look for her desperately. More people float past him. He comes across big flowers. There are a lot of them but he feels he will see Geet if he gets past the flowers that feel like a threat to him. It is with some struggle that he goes past them but where is Geet? The water fills up all space—it is crystal clear. It is all pervasive, it is empty, so it must be space itself. 'Give me space to breathe. I am choked.' Fire, Water, Air, Earth—what is the fifth? The fifth is death. Geet is dead.

'I see her there—so far away, as she glides with the other paragliders. I call out to her but my voice refuses to reach her.'

It is just 8.30 a.m. but Moksh leaves for the tea shop. He is happy to see Olivier already there.

'I have decided to take your advice,' says Moksh without preamble. 'I have to meditate.'

'I was sure you would come back to say that. I already spoke to the White Lama. Let us go to him right away.'

15. O

Summer – 502

'Ratna, I must leave immediately as I have a meeting with Maitreya after dinner. He sent a message that said it was urgent,' said Ajita, addressing Ratna. 'I will be late returning.'

'Certainly, Ajita,' said Ratna. 'I have an early start and will be up early. Is everything all right?'

'All his message said was that there was an incident which made this meeting necessary.'

Like Ratna, Ajita had felt that Maitreya was agitated. The Cārvākas had met recently, and if Maitreya had wanted this emergency meeting despite that it must be a grave matter, he felt.

When he reached the venue, he saw that all the members had assembled and there was a palpable tightness in the air. When they had all settled, Maitreya started speaking, 'Friends, I have received bad news. My dear friend Makkhali was mercilessly beaten yesterday. He was in a debate and, yes, as always, his manner was aggravating. We are aware that he is matchless in debate despite his brashness that makes an appearance at times. My first guess was that it was his invincibility and manner that elicited this savage attack. But I think there is much else that is happening here. It is a threat, a warning that they will use brute, physical strength against the Ajivikas and us. We must be careful and guard against attacks directed at us. But we must dig deeper and understand what is happening, which means a meeting with Makkhali is necessary. If Ajita agrees, we will meet Makkhali, discuss what happened and plan the path ahead.'

'Any idea what the attackers' identity was?' asked Ajita.

'That is still unclear, Ajita. But, as I said earlier, these are turbulent times. With new systems challenging the existing and archaic, it is inevitable that there will be great disturbances. I had anticipated that this will start getting savage but I didn't expect it this early.'

'We must leave as early as we can and meet Makkhali. Where is he staying?' asked Ajita.

'He is in an ashram near Panchala. Let us wait a few days. Let him recuperate and regain his strength. We can leave early next week,' said Maitreya.

The next evening when Ajita was with Japa, he appeared withdrawn. Usually, even if he was disturbed, he shared his feelings with her, but that evening he was silent. Despite their lively debates, at times Ajita and Japa were exhausted by speech. At such times, physical intimacy was what helped. It became their language and helped navigate a realm where all ideas were absent—a language which, with all its frenzy and fury, was ultimately tranquil. When they lay in bed later, exhausted but satisfied, Ajita started talking.

'I think this will be a difficult phase. The Cārvākas as well as the Ajivikas, Jains and Buddhists are all gaining in stature. This has shaken up the existing structures badly. That is causing this backlash. When I discussed this with Maitreya privately, he said that it is a tangled mess. His feeling is that there is great bitterness and resentment even between us. The Ajivikas and Jains have their issues, the Buddhists find us difficult and, frankly, we Cārvākas have been negative and disruptive in the ways we have attacked the rest. These attitudes must change and we must unite.'

'Like that incident in Rajgriha?' asked Japa.

She was recalling the time when Ajita was lecturing in Rajgriha, and he was verbally attacked and insulted by three men.

'What happened there was a bit different. I was attacked because they were upset with my arguments, but it was directed at me as an individual. What is happening this time is different. Their established ways are clashing with the new ideas we preach. This time the stakes are higher and it is a war.'

By the time Maitreya and Ajita reached the ashram where Makkhali was staying, it was very late and they were exhausted.

'Let us get a night's rest and meet him after that,' suggested Maitreya and Ajita agreed.

When they met Makkhali the next day, they were quite taken aback at seeing him as badly injured as he was.

'It was quite a thrashing, Maitreya,' said Makkhali, laughing at himself.

'This is bad, Makkhali.'

'Yes, but it is evidence that I upset them greatly and that makes me happy,' Makkhali said with a smile.

'And their identity? Was that at all apparent?' Ajita asked.

'All I can say is that they were allies. I was engaged in a debate with them when this happened. We have mutual differences, sure, but we are all united in the struggle against the existing archaic systems. That is why I was surprised by the attack. Between allies, we can debate, disagree and even abuse, but this? This is unacceptable.'

Ajita and Maitreya were stunned by what Makkhali had just divulged. There was silence after which Maitreya said, 'It is entirely unacceptable. I think a meeting with Gautama and Mahavir is necessary. Between us, we can represent the Ajivikas and Cārvākas. This is urgent.'

'I agree. Let us plan a meeting in Rajgriha in ten days' time. I think I will be fine by then,' said Makkhali.

The meeting day arrived. It was Mahavir and Gautama, each with a few disciples, and Makkhali and three Ajivikas. Maitreya represented the Cārvākas with Ajita and Priyasi. As Ajita sat there, watching the rest settle in, he had a sense that this meeting had immense significance. 'But will it be remembered many years later,' he asked himself. He knew that these were pre-eminent thinkers, the greatest minds in the land. He accepted their greatness even if he had intellectual disagreements with them.

But what is remembered is what is created, archived and kept alive by retellings, he realised. In the retelling and the remembering, usually the event get warped and twisted, details are erased and invented, and eventually presented in a manner that safeguards certain interests. 'Which man present here will be remembered centuries later,' he asked himself. 'Which man will leave behind a legacy, a sect, a system that will find disciples and enthusiasts centuries later? What the future discards and what it retains will decide the way the present is viewed by the future but, strangely, reflected in that view will be the future's self-image.'

Ajita was immersed in his reverie when he heard Maitreya speak. 'We all understand why we are gathered here,' Maitreya began. 'We are aware that Makkhali was attacked and beaten up during a debate, right here in Rajgriha less than three weeks back. That an intellectual disagreement can result in such savagery is a crying shame. I am least interested in seeking the attackers' identity. Instead, I think the deeper malaise, which lies underneath the sagacity, percipience and acuity that we thinkers take pride in, needs be addressed. It was Makkhali's wish that this meeting be called. We have all revered him as a teacher and a thinker, and despite the differences we have had with him, we still respect him and treasure the time we spent with him. Further, what unites us is the stand we have taken against the rituals and sacrifices and the mindless animal slaughter during these sacrifices. Even if we differ in significant ways, it is my belief that by taking a united stand we will find the strength that will help us fight these ritualists.'

'I agree with Maitreya,' said Makhhali. 'I thank him. He has said many kind things. But let me say this; this isn't the first time I was beaten up. And it will happen again. And again. New thinking, new ideas are always a threat, the biggest threat because ideas can shake empires. They can shake existing systems and that is why these fights are bitter. I have never been scared, I laugh at these injuries but I will fight like I always have—single-handedly.

'But I am happy when friends take up the fight by my side. Even if the dream that we may affect a change remains unrealised, it is beautiful when friends share that dream. It is in a place where these dreams intersect that we may find the truth. And that is why I value friendships. With the best friends, we share what we want, imagine and dream.

'What are we up against, then? Yes, we are fighting archaic practices, blind faith, meaningless rituals and all that. But, at a deeper level, I can let them be.

This may surprise, even appall, this gathering but I can let the brutal rituals be because that savagery is, within a larger perspective, actually as insignificant as kindness. What matters, at that level, is empathy and mutual respect. The issue is that these men find me difficult simply because they feel threatened by my thinking, by my ideas. Just the fact that I think differently induces anger and rage in them. They feel threatened and they react.

'Maitreya said rightly that there was a time we walked the same path and then we walked away. When we walked the same path, I didn't lead the way. At times, we sat mid-way and discussed which the right path may be, if it even exists. We agreed and we went ahead. Then came a time when we didn't agree. But, I believe, we still shared a dream and that is why we were friends. We always carried mutual respect.

'But after I was beaten up, I think that respect and that empathy has disappeared. Maybe the well was never deep and that is why it dried up easily. But dried, it has. When that happens between friends it is very disheartening. That is why I felt we must meet and talk. And maybe start afresh.'

There was silence after Makkhali's speech. Ajita was truly stunned.

Maitreya and Makkhali had said very similar things in essence but while Maitreya was terse and precise, Makkhali was magical. He did reiterate what Maitreya said but he said much else and placed his speech in a much bigger frame.

After a while, Mahavir began speaking: 'I am deeply saddened by the events that have necessitated this meeting. This gathering is aware that my beliefs are simple but my principles are unwavering. I respect each and every living creature, big and small, and I am strictly against injuring any living being. I will never hurt the tiniest insect. Hurting a human being is unimaginable. Makkhali and I have been friends since many years and I respect him as a thinker. Yes, we have had differences but these are insignificant when measured against what we have shared. Even as I heard Makkhali speak I felt I disagreed with him in the way he thinks cruel animal sacrifices can be permitted if viewed differently. In my understanding, whatever perspective we take, these sacrifices are unacceptable and unjustified. But what if we disagree? Can I attack him, threaten him and beat him because he thinks differently? That is equally unacceptable. I agree with Maitreya that we must put behind any differences we may have and unite in the fight we are all engaged in.'

There was a gravity in the way Mahavir expressed himself and the gathering went silent after his speech.

After a pause, Ajita felt he must say what he had in mind. 'I am happy,' he said, 'that we are in agreement. But we must clarify what we mean when we say we want unity. We must understand that we will still have, and must have, disagreements at an intellectual level. It is by debating and disagreeing that we can sharpen the ideas that we have. That intellectual space must always be available. Where we must stand united is in the streets, in the struggles we wage against the system. In all dealings with the state and the rulers we must be undivided in the stances we take. If we display any weakness with the rulers, they will use it and drive a wedge between us.'

He saw Gautama smile as he said this. 'This is very true and I agree,' he said. 'In fact, everything that has been said here is very well articulated and I am in full agreement.'

When they later walked in the garden, Ajita asked Maitreya, 'It was a successful meeting, wasn't it?'

'It was. It was critical that we all meet and discuss these issues. We will wait and see what impact it has,' said Maitreya, but Ajita felt Maitreya was a bit unsure.

'What is the matter? Is there any difficulty?' he said.

'It is fine. I am happy with the way things went in the meeting,' said Maitreya. 'Mahavir is unwavering and dependable. But Gautama . . . I am a little unsure. Maybe I am stuck, seeing him the way I knew him way back. I am sure he has changed.'

Even as he said this, they saw Gautama sitting under a tree, resting. Having exchanged pleasantries with Maitreya, Gautama said, 'I assume this is Ajita. We have never met but his fame precedes him.'

Ajita smiled.

'Let's sit here and talk,' said Gautama. 'The Cārvākas are being discussed everywhere but it will be nice if Ajita can present us a summary.'

Ajita smiled. 'It is my pleasure,' he said.

Ajita, fully aware that this was a chance he may never get again, presented a detailed talk in which he deftly tied up the different ideas that he had arrived at and presented it as a single, unified system. Even Maitreya was surprised at the edifice he saw Ajita erecting.

'Ajita,' said Gautama, 'this is impressive. And while I see and admire the skill and craftsmanship that has been used in establishing matter as primary, we all accept that there is the mind, there are mental states, feelings and will. Where is all this in this materialistic picture?'

That hurt Ajita a bit and he replied, 'Yes, I am aware that there is a thing called the mind and that there are mental states. I have spent time understanding where they are in my picture. When I say everything is matter, I mean that at an elementary level everything is matter. When elementary matter is synthesised and structures are created, then the mind and mental states and, indeed, life itself emerges. The magic is in assembling tiny bits and in synthesising aggregates. That things can have features and qualities that are absent in their parts is the biggest magic ever.'

'I think that is a metaphysical sidestep. The issue is just stated differently,' said Gautama.

'I disagree. I think this idea—that qualities emerge in the way things are synthesised—will survive everything else that we will all ever say,' replied Ajita.

Gautama smiled. 'The self-belief that I see is heart-warming. But, tell me, the Cārvāka system rejects karma, its cause and effect. Then what is ethics in this system? What is it that incentivises an upright, ethical path? The Cārvāka system, as I understand it, discards the self, the divine, heaven and hell, and past and future lives. If it all ends right here with this life, where can we place ethics in this picture? And is there a higher intent—an attempt even at deliverance? When all this is missing, why will there be spiritual practice? A pleasure-seeking, self-indulgent existence is what will naturally be prescribed by this system in my view.'

Ajita remained silent.

Gautama added, 'Therein lies my issue. Human beings will act rightly if they understand what they will gain by it.

I myself struggled with this and then accepted karma as a principle and, as a result, the idea that there are several lives even if I reject a stable self. And, in the Cārvāka system, where is suffering? Suffering is universal and its end is what human beings seek,' said Gautama.

Ajita realised that Gautama was right but, rather than accepting that, he started attacking Gautama. This surprised even Maitreya.

'I agree the Cārvāka system can be enhanced. But I have issues with the exaggerated manner that suffering is dealt with in Bauddha thinking. We experience suffering and happiness—neither is eternal. With death, suffering ends. Everything ends. Suffering is real when it exists. If we claim that attachment is its cause, as the Bauddhas say, we are taking away its legitimacy. The starving child can feel suffering as much as he feels hunger. He is suffering because he needs a meal and it is right that he craves and desires it. Feeding the starving child is every human being's duty but as thinkers the duty is in finding what it is in the system that keeps the masses hungry.'

'This is suffering at its simplest. Suffering exists at many levels. But we shall let it be.' Saying this Gautama shut his eyes and became silent, making it clear that the debate had ended. Ajita felt restless because he hated leaving an exchange unfinished but Gautama had made his disinterest very apparent.

The first evening after Ajita had returned, Japa saw that he was again distant and restless, like he had been when he had first heard that Makkhali had been attacked.

'What was the meeting like? Was it successful?' she asked.

'Yes, it was fine,' said Ajita, but then went silent again.

'Tell me all! There were all these great men present there. What was it like being with them? Exchanging ideas? What did they say?' Japa persisted.

Ajita pulled himself up. 'I realise I have been sulking, but I am fine. The meeting . . . it went the way we wanted it.'

'And what did they all say?'

'Well, they all talked—Maitreya, Makkhali, Mahavir and Gautama. It was quite a special setting and I felt grateful that I was there. I did say my bit in the end.'

'That's great. But then why the sulk?'

'It wasn't the meeting, really. It was what happened after the meeting. I was with Maitreya and we saw Gautama sitting under a tree. I gathered the different ideas I have been grappling with and presented it as a seamless system. It was the first time I was assembling all the different strands in a systematic manner and it was the first time, I think, that even Maitreya was seeing the larger picture.'

'A meeting with the Buddha himself! That must have been great! But then, why the dispiritedness?'

'Alright. I must admit that meeting him was bigger than meeting the rest. As I said earlier, I am greatly impressed by Makkhali. Even this time when he talked in the meeting, I was awestruck. But meeting Gautama was different. It was huge in my mind. When I started explaining the Cārvāka system, I was happy because I was lucid and clear. I think even Gautama was impressed with my talk. But then he suggested that there may be a lacuna in my system. When he said it, I saw it—a massive gap staring at me. I had made an attempt at great clarity when I presented my ideas and that just made the gap apparent. I felt shattered.'

Japa, taking his hand in hers, said. 'Keep at it. The answer will appear.'

'When I argued with Makkhali the first time and he indicated what may be lacking in my ideas, I wasn't shaken. I was sure that I will find the answer and I did. I think it is really because I have made Gautama such a large figure in my head that I am struggling,' Ajita said.

Japa gazed at him. 'Banish that image—that large figure—and I am sure we will get past this.'

16. P

May 2009

'I am so glad to see you,' says Dolma, as she hugs Moksh warmly. 'You know you are my favourite tenant, right? I don't like to rent out the cottage to anyone else. But how long are you here for this time?'

Moksh has just returned to Bir after visiting Bombay for a few months.

'Oh! I would give anything to be here all the time. But I have to go back to make sure they don't throw me out of my job. This time I am here for four months. I managed to get some study leave granted and that when added to my vacation gives me four months. I wish it could have been longer though.'

'And it can't be any longer?' Dolma asks sadly.

'I had initially taken two years off. But then I requested my influential friend to have it extended for another year. That is how I stayed here for three years. But I am afraid I cannot continue doing that. I cannot bear to live in Bombay for long, so I will need to go back and forth.'

'As long as you come back!' said Dolma, with a big smile. 'But what does your White Lama say? Does he not want you to move here? Be here all the time?'

Moksh laughs. 'You know him well. He did try to convince me to leave my life in Bombay and just move here. But I managed to convince him that I need to be in Bombay for a good amount of my time so that I can continue in my job and earn a living. He is very satisfied with the strides I have made with my meditation. He knows that I can do quite a bit of it on my own. He always says that the techniques can take us to some level—from there it is our own journey.'

Dolma nodded before asking, 'And when you are teaching in the university in Bombay, do you get enough time to do your writing?'

'Yes, Dolma. Maybe not as much as I did here but I have managed to work out a routine and I follow it very strictly.'

'I don't doubt it. I have never seen anyone follow a routine as strictly as you. I admire that about you,' she says, as she takes her leave.

When he is finally alone, sitting in his favourite chair and looking out of the window at the mountains in the distance, he thinks of what he told Dolma about his routine. It is rather odd, he tells himself, that when you follow the diktats of time rigorously, you somehow become free of it. It is like moving with the same rhythm as time so that it seems to be not moving at all. He had worked hard on achieving this state but he felt that he had finally achieved what he desired—the freedom from the earth and the sky that he had once achingly longed for as he watched the gliders when he first came to Bir. But even as he thinks this, he realises that he would never have achieved this sense of freedom without the White Lama. The lessons in meditation and inner healing that he has received from the White Lama have been more transformative than anything he has ever encountered. The Lama's training has enabled him to navigate his inner world confidently.

It is about two weeks after his arrival in Bir that Moksh visits Lhasa. He is glad to see that he is recognised and welcomed warmly by the staff there. His regular table is made available for him and he waits, over a bowl of well-brewed tea, for Olivier. Olivier is unusually late and Moksh has already looked out of the window several times to see if he is coming. After they first met, Olivier had been in Bir for about a year. He then moved to Berlin on a work assignment.

When he finally arrives, they greet each other like long-lost brothers.

'I am sorry for being late. But my bus from Delhi got delayed.'

'You got here by bus? You must be tired,' says Moksh.

'I am quite used to it. So, tell me, how are you? You are looking well.'

'I am fine. Less anxious and more rested than I was when you first met me.'

'It has been quite a while since I left for Berlin. More than three years now,' said Olivier.

'And how is Berlin? Do you like it there?'

'The job is interesting and I have found friends there with interests similar to mine—meditation, healing, you know? I quite like it. And you, how often have you been coming here?'

'I was here for a stretch of three and a half years and then I went back to Bombay. I was there for almost a year before returning. I will be here for about four months this time.'

Moksh inhales audibly before he continues. 'I must thank you, Olivier, for what you have done for me. My time with the White Lama has really brought me back on track. I was lost.'

'Oh, come on. I did nothing. And anyway, you have thanked me before.'

'I feel the need to thank you again and again because this has been invaluable for me. What I have gone through can only be described as enantiodromic—a word I guess you are familiar with because of your line of work. All these years, I held materialism so close to myself, but the intensity of meditation has unfolded that materialism for me. It has revealed its own negation at the very core so that what I have left is not materialism but its obverse. With my materialism I had deceived myself into thinking that I was committed to the here and now, but it is only through meditation that I have found that I can actually inhabit the here and now—the moment. And when that truth is revealed to you, you feel liberated from it. Every object contains a universe within itself and every moment contains a whole history. To settle for the given object and the given moment is the mistake we make when we are naive and do not see things in its entirety. I know that what I say must be familiar to you but I felt the need to articulate it,' said Moksh.

'Enantiodromia . . . hmm. I may have felt it but I could never articulate it. My own trajectory was not very different. I was trained in hard science and only believed the rational. I too moved away from that line of thinking. But, yes, I didn't know how to say it in words. I can see that you have reached an advanced level in your meditation. You are on the threshold of bigger things, Moksh. Go forward and go where the road takes you.'

'At least I have moved a little along that road,' Moksh says with a laugh. 'Will you get time to see the White Lama? How long are you here for, by the way?'

'I will definitely meet him but I am here only for two days before I go to Dharamshala where I have a few meetings. I will leave for Berlin by early next week. But, Moksh, I want you to know that, I am so glad we could meet. I don't know when we will meet again. But take care and write to me when you can.' Saying this, Olivier left.

Moksh is back in his flat on Laburnum Road after his four-month stay in Bir and he feels glad to be back. Bir does Moksh a lot of good and he likes to be there—his routine of writing, meditating and walking rejuvenates him. But, no matter what, Bombay is where he feels at home. Mr Lotvala had once said, 'You know, Moksh, we are such Bombaywalas. The clean, fresh air of the mountains gets too much for our lungs after a while. We need to come back to breathe this city's contaminated air to feel normal.'

Over the years though, Mr Lotvala has grown irritated with Moksh's newfound beliefs.

'I don't know where this is going, Moksh. You don't really want me to believe this mumbo-jumbo, do you?' he says, when he meets him on his return.

Moksh does not defend himself. He smiles instead.

'This is another thing that infuriates me about these religious sorts—their self-assurance and smugness,' Mr Lotvala says with a hint of scorn.

'You said one thing and listed two,' says Moksh, continuing to smile.

'Oh, come on, Moksh!'

'All right, all right!' Moksh raises his hands in surrender. 'But seriously, Mr Lotvala, I am committed to our cause. I have discovered the other end of things recently but that is more an internal rearrangement—that is about me and myself. My connections with the world are still mediated by ideas that you and I stand by. Don't ever doubt that. In fact, by clearing my inner self I am able to relate to the outer world without much clutter.'

'I detest all this talk of "inner self",' says Lotvala, angrily.

'I think you should also be devoting some of your time to yourself,' says Moksh. 'It will make a big difference.'

Mr Lotvala remains silent.

'Fine, I will make sure not to discuss my Buddhism and my meditation with you. We will limit our discussions to our journal and the other activities of our society,' says Moksh, with an air of finality.

'I never imagined there would be a day when I'd be saying this to you, but when did you start thinking that you could dissociate your religious beliefs from the larger ideas that we use to understand society? You are not naive—you know what religion is about. Just two years ago, a twenty-five-year-old civil war ended in Sri Lanka. It has been described as an ethnic battle—between the Tamils and the Sinhalese—but do you really think that there is no way religion enters this war? I chose to talk about Sri Lanka because the Sinhalese are mainly Buddhist. Even I had trouble reconciling that fact with the non-violent face of Buddhism but one cannot ignore it. I hear from friends that trouble is brewing for Muslims in Myanmar and they are beginning to be targeted by militant Buddhists. Even for a communist and an atheist like me, 'militant Buddhists' sounded like a contradiction in terms. But again, that is because of the way we have constructed Buddhism in our heads. Of course, not just Buddhism but all religions have a history of violence. You have to see this larger form of religion. You cannot avoid this by trying to hide behind mysticism and refusing the label of religion.'

Mr Lotvala seems agitated and Moksh waits for him to calm down a bit before he says, 'Mr Lotvala, I am sorry but when did we communists start getting righteous about violence? I don't think we have much of a locus standi on that, do we?'

Mr Lotvala calms down somewhat and Moksh continues. 'In any case, I am acutely aware of the contradiction that you have alluded to and I admit I don't have any resolution to offer. But I have a few thoughts about this which I would like to share with you. You know very well the kind of atheist my father was and I have shared with you the fact that my mother was religious.'

'Well, I knew your mother was a believer. Even Sanjay has talked to me about it,' says Mr Lotvala.

'I guess he must have shared that with you,' says Moksh. 'But I wanted to share with you an incident from the time when my mother was terminally ill with cancer. The doctors had informed us that there was nothing they could do to save her and my father was very distraught. At that time, some friend gave him the contact details of a faith healer of sorts. I was around when he told my mother about the faith healer. What was interesting was that it was my father who was willing to give the faith healer a chance but my mother would not hear of it. Of course, there could have been a variety of reasons at work behind these decisions: my father was so scared of losing my mother that he would give even something that did not conform with his rationalism and aetheism a chance and, at the same time, my mother was so aware of the finality of her disease that she did not want to waste her time on any treatment. Nevertheless, neither of them would have made the decision they made had they been wholly committed to what they claimed to be following.'

He takes a moment to catch his breath and then continues. 'And this is exactly what interests me—the tight corners that we get into in life—situations that make us act in ways contrary to our touted beliefs. And that is what exists in actuality—we hold inside each of us several strands of different ways of thinking, many of which may contradict each other. Take Yusuf Chacha, for instance. Here was a man who was a strict Muslim and a committed Marxist. Or Geet—who was a left-oriented feminist but wanted to go to some mandir in Wimbledon when her mother was sick. Or Maya—who is a firebrand Dalit Marxist but is also Buddhist and for whom Buddhism is a lot more than a religion or belief system. It is integral to her Dalit identity.

'I don't intend this to be a defence of my own contradictions. I only know these contradictions exist in others as they do in me and I need to bring these strands of thought together in me so that I can continue to breathe.'

Ono settles comfortably into the low-slung divan, balancing the glass of wine that she is holding in her hand.

'So, tell me everything. How long were you in Dharamshala?' she asks.

'I went there in December 2005, Ono. I remember how cold it was. It is not exactly Dharamshala. It is a small town called Bir about sixty kilometres away. Small but quite lovely,' says Moksh.

'I am sure it is lovely, else what could tear you away from Bombay? When you are there next time, I should try and visit you.'

'Yes, you must. Though you may want to stay in Dharamshala because a tourist can do much more there.'

'And what have you been doing in Bir? I guess you must have had a lot of time for your work and for your writing. I want to hear more about your book. And, when did you decide that you should be writing a work of fiction? I remember you talked to me about it a few years ago.'

'Yes, that was just two months before I went to Bir.'

'How does it feel to write fiction? This is your first time with it. What are the challenges that you face?'

'It almost feels like you are interviewing me,' says Moksh, smiling.

'Famous writers of fiction like yourself can only talk through the medium of interviews, I imagine!' Ono joins in.

Moksh laughs. 'Well, Ono, you know exactly why I decided to rewrite this book as fiction. I wanted to drown myself in it and that is what I did. But there are a lot of issues that one encounters only when one is writing fiction. If I were writing an academic book, I would never have come across these kinds of challenges.'

'What do you mean?'

'As I was telling you even then, fiction lets you get under the skin of the characters and in touch with their lives. But when a story is set, like mine is, in a historical moment two and a half millennia ago, you are left struggling with understanding the minutiae of these lives—how they lived, what they did, what the rhythm of their days and nights was, what they ate and what they wore. As a writer, one may choose to be clever and not refer to any of these details but that is never going to work in fiction. Because these tiny elements are always around. One can't tell an authentic story without them.'

Taking a break only to catch his breath, Moksh continues. 'How did my characters talk to each other? How did they show care or concern? How did a little boy address his father? How did his mother show love? We are well aware that none of these are articulated in a uniform manner even across coexisting cultures; then how do we even begin to think of something that far back in time? Historical texts obliterate these minutiae so there is no way to go back and find out.'

'So, how did you handle these questions?' Ono is intrigued.

'I decided to do it my own way because I doubt there is any one way to handle it. So, I threw caution to the winds and modelled their modes of thought, behaviour and actions on our own times while retaining a flavour of that time in the story. Very broadly, I think my nouns are from that time but my verbs are what we currently use. I have tried to not become anachronistic by bringing in 'things' that are modern into the story, but when they reason or argue, when they show rage or love, when they ache or cry, I make them do it like you or I would. I am also stressing the fact that this was the time the first truly urban cultures came to be, and a sense of freedom and broad-mindedness came with it. In my mind, it is this urbanity that somehow makes them not very unlike us. It works for me only if I see some of myself in my character, only if I ask myself what I would do in certain situations or circumstances—fashion him in my own image, somewhat.'

Ananya smiles. 'I can see many readers may have issues with this but I find it quite interesting. I would love to read it the moment it is ready.'

'Yes, of course. I want you to read it.'

'And when you called me the other day, you were telling me about your new interest in Buddhism and meditation. I must admit, I was quite amazed. Does that still hold?'

'It is more than just an interest, Ono. It is something that has taken over my existence now.'

Ananya looks at Moksh a little worried because she feels his voice change when he says that. It is almost as though a new Moksh has entered the room with this subject.

'That does not sound like the Moksh I know.' Moksh smiles but does not answer.

For a few minutes, they sit drinking their wine in silence.

Then Moksh says, 'When I was in Bir, I went to Dharamshala often for my library work and, at times, I would stay there for two or three days. There is a Tibetan Government-in-Exile in Dharamshala and they also have a library where I often went. One of the things that attracted me to it was their archives which has a great collection of Mahayana Buddhist texts, all of them translated from Sanskrit, in which they were written originally, into Tibetan. These translations were done more than a thousand years ago and these texts have been carefully handed down the generations. However, some of the Sanskrit originals have been lost and we have only the Tibetan translations available. So these archivists have started doing this work of recreating the Sanskrit originals from their Tibetan translations.'

'That sounds fascinating,' says Ono.

'It is, but that is not the reason I am sharing this information with you. You see, this reverse translation, if one is allowed to coin a term, is unlike my work with writing fictional history where I am using historical information from that time, whatever may be its limitations, to create a fictional narrative. In the reverse translation, what exists now is used to create something that existed earlier. But one of the things that meditation allows you to understand is that you have the ability of reverse translation locked within you.'

'What do you mean?' asks Ono, confused.

'I am writing, through this method of reverse translation, the lives that I have lived earlier.'

'What! You can't be serious,' says Ono.

'I am—very serious. Meditation has revealed to me, through the sorting out of the inner self that I am now, events and incidents from lives I have lived earlier. It is through this that it becomes crystal clear that this life, which we take to be everything, is just one instalment of a serialised narrative. But because what we are now is a result of our actions from some earlier time, an understanding of ourselves through meditation throws light on what we were earlier. I am taking these insights into these earlier lives and stringing a narrative thread through them.'

'So you are writing another book? Something on lives lived before?'

'Another book? All I know is that I am writing Ajita's story and I am writing my own story and these are being written in two books—Ajita's story in the blue book and mine in the brown,' says Moksh, gesturing to two books lying on his writing table. 'But that is only at the obvious level. At another level, I really don't know if there are two books. Where does one end and the other begin? I don't know. I don't know whether I am a writer or a character in the book—and if I am a character in the book, then what of this moment? Are we to think we inhabit reality as we sit in my living room drinking wine or making our way through a fiction?'

'Moksh, I think you may be a little drunk,' says Ono. 'I am not sure I am fully with you here. But I do want to read your book on Ajita. I will be glad to read it as an editor since I have been doing that kind of work for years now. So, your blue book, yes, definitely. Your brown book? Well, frankly, I am not sure. I see it as a kind of diary you are writing and I feel it is best no one else reads it. Not me, certainly.'

'I don't know why I am so sure of this but I think you will be curious to find out what is in the brown book,' says Moksh.

17. Q

Summer – 492

It was only a few days after the celebration of the harvest festival that news reached Vaishali that Ajatashatru had crowned himself Emperor of Magadh. It was not just his succession that was making news but also the manner in which it had purportedly happened. As various stories were reaching Vaishali, the common thread that ran through all the accounts was that Ajatashatru had taken his father, Emperor Bimbisara, captive by carrying out a surprise attack on his palace and put him in prison. The rumours also claimed that he had either imprisoned his brothers or killed them. Whatever the truth may be, he had certainly managed to get them out of his way. The news caused a furore in Vaishali.

Emperor Bimbisara had built his empire through war as well as marital alliances. He was as generous with his friends and associates as he was firm with his enemies. He had married one of the daughters of the Lichchhavi rulers of Vaishali and had very good relations with them. For the people of Vaishali, Bimbisara had assumed a larger-than-life image because of the power he wielded but, at the same time, he was seen as a friend and supporter of the kingdom.

At a very young age, Bimbisara had defeated the king of Anga in a cleverly planned campaign and annexed his kingdom. When Ajatashatru grew up, Bimbisara made him the governor of Anga, and so the young prince moved to Champa, its capital, with ideas in his head and ambitions in his heart. He also brought along his ruthlessness and the result was lethal. More than anyone else, it was the people of Anga who were witness to the cruelty of their new governor. Away from the watchful gaze of his father, Ajatashatru could have wasted his time on wine and women, like the other princes of his time. But this young man was burning with such ambition that even his father's large empire was too small for him.

As he spent his days in Champa, fanning the fires of ambition inside him, he developed strategies and game plans to reach his goal.

He pursued varied interests. He was a fine horseman and he prided himself on possessing the best horses anyone had ever seen. He took a personal interest in supervising their health. The young prince also liked spending time doing the rounds of the blacksmiths and the foundry, and took a great deal of interest in the weapons they made. He incentivised innovation and his workmen tried to outdo one another in producing new and effective weapons of destruction, the likes of which no other kingdom across the land possessed. The prince spent the rest of his time with his ministers, discussing the functioning of their ministries in great detail. It was only late in the evenings that he would retire to his pleasure gardens and indulge in the best that his kitchens and wine cellars could offer.

After spending six such years in Champa, he felt he was ready to take over from his father and become the emperor of Magadha. He set about executing his grand plans of making

Magadha the largest empire that had ever existed. Over time, he had cultivated a faithful inner circle of ministers and advisors, both in Magadha and in Champa, and their loyalty to him was much greater than to Bimbisara. With their counsel, he worked out the details of attacking Bimbisara's palace. The coup was planned to such precision that Ajatashatru knew that he could carry it out with just a handful of armed soldiers with him. He arrived in Magadha late one night with a small group of his most trusted soldiers, and in less than an hour he had gained access to Bimbisara's inner chambers and taken his father and stepmother captive. His inebriated brothers were picked up from their palaces, clueless and complaining. The swiftness of the attack and their own hapless state resulted in them offering no resistance.

In the months that followed, Ajatashatru assumed complete control of his father's empire and firmly put out all attempts at resistance and revolt that came from some small sections of the land. He was now ready to unpack his imperialist ambitions and started planning the first of his big military campaigns. The size and might of the army of Magadha and the superior weapons of war that they had at their disposal meant that this task proved to be even easier than Ajatashatru and the ministers of his council had anticipated. Very soon, the empire had grown and taken within itself most of the kingdoms stretching from the distant east to the farthest reaches of the north-west. There were still a few kingdoms in between that had not succumbed to Magadha's might—some too small and weak to be of immediate interest to Ajatashatru and some too powerful, against whom the campaigns had to be planned and executed more carefully.

Somewhere around this time Bimbisara and his wife died in prison. It was not clear whether it was suicide or if Ajatashatru had had them killed. Thus, it came to be that the much venerated Emperor Bimbisara died a lonely and unsung death.

Winter – 487

One evening, when Ajita was still busy with his last patient, Maitreya dropped in to meet him. Noticing his friend was still busy, he said, 'I have something to tell you and it is very important but I will wait till you have completed your work.'

When Ajita was finally done and came out to meet him, he could see that Maitreya was being barely able to contain his excitement.

'I have some very interesting news. I have a friend in Rajgriha who is close to some of the senior ministers in Emperor Ajatashatru's court. He sent a messenger over to deliver word to me today. We will get formal intimation from the court of Rajgriha, of course, but he was so excited on finding out that he wanted to share it with me as soon as possible,' said Maitreya, bubbling with excitement himself.

'But what is the message?' asked Ajita, smiling at Maitreya.

'What I have been told is that Ajatashatru is apparently going through some sort of crisis. I hear that he has been traumatised by his father's death; rather by the fact that he was responsible for it. He has not been himself for several weeks now and his ministers are worried. This is not something any of them anticipated. They have suggested that he seek out a teacher who will help him navigate this crisis, and even though the emperor was initially hesitant, he has now agreed. Seven names have been suggested and you are one of them! Can you even believe that?' said Maitreya in an ecstatic burst.

Ajita smiled. 'I am happy, Maitreya, but not overjoyed like you are. Pardon me, but your exultation is unbecoming of a revolutionary leader!'

Maitreya laughed and said, 'No revolution has been wrought by people who shut themselves up in a cave. It is important to be heard and to convince people. For that one needs access to the strongholds of power. And when I see a chance of that, I am happy. Don't be so staid, Ajita! The emperor of Magadha asking for an audience is something to be jubilant about. It is an acknowledgement of your growing fame as a philosopher that is making me so happy.'

'Yes, I am happy about that too, though I would like to think of it as recognition for the Cārvākas and not of my fame.'

'It is the Cārvākas but you are the philosopher amongst us. There is no doubting that, which is why the emperor's counsel would like to invite you and not any of us.'

'But we have to tread carefully, Maitreya. Who are the other philosophers he has invited? I am sure Gautama and Mahavir have been invited too.'

'Yes, they are and, of course, our friend Goshala.'

'And I guess there will be some Vedic philosophers who have been invited as well?' said Ajita.

'The three others are Sanjay Belatthiputta, Purana Kassapa and Pakuda Kaccayana.'

'But they are all Ajivikas, are they not?' asked Ajita.

'No, Sanjay is not. I have known him for a very long time and he is a great ascetic. But he is committed to being a rigorous agnostic and does not want to align with any of the systems.'

'And the other two?'

'They are Ajivikas. There are differences between Makkhali and these two but not any that are significant. I can say with some confidence, though, that it is Makkhali who is the backbone of their system.'

'Maitreya,' said Ajita, 'I still think we need to be cautious and tread carefully. In savouring the feeling of vindication, we forgot to pay attention to some curious details. Do you see that not a single Vedic philosopher is on the list of invitees? One would have thought that they would certainly want Mimamsaka there or at least Samkhyaika. In fact, there are several eminent names they could have included. The fact that they are missing is clear evidence of what you have been saying all along—that there are huge political changes afoot. These changes are altering the relationship of religion and philosophy with society in general and the state in particular.'

'The tributaries are becoming the rivers,' said Maitreya.

Ajita smiled. 'Indeed. I must say that at the level of philosophical thought, I feel that common people should come to accept ideas on their own through a process of reasoning, understanding and even arguing. Through any way, in fact, except imposition. This applies to our thought as it does to any other. So I do not want a situation where an emperor or a king or a landlord becomes our patron and imposes our system on people over whom he has power.

'I am happy our system is thought of as a big river and not as a tributary but I will go along with this only up to a point. To become so mainstream will run counter to our revolutionary ideals and we cannot bring about a transformation by allying with people in power.'

'But . . . but you cannot refuse this invitation!' said Maitreya, somewhat agitated.

'Well, that is true. It is a tricky situation. But my suggestion is this: if we can build a consensus between the seven of us who have been invited by the emperor then we can attend the meeting, say what we have to but get out of there without any commitment. All seven of us must adhere to this so that it is unfair to no system.'

'I am in complete agreement. We had already discussed the issue of co-operation in our meeting with the other thinkers in Rajgriha. I have no doubt that Makkhali will be with us in this and, from what I can guess, Mahavir and Gautam should also support us.'

'That is what we need. And through Makkhali we can make sure that Purana Kassapa and Pakuda Kaccayana also lend their support to this line of action.'

'That will definitely strengthen our case. And, as I said, Sanjay Belatthiputta is an old friend of mine and I will talk to him about this. I do believe he will need little convincing because he is so sceptical of everything. Allying with the state goes against his very nature.'

Ajita looked buoyed. 'Now we will wait for the official invitations to come and then get in touch with all of them to call a meeting. Maybe we should all meet in Rajgriha before the meeting with the emperor is scheduled. I defintely want you to come with me to Rajgriha, Maitreya. Your presence at this meeting is all too important.'

'I wouldn't miss it.'

As Maitreya had said, the invitation soon arrived. Ajita set off with Maitreya for Rajgriha a few days in advance, so that they would have ample time to meet the others before their meeting with the emperor. The meeting with the six philosophers was fixed two days before the big day.

When they met, it was Maitreya who took charge and laid out clearly what he and Ajita had discussed. They had already briefed Makkhali and he was in agreement with their planned course of action. In turn, Makkhali had talked to Kassapa and Kaccayana about it and both of them had expressed their support.

Kassapa had an important suggestion to make. 'In my opinion, we should make sure we make an incoherent and abstruse presentation of our ideas before the emperor. If we present it in a clear and coherent fashion, there is a danger that he may actually like what we are saying and we will then have no escape.'

Ajita looked at Kassapa admiringly. This was clearly someone after his own heart.

Sanjay, who had remained silent till this point, said, 'I agree with everything that is being said. I prefer the solitude of my home in the forest and will not give that up for anything. So it is very much in my interest not to make any kind of commitment to the emperor.'

'I too am not in the frame of mind right now to make any political alliances,' said Mahavir. 'At the same time, it has to be said that these are difficult times we live in and I am worried about the safety of my followers. I do not want to make an alliance with the emperor but that does not mean I want to incur his wrath either. I will be brief about what I say and I am sure it will not make any impression on him.'

Maitreya beamed with satisfaction. 'So, do I conclude that we are all in agreement with the proposal?' he asked.

'I have not spoken yet,' said Gautama.

'Oh, I apologise, Gautama. I took your silence for agreement. But, please, tell us what you have in mind,' said Maitreya, contrite.

Gautama waited till there was absolute silence in the room and then started speaking. 'I appreciate the spirit in which the proposal in today's meeting was made and I can see the logic behind it. But I am not entirely sure that I agree with the way this is going to be actualised. If we do not want an alliance with the emperor, we should make that clear to him and not worry about the repercussions of turning him down. I expect he will be reasonable in dealing with a refusal. For me, he is a human being first and an emperor later. If he approaches me, I will speak to him. I will share with him the thoughts I share with any person on the street. If he is in a position to accept what I say or see some merit in it, he may act upon it or else he is free to move ahead in peace. That has been my way and it will continue to be.

'Having said that, I do respect the fact that between all of us here, we share a world view to some extent and we did make a commitment some time ago in Rajgriha to work in co-operation. It was Ajita's suggestion, I remember, and even at the time that he made it, I thought it was a good idea. I have great respect for his thinking. But do we share only a world view or a value system too?'

He paused for a moment, and then continued, 'Anyway, let me not take too much time over this. I believe that for me the right course of action is to not meet the emperor at all. I will be sending him a message this evening, apologising to him for my absence at the meeting.'

There was a stunned silence in the room but every one there knew Gautama would not budge from his position. So it was decided that only six of them—Makkhali, Mahavir, Sanjay, Kaccayana, Kassapa and Ajita—would meet Ajatashatru.

Two days later, the emperor's distinguished guests gathered in a grand hall in Ajatashatru's palace. The emperor took his time to make an appearance and it gave them enough time to settle down and appreciate the beauty of their surroundings.

Finally, when Ajatashatru made an appearance, he looked every bit as formidable as he was made out to be. People in the room felt dwarfed in his presence. His minister went through the formalities of introducing the guests to the mighty Ajatashatru and then it was the emperor's turn to speak. As he spoke, Ajita felt a pang of guilt. To hear the emperor speak was to hear a young man express his confusion and disenchantment. A young man who was uncertain of his place in the larger scheme of things and his disillusionment with the purpose of success and achievement. Ajita felt he had already convinced himself and the others, well before meeting the emperor, that the ruler's intentions in arranging this meeting were purely political. He now realised he'd been unfair.

He remembered how Makkhali had told him in their first meeting that people's goals are primarily soteriological and that is the reason they wish to speak to philosophers or religious leaders. It was clear that the emperor was also seeking something similar and, in that moment, Ajita wondered whether he should soften his prejudiced stance and speak from his heart to the emperor, as he would to a disciple. He realised, however, that it was too late to do that because the others were already prepared to act according to their previous plan. He would be betraying them if he were to now deviate from that game plan. But close on the heels of this another thought followed—he reasoned with himself that even if it was the emperor's current aim to seek someone, maybe a religious guide who could offer him advice and solace in his moment of crisis, the relationship that he would forge would eventually become a political arrangement. He would be an earnest disciple but an emperor is much more than the individual he appears to be in this moment—he is inseparable from his empire and his state.

Ajita's thinking was interrupted by Kassapa's voice, who was just beginning to speak. After some prefatory remarks, Kassapa discussed in detail the ideas of sin and virtue. When he began his words seemed to be making an impression on the emperor but when Kassapa went about taking up an extreme relativist position on good and evil actions, the emperor seemed to lose interest. Ajita was impressed with the kind of illustrations that Kassapa used to justify his extreme position—'Even if a man destroys all life on earth, he commits no sin,' he said, for instance. He left the emperor decidedly sure that he would not want to have anything to do with him.

When Makkhali spoke, Ajita realised that he had taken on the task of painting himself in the colours of his caricature. He had often been dubbed as a fatalist and he hated this image that had been created. But he decided that it was the day to fully assume this position in the manner of a self-parody. He spoke at length with his customary flair and as he went on, he tightened the noose of fatalism further. By the end of his speech, people were literally gasping for breath.

Ajita was still reeling from Makkhali's presentation, when he realised it was his turn to speak. He decided to talk about the finality of death in his materialist conception of the world, his arguments against afterlives or previous lives and his rejection of karma. In fact, he did not have to present too much of a caricature—he talked in a non-technical way about the major tenets of his philosophical system, choosing to pepper it with a couple of very hard-hitting examples. That was enough to ensure that it would offer no comfort to the emperor.

Kaccayana chose a somewhat different strategy—he went along with abstruseness. He talked of the seven elemental categories that were fundamental to his system of thinking but then went about discussing it in such a recondite manner that not just the emperor but all the others present were left clueless about what he was getting at.

Mahavir was the very opposite of Makkhali—he did not enjoy a situation of this kind. He could not parody or caricature, he could not bring himself to take on any extreme position because that was not true to his system and neither did he want to create cobwebs of confusion by talking about abstractions. He instead chose to speak of a truth—a single truth from his philosophical edifice—which he knew would make deeper sense only when looked at in the context of the larger system of thought that he and the earlier masters in his tradition had developed. He talked about restraints that he claimed were important in spiritual practice. But since Mahavir presented it to the emperor without reference to anything else in his system of thought, the emperor could not make much of it.

Of the six of them, it was Sanjay Belatthiputta for whom the task at hand was the easiest. Sanjay was an agnostic to the core and he went on to take up several issues about life and death, heaven and afterlife, good and evil, and treated each of these binaries with the deep agnosticism that characterised his thought.

Because it was already planned and was also part of royal custom, the emperor went through the motions of engaging them in conversation over a grand meal that followed but it was clear that he had come to the conclusion that he had gained nothing by meeting these six thinkers.

Ajita and Maitreya returned to Vaishali the very next day. Ajita had been too busy to devote any time to the archives that he was working on and so he decided to do so on his return. Three days later, he was still busy in the archives dictating to one of the scribes, when Maitreya came in.

'I am sorry to interrupt, Ajita,' he said, 'but I need to speak to you. Alone.'

When the scribe left, Ajita turned to Maitreya. 'What is it? What's the urgency?' he asked.

'I have some news which will surprise you. It appears that two days after we left Rajgriha, Ajatashatru met with Gautama. Gautama talked to him at length and the emperor has now committed himself to Gautama's path.'

18. T

November 2010

When Ananya reaches Moksh's home, only Mohini is around.

'Sa'ab said I should give you a number and you should call him.'

'Moksh will never buy himself a mobile phone. He is so annoying,' Ananya says, as if she were reminding herself, while she calls him.

'Ono, sorry. A friend is undergoing an emergency surgery. So I am in Bandra. I will come as soon as his surgery is over. Can you hang around or are you busy?'

'No, I made sure I am free all day. I will be here and Mohini can cook me some food. Come when you are done. I have read your book and have views we should discuss. So come prepared.'

As Mohini prepares some coffee for her, Ono browses Moksh's bookshelf. She looks for a book which can engage her for a couple of hours—should be easy since Moksh has an impressive library. Her eyes fall on a brown book in a corner—Moksh's diary, she remembers.

She had once declined reading Moksh's diary. However, she is curious now and convinces herself she will read a few pages and make some sense of Moksh's mad obsessions.

She feels a sense of pleasure and power as she plonks down on a chair, readying herself for Moksh's diary which he hopes she will help her know his inner world.

July 1917

Dr Singh leans back in his chair and closes his eyes. For years, he has been an early riser, waking up well before dawn. He realises he is middle-aged now, for sleep weighs on his eyes as soon as he has had his lunch. He is nearly dozing when he hears his younger colleague, Vinodini, come in.

'Sorry, sir, were you asleep?' Vinodini asks.

'Well, no. I may have been very soon.'

'A family is here . . . asking for you.'

'A family? Yes, of course. Mr Yograj Singh,' he says, checking his diary. 'Please send him in.'

Yograj Singh's huge presence dwarfs his wife who walks behind him. She is holding her son by his hand, nearly dragging him inside.

'Vinodini,' Dr Singh says, arranging some papers, 'I will need you around.'

When he looks up, he sees Yograj's eyes focused on him.

'Dr Singh?' says Yograj. 'From your name, I imagined you were Sikh. I now see you are Hindu.'

'Well . . . I am Dr Samuel Singh. You can guess my religion now,' Dr Singh smiles. Yograj looks confused.

'You have come here for your son's medical care and my religion will hopefully be of no consequence?'

Yograj Singh has no reply and can barely nod.

'Dr Singh, I am Rajjo. Our friends spoke very highly of you,' Yograj's wife jumps in. 'We hope you will help us, help cure our son.' Yograj Singh, by now, can only agree. 'Haan-ji, please give our son his leg back.'

'Singh sa'ab, I will do all I can. For now, I will examine him and give you my opinion,' Samuel Singh says. Handing Yograj's son a candy, he says, 'May I know your name?'

'Arre bolo! He is asking you your name. Reply!' Yograj says roughly.

Rajjo holds her son's hand. 'Kake,' she says, 'please answer.'

'Bhisham,' he whispers.

'Bhisham? Such a nice name,' says Samuel Singh. 'However, I like Kake more. When I was small, everyone called me Kake. Can I call you Kake?'

Kake smiles.

'Come, son,' Samuel says. 'Lie down here and I will examine you. Vinodini, will you help me?'

Kake is nine years old, Samuel learns as he examines his limbs.

'He was fine, like any child his age. A few weeks ago, he came home from school. He was running a fever. His fever remained for a few days and his legs were aching. He would cry because he found his pain unbearable. And in a week or so he had problems walking. His leg . . . ' Rajjo pauses and Samuel sees she is crying.

'We have come here hoping you will cure him,' Yograj says. 'He is our only child.'

'Singh sa'ab, your son has polio. We have no cure for polio and I will make no false promises. If we give him good care, he may recover. However, a full recovery is unlikely.'

'You mean, he will never walk normally again?' Yograj asks.

'If you ask people in my profession, many will say no. However, I am hoping he will, helped by good medical care. A fusion of medicines, massages and exercises may help him recover a good deal. However, be prepared for a long haul. Maybe years.'

'Do you really feel he will recover?' Vinodini asks Samuel when she finds him alone.

'You mean Kake?' he asks. 'He is young and in good physical shape overall. My guess is he will recover a good deal. Of course, one can never be sure. I have come across some new research papers on polio, especially in some American journals which may be useful for our purposes.'

'You will become famous if you can make him well.'

'I hope I can make him well, and I hope my reason will be nowhere as selfish! I am happy being unknown, if I can do some good.'

'You sound like a religious man even if you declare yourself a non-believer,' says Vinodini, smiling.

Samuel has made good use of his club membership by making sure he manages four days of squash or swimming every week. Now, as he sips his whisky following a good game of squash and a shower, he dwells on Vinodini's remark of how he is seemingly religious. His self-discipline, he is aware, can appear as zealousness and his immersion in his work like religious fervour.

'How're you, Samuel?' says a familiar voice. 'Mind if we join you?'

'Oh, sure. How're you, Mark?'

'I am fine. Has been a while since I saw you.'

'Yes, I hardly see you here.'

'I have been so busy,' says Mark. 'However, I love being here. Lumsden has done us a huge favour by building a very good club. You know Reverend Graham Ross, I presume,' he says.

'No,' says Samuel, reaching for a handshake. 'Are you new around here?' he asks Reverend Ross.

'Yes, I arrived four weeks ago from Glasgow.'

Mark orders a round of drinks and having had a couple of sips, he says, 'Graham and I were class fellows in school. We go back a long way. And, Graham, Samuel is a very close friend and, I should add, a well-known surgeon.'

'Oh, come on!' says Samuel. 'I am hardly well-known and where I work one can hardly be only a surgeon. One ends up doing all kinds of work.'

'When I was young I was keen on pursuing a career in medicine as I saw medicine as a very noble profession. By helping cure people of illness and disease one is doing work which is as valuable as someone in a church does,' says Graham.

Samuel's eyes narrow on hearing Graham's remark.

'I find many of my colleagues wholly devoid of any concern or love for fellow beings,' he says. 'No, medicine is no longer a noble profession. However, your comparison is amusing. I am sorry I am irreligious.'

Graham smiles. 'A man of medicine cares for a person's body, a man of God for his soul.'

'A compendious epigram, if I may say so. A carer of souls!'

'Surely you believe we humans possess souls?'

'Yes, I do, Reverend. I see human souls every day and I find souls revealed in deeds of kindness, compassion and care. When I cure a body, I see a soul come forward smiling. I see a soul in an old woman when she holds my hand for having relieved her of her pain. I see a soul in a child's smile. Nowhere else.'

'We may shower love on someone and, indeed, glimpse his or her soul. However, we are deluded if we convince ourselves of our powers. Of course, we can care for old people or for children and we can nurse sick people. However, our medicines, surgeries and cures will lose all efficacy if His grace is missing. We can only show kindness, compassion and love—all else is in His hands,' says Reverend Ross.

Samuel shakes his head. 'No, we have some power and agency. Even your God would be happier if we could do all we can, on our own and leave him alone. Of course, in many areas, science has hardly made any progress. However, where we know, we know a good deal and such knowledge helps in achieving desired ends.'

'If only we could be sure of which end will be achieved, we would have no need for God,' Reverend Ross shrugs.

'Even when we believe in God, we can scarcely be sure,' says Samuel, wryly.

When he goes back home, Samuel lies wide awake in bed. Memories of his grandpa, his dada-ji, flood his mind. As a child, he loved his dada-ji like he did no one else, and dada-ji loved his grandson, whom he called Kake, deeply. Dada-ji had worked all his life as a gardener, and even when he grew old he would spend a couple of hours every day doing gardening. He had begun working in a church garden as a very young boy—a place which was his only refuge when he was orphaned, a place which provided him care and which he made his own. Because of which, from Gurdayal Singh he became Francis Singh. When he grew up, he married Neena, Samuel's dadi. Samuel had never seen her because she died a year before he was born. When she died, Francis was overcome by a feeling of hopelessness. Only when Samuel was born did he feel like his usual self again.

Francis had worked hard all along, and made sure his son, David, received good schooling. He had always hoped his son would find work in an office as a babu—for a gardener like him any office job was special. Francis's joy had known no bounds when David had become a clerk in a new railway company called Scinde, Punjab and Delhi Railway. When David married Nalini, he had married a woman who came from a class above his own, ensuring his family's upward passage. As a consequence, Francis had big dreams for Kake, his beloved grandson. He hoped Kake would pursue a career in medicine and become a famous surgeon one day.

Dada-ji did all he could for his Kake: he ironed his school uniform, polished his shoes, combed his hair and scrubbed his face as he readied him for school every day. When Kake did his school work, dada-ji would help him in any way he could. One lesson Kake did learn from dada-ji was of prayer. Love for God, love for our family, love for our friends, love for our fellow men was dada-ji's simple maxim which he believed in and lived by. He hoped his grandson would follow him. Kake's love for his dada-ji made him believe every word he said.

One day, when he came back home from school, Samuel found his dada-ji in bed, gravely ill. Nalini had gone in search of medical help and he was alone. Dada-ji could hardly speak and Samuel realised he needed sleep. Since Samuel would be alone, dada-ji remained awake, such was his concern for his grandson. Only when Nalini came back did dada-ji close his eyes.

Dada-ji's sickness only worsened as days passed. He remained ill for nine days, and Samuel prayed fervidly. He knew his love for dada-ji was pure and he knew his grandpa would be saved by God. However, no prayer could save dada-ji. Samuel's world came crumbling down. He made himself a couple of promises. He would become a surgeon like dada-ji had desired and never again would he pray or believe in a God who was no help. He also decided he would have no family, no wife and no children so he could spend his life serving people who needed his care as lovingly as dada-ji cared for his garden.

Lying in bed now, Samuel remembers his childish and courageous decisions. He also realises how closely his life resembles his dada-ji's. His grandpa based his life on principles of love and care, like he himself does. Dada-ji's belief in God and his own lack of belief made no difference.

He remembers Reverend Ross.

'Ross seeks God because he sees deficiency in human endeavours,' Samuel muses. 'I believe we should improve ourselves and overcome any deficiency. God is no answer.'

February 1919

Vinodini checks Samuel's diary and says, 'Kake will be here soon. He has been penciled in here for 4 p.m.'

'Yes, I know,' says Samuel. 'I see him every four weeks now, unlike earlier when I was seeing him every week.'

'I remember Kake from when he came here a year and a half ago. He has made so much progress. Now he can move on his own.'

'Yes, Vinodini. Even now, while he can only drag himself, he can do so on his own. His knees are also seeming more flexible now. I am happy Kake has reached where he has. However, I imagine a couple of years more will be needed.'

'I admire your perseverance. No one else I know can be so caring.'

'I care for Kake and for people like him who need my help. My ego has no place here.'

Very soon, Kake and Rajjo arrive.

'Hello! How're you, my prince?' says Samuel, beaming. 'How's he doing?' he asks, addressing Rajjo.

'He seems fine. He is doing his school work well. Of course, he misses playing games like his friends do. However, we have been walking every evening. He likes open spaces so we do our walks in a garden.'

'Very good. Exercise is good for you, Kake.'

Kake shows his approval by nodding vigorously.

'How much longer, you feel, before he can walk?' Rajjo asks. Dr Singh inhales deeply. 'He is doing well and you are really giving him very good care. However, he will need a couple of years before he can walk.'

'A couple of years!' Rajjo's face falls.

'Rajjo-ji, he will walk only if you give him courage. So keep hoping and also give him hope.'

'Yes,' she says, wiping her eyes.

When he is done examining Kake, Samuel says, 'You are looking good, Kake!' He faces Rajjo. 'Give him his medicines regularly and make sure you go for your walks every evening. I will massage your legs now, Kake, and you can go home when I am done, okay?'

Kake smiles.

April 1919

Vinodini leans back in her chair and says, 'I am done. I have no energy and no will anymore. How many more people will die on our beds? How many more injured and bleeding will come in?'

Samuel holds her hands in his own. 'Calm down, Vinodini,' he says. 'We are doing all we can and more. As far as I know, all wounded people are now being cared for and no more are coming in. And we will save many, even if our resources are less, as long as we have our will and courage. I feel you should sleep a while now and come back refreshed. I myself will close my eyes briefly and go back.'

Vinodini agrees and closes her eyes. However, Samuel lies awake in his chair. When he does close his eyes, he sees gruesome images of mauled and bleeding bodies. He sees lines of corpses and piles of bleeding humans.

'How can anyone indulge in such savagery? How can he open fire on human beings? So cruel!'

A week passes by before even a semblance of normalcy comes back. Samuel is in his office when a man comes carrying a message from Yograj Singh. Samuel's week has been so harrowing even Kake has escaped his memory. Yograj Singh's message has a sense of urgency: he calls Samuel home. Samuel decides he will go.

Yograj's home is an old haveli housing a large family of uncles and cousins. A young man, possibly a nephew, gives Samuel a chair in an open veranda. When Yograj comes, he is speechless.

'Yograj-ji, where is Kake? And Rajjo-ji? Is all well?' Samuel asks.

'Kake and Rajjo were in Jallianwala on Baisakhi,' Yograj says and breaks down.

When he can finally speak, he says, 'Jallianwala was where Rajjo and Kake would go for a walk every day. Kake liked walking in Jallianwala. Before Baisakhi, Dyer had imposed a curfew. I was worried Jallianwala may be crowded on Baisakhi. However, Rajjo said, "Kake will enjoy himself. We will be careful, in one corner away from everyone." My guess was our local police would be used in chasing people away which was already scary. I was worried, especially because of Kucha Kurrichhan.'

'Kucha Kurrichhan?'

'Yes, an English memsahib was walking somewhere near Kucha Kurrichhan—she was from a church—and some of our people pounced on her. She could have been killed. Luckily, she was saved, again by our own people, and given refuge in a safe place. However, when Dyer was informed, he was so angry we knew he would plan his revenge. We knew he would impose a curfew. However, no one could imagine he would kill people mercilessly giving no warning,' Yograj says.

Samuel is surprised by how composed Yograj is, while speaking of Jallianwala. How calm. As if reading Samuel's mind, Yograj pauses and says, 'Kake!' and breaks down crying. Samuel is helpless and has no words of solace for Yograj.

Since his dada-ji died, Samuel has never been inside a church. He is awkward; he has no idea why he came here. Some force from inside him, working unconsciously, has dragged him here. He finds a place in a back pew and closes his eyes. He is all alone so when he hears someone coming, he is surprised.

Reverend Ross looks down and says, 'Why! Fancy seeing you here. I would have never—' A look of hopelessness in Samuel's eyes makes him pause.

'Are you well, Dr Singh?' he asks.

Samuel can find no answer. 'I am vanquished,' he says, finally.

'Vanquished?'

'Yes, vanquished by your God. I give up. I believed we have agency, we have power. No! We are powerless and unavailing.'

'Did you lose somebody?' Graham asks, placing a hand on Samuel's shoulder.

'Yes, someone I was caring for and helping recover from a crippling disease. A child who had a whole life ahead of him.'

'And?'

'And? I was hoping he would walk, Graham. I was doing all I could. Of course, one knows success in such endeavours is never assured. One can only hope for success and prepare for failure. However, how can one prepare for failure if one has no idea how one can fail? If he could never walk even when I had done all I could medically, I would say I have failed and would have been equanimous in my failure. No, here I am doing all I can and am approaching my goal inch by inch, and suddenly he is gone. Someone fires a gun and kills him. Which makes no sense!'

He pauses and adds, 'I was eleven years old when I asked God for his help. Someone I loved dearly was dying and I prayed for him. For nine whole days, I prayed. My prayers were useless. My loved one died and alongside him God died for me. I became a man of science, believed in science and looked for hope in science. Now, I see no hope—in religion or in science, in belief or in reason. I can see only an absurd face mocking me.'

19. R

Ajita was seething as he paced up and down the hall. Japa sat, quietly waiting; she knew he would only speak when he wanted to.

'It is unbelievable,' he said, finally, 'that Gautama should do this. He told us he would not meet the king but then the moment we get back, we find out that is exactly what he did. This kind of duplicity is unacceptable.'

'Maybe some developments took place that you don't know of?' said Japa, tentatively.

'Such as what?'

'I don't know. I am suggesting that you may be too hasty in judging him. Maybe the king himself went to meet him. And, Gautama had told you, he was willing to meet the king like he would meet anyone else. So, maybe it wasn't duplicitous at all.'

'That is a naive view. I am positive that Gautama had hidden motives all along, and he planned this in advance. Now he has a mighty king as his disciple—a disciple who will be willing to do his bidding.'

'So what, Ajita? Why do you feel upset about that? All six of you who met the king decided you did not want him as a disciple. You planned it and spoke to him in such a way that it would be evident and he would not want to have anything to do with any of you. And then when someone does take him as a disciple, you get upset about it? That does not make any sense.'

'Japa, the issue is of unity. We had pledged that we would act as one and Gautama went back on that.'

'I don't see it that way. If you thought the king's backing would be beneficial, you could have had him as a disciple too, but you did not want that. The Buddha is happy to have the king as his disciple. The king is happy being a Buddhist. What is the issue?'

Ajita did not say anything but he did not look pleased.

'Think about it, Ajita,' said Japa. 'The king wanted to meet all of you because he genuinely needed advice on handling his own wounded self. He was so blinded by ambition that he caused the death of his own family. He may have become king, but he most likely found it difficult to live with his guilt. I believe he summoned you all in the hope that one of you could give him the salve he needed to alleviate his pain. In Buddha he may have found that much needed absolution. It is not the case of the sage seeking the king; instead it is the king who wanted the sage to guide him.'

'So you believe that Gautama met the king as he would a common individual?'

'Yes, I think the king went to him to seek his guidance. I also feel that in choosing the Buddha as his guide, the king did the best he could have.'

Ajita gazed at Japa in shock and said, 'What!'

'Yes, Ajita. I got a chance to listen to him speak a few months ago when he was visiting Vaishali. I went with a completely open mind to listen to him and sat, as one among so many, in that huge audience. But when he spoke, I felt the audience vanish. I felt I was alone with him and he was speaking only to me. Listening to him speak filled me with a feeling of calm and peace that I have not felt in decades.'

'But why did you not tell me about it?'

'This was when you had gone to Champa. I thought of telling you when you came back, but then I hesitated. You won't admit it, but I know you have an issue with him. It is something close to envy; that's how I see it, at least. So, I thought it best not to upset you by telling you about it.'

'I can't believe you can say this!' said Ajita, agitatedly.

'I say this because while you may find it unpalatable, deep down you know that I am not lying. It is only with the Buddha though that I find you to be like this. The poise and the confidence that you usually exude fades away when you talk about him. It may be that you know he possesses something you don't. If I have to guess what that is, I would say it is the Buddha's innate ability to instil a sense of peace in his disciples. People find his philosophy to be accessible. That is not the kind of philosophy you put out. People feel intimidated by what you put out as philosophy, they find it difficult to follow. And the bits that they can follow give them no hope of salvation. Common folk look to people like you to show them something beyond all this gloom, but you withhold even the slightest indication of hope. You insist that it will all end with this one life,' said Japa.

'I have to be honest with myself. I follow the logic of my system and let it take me along. If the conclusion it leads me to is dismal and gloomy, as you say, then so be it. I am not going to put up illusions that people can amuse themselves with, just to help them cope with gloom. I find optimism in the act of living, in the challenges we take up and deal with successfully, in going about the business of life. My view of life is not gloomy and dismal. That is one aspect of it but that is accompanied by light and lightness. In fact, what I find unacceptable about Gautama and his ilk is that they make too much, to begin with, about life as inescapably sad and desolate and then they suggest ways to find hope and salvation.'

'It is not so much what you say, Ajita,' said Japa, 'but the agitation is palpable in the way it is being said. I want you to pay attention to that and find out its cause.'

Ajita looked at Japa closely. In spite of all the defence he had put up, he knew Japa had touched upon something deep.

Autumn – 486

It meant a lot to get invited to the Vidwat Sabha in Kashi—a symposium that took place only once in a decade. Only the most well-known minds got invitations to speak and debate at this symposium. The Kashi Vidwat Sabha was the biggest and most esteemed of all such sabhas and an invitation to attend it was an acknowledgement of the invitee's eminence. But Ajita's joy on getting invited was dampened because Japa's comments had made a deep indentation on his mind and he had become somewhat negative in his thinking. But the Sabha was still six weeks away and Ajita hoped that by then he would be able to put those comments behind him.

Japa was genuinely happy to know that he had been invited to the Kashi symposium.

'It is such a distinction to be invited to something as big as this Sabha, Ajita. You don't even have to win; it is enough to just be invited to an event of this kind,' she said, happily.

'So you think I may not win any debate?' Ajita asked.

'You know I didn't mean that. You should know now that you have found a place amongst the best and the wisest that this land can boast of. And when you occupy that exalted position, you should not be as childish as this.'

'I know,' said Ajita, sheepishly, 'I am being stupid.'

'I wish I could come to Kashi too. But the shop needs me most in this season, with all the big festivals coming up. I just won't be able to get away.'

'I so want you to come with me, Japa. But I know you can't, so I will not insist.'

'I will be by you, Ajita—in the symposium, when you talk, when you debate and defeat the opponents. I will also be with you when you go into the city to take in its sights, sounds and smells,' Japa said with a delighted laugh.

Ajita had no time to settle in. All he had managed was a night's sleep and now he was off to the opening function of the Vidwat Sabha. On his way to the venue, he managed to get a few glimpses of the fascinating city and decided he would stay back and get to know Kashi in its depths post the symposium.

The Vidwat Sabha was to last a whole week and a demanding schedule lay ahead of all of them. Two days of talks had been scheduled ahead of five days of debates. Ajita was to talk on the second day. Despite his calm disposition, he was pleased to have been asked to speak, because only the best of the best could hope to give a talk in this Sabha. When he got up to the podium and saw the big audience, he somehow became calm and felt totally in command. His ideas flowed like the Ganges did just outside the venue and they flowed deep. A section of the audience, not acquainted with Ajita's thought, had come expecting a banal talk lacking in philosophical sophistication, but when he spoke, he held them spellbound. It was evident that he was fully knowledgeable about the systems of philosophy that he chose to attack. He had delved into the subtleties and nuances of these systems and his elenchus was so elegantly fashioned that it left the sceptics stunned. Many in the audience knew that they had witnessed something momentous.

Buoyed by the success of his talk, Ajita went into the debating sessions high in confidence. One by one, he debated and decimated five opponents with such ease that it seemed he was unstoppable. It was as much his intellectual capability as the fact that his philosophical position was completely novel that helped him outdo his opponents.

Having won five debates, Ajita was now in the final. He was now up against Nityananda, a Mimamsaka who, in fact, lived in Kashi and had a huge following in the city. To debate him was a daunting task in itself but to do it in Kashi, his hometown, was deeply disquieting.

Nityananda's height did not quite match his eminence; he was a small individual. But when he began speaking, Ajita knew immediately that this was no insignifcant opponent and that it would not be an easy debate to win.

A good fifty minutes into the debate, Ajita and Nityananda had moved into the nucleus of the debate and took up the fundamental issue of what it was to know and what made knowledge possible. Nityananda took up a position on modes of knowledge that he called non-factual and on the impossibility of establishing its validity by usual human means. He went on to claim the limitations of language in establishing such claims. Instead, he said, one must seek to show evidence of the negations of such claims and the inability to do so should be thought of as equivalent to being the validity of the claim. It was just the kind of muddle-headed logic that Ajita detested but even he had to admit that this was possibly the only time that he had seen muddle-headeness so deftly cloaked in lucidity. In the beginning, he wasn't confident about which end of the tangled mess he should unknot. He went about his task slowly, but then the knot began to show signs of loosening and he became confident. It was still an uphill task but he stayed steadfast and ultimately won the debate.

Ajita was ecstatic. This was his life's pinnacle, the apex, but often such dizzying exultation is followed by a feeling of emptiness, and Ajita felt it even as he was getting up to leave the podium.

People came up to him and wanted to speak with him, but all Ajita wanted to do was spend some time by himself. The king of Kashi had invited all the guests of the Sabha to a magnificent feast that night. Ajita excused himself and walked out to find a secluded spot to settle down by the Ganges.

The sun was not yet close to setting but the late autumn evening was cool enough to be enjoyable. He watched a few boys at a distance, diving out of a boat to swim in the Ganges. It must be cold, he thought, but then his thoughts went back to his own childhood when he and his mates would splash about in the pond even in the coldest months. Even at this distance, Ajita could see only joy on the boys' faces. He longed to be like them, happy and with no anxiety. He decided to climb down and move close to the bank. As made his way, his eyes fell on a woman so old that she was bent with age. The old woman's eyes seemed to speak of loss and pain. The old woman seemed to convey a hopelessness that touched something deep inside Ajita. He moved away and looked up to see a dead body being laid on a pile of wood. A young man standing by him with a pot in his hand, most likely the dead man's son, had a look of devastation on his face that seemed to be speaking the same language as that of the old woman's eyes. Feeling helpless himself, Ajita sat down and looked at the Ganges. In Kashi the Ganges did not just flow. It was the city that moved and in its vast motions took the mass of people along. The Ganges was an unmoving witness and, as Ajita noted, maybe even an unmoved witness.

The spot that Ajita occupied at that moment was the dividing line between the tumult and intensity that was Kashi and the stillness that was the Ganges—that twilight zone that evokes doubt and questioning. Ajita had won the debate in the Vidwat Sabha and it was his life's biggest moment, no doubt. But as he sat by the banks of the Ganges, Ajita felt that moment belonged to the tumultous activity of Kashi. The Ganges had its own time-keeping, and, in that estimate, the Sabha, the debate and the win all dissolved into nothing.

'What have I achieved? Nothing, absolutely nothing,' thought Ajita. 'My philosophy is just a game. Today's win in the Sabha only tells me that I am good at playing this game, that is all. Nothing I have done touches the lives of people—not the boy's joy as he was diving into the Ganges today and definitely not the woman's, whose depth of pain I could not even fathom. I thought I was doing something valuable in setting up a system of thought committed to the actual and the given but who can deny that the joy and sadness, elation and dejection that people feel is also in the domain of the given. And I don't even come close to talking about any of this. The Mimamsakas and the Samkhyayikas, the Buddhists and Jains focus on the human subject and they talk to them about ultimate goals, salvation, utopia and all that. These may be myths—I have exhausted myself, shouting about that all the time—but it is these myths that give people hope. This is exactly what Makkhali was telling me. I did not pay heed to it because I thought, at that time, that I wanted to follow the path of knowledge alone, even if that knowledge was not easy to digest. But that is not what people want. They don't want to be told that this is the only life they have; that they should not expect a god to save them; that, to begin with, this god will have nothing to save because this body will die and decay and the soul is a falsehood; that one's good actions may not always yield good outcomes and bad actions may not be punished. Who is going to find any of this useful in getting any solace? The common folk, weighed down by despondency and desolation, seek some hope they can live by. If I take away even that hope, what do I leave them with?'

The sun was going down in the distance. Ajita got up. He made his way to the palace to attend the night of festivity. In this moment, that was the last thing he wanted to do but he knew he could not excuse himself.

The king of Kashi and his people had gone all out to make the evening special. The function was held on the imposing lawns of the palace which was by the Ganges. The whole place was lit up by what looked like a thousand lamps and the effect was beautiful. Having won the debate, Ajita was the guest-in-demand that evening. But having exhausted himself with the unending polite exchanges, Ajita decided to find a place to sit down and be on his own. He chose a spot that was hidden by a tall bush, so he would not be visible to too many people. But, in a little while, he could see someone coming his way. It was an old man, small and bent, walking with a stick in his hand.

He sat down by Ajita's side and said, 'I could not find you and then someone told me he had seen you come this way. I wanted to talk to you.'

'I see. Well, I am Ajita.'

'Indeed, I know that. I was in the audience today when you debated my son and also when you spoke on the second day of the Sabha.'

'Son? Do you mean Nityananda?' Ajita was confused.

'Yes, he is my son. My name is Jeevananda.'

'Jeevananda? The famous Mimamsaka?'

The old man laughed aloud. 'It has been a long time now since I was anything like famous,' he said.

'How amazing! I apologise that I could not identify you. You see, we met a long time ago when I was a student. I was a student of Vishwanatha of Kamboja.'

'Yes, now that you say it, it all comes back. I went to conduct some yajna that he wanted me to teach him. So, you also studied with a Mimamsaka?'

'Yes, but close to the completion of my studies, I became disenchanted with what he was teaching me. And once I was done with my studies, I did not continue with Mimamsa myself. I decided to follow my own path.'

'And you went on to set up this system of philosophy that we now know you by! That is quite an achievement. Nothing Vishwanatha and I did can come close to it,' said Jeevananda.

Ajita smiled. 'I am happy that someone as famous as you is saying this. But my achievements, in actuality, do not add up to much.'

'I don't believe that,' said Jeevananda. 'People like me could only follow systems and schools. I took what was passed on to me by my uncle and blindly followed it all my life. Yes, it seemed a lot like knowledge, but, in fact, I was only echoing what had been said. I did not know and I was not taught that philosophy is about making one's own investigations, asking one's own questions. Yes, textual testimony is also a valid means of knowledge but not the only one. Without an examination of facts and analysis, one cannot accept anything as knowledge.'

Ajita could say nothing. He simply watched in awe—that one of the most famous minds of his age was saying this was unimaginable.

Jeevananda continued, 'And what of the knowledge that was handed down to me? What use was it? Its attempt was to conceal, not to illumine. That knowledge was a compilation of what seemed like meaningful statements about things that did not exist and so, in my opinion now, these statements too have no meaning.'

Ajita was quite speechless, when Jeevananda spoke again. 'Ajita, I am old and unable to do yajnas. I have no students, no disciples. I am on my own having handed it all to my son. My body is not what it used to be but my mind is still active and I have plenty of time to think. It is inevitable that such questions should visit me now. These doubts should have, ideally, come to me in my youth but, as a young man, I was the total image of confidence. I had such vanity and conceit in the knowledge that I possessed that I did not let the slightest doubt affect me. When youth left me, so did its companions: vanity and conceit. Instead, it is self-doubt that has come to stay with me now and I pass my days and nights in its company. Not too long ago, a young nephew of mine told me about you. He had attended a talk by you and was completely taken with it. And then I got to know about this talk at the Vidwat Sabha and came to assess you myself. And I am glad I could listen to you myself.'

Ajita had been silent all this while because he was soaking in all that Jeevananda was saying.

'I cannot tell you how much this means to me. I feel genuinely humbled,' he said at last.

'Ajita, you have been blessed with scepticism, intelligence and wisdom. Anyone who wishes to build a philosophical system ought to have these. But, in addition, I can see that you have the boldness and the mettle that is needed to follow the path that you have chosen. I can imagine that, at times, you may feel diffident and unconvinced about what you have built. But don't give up. Keep at this and you will leave behind something valuable.'

20. U

April 1317

Kami sits cross-legged on the rock, her lower garment spread across her lap perfectly to hold the berries she has gathered today. A beatific smile spreads across her face as she assesses her loot. She likes afternoons the most, even when it is hot, for that is the time she spends with her friends, playing games, climbing trees or swimming in the river. On most other occasions, there is a lot of work to be done at home and no time for anything else. It is the same with her friends. Biji and Ragini work at home, while Rajan and Karma are engaged with all the reading and writing they have to do. At times Kami feels it is good that she is a girl—she does not think that she has it in her to spend the kind of time Karma does with his reading.

However, she knows Karma is not an ordinary boy. His commitment to learning is great and he is clear that he wants to be a learned man. He has already shown a lot of promise and the fact that people have faith in his abilities makes him want to work harder. In fact, he works so hard that there are times he does not come down to play with his friends in the afternoons.

'Why does Karma want to tie down his mind to books?' Kami wonders. 'When I work, whether it is cooking the vegetables, grinding the rice or washing the floor, I still have my mind free to think of what I want. Karma, meanwhile, is so involved in his books that he forgets all else.'

Kami has a very active mind and is always eager to get to the why and how of things: Why does milk boil and flow all over when water does not? How do worms find their way into a closed jar of grains? How does a newborn calf stand on its feet so soon after it is born?

Kami is very eager to know, to learn. However, it is not bookish knowledge that will do for her, it is the light of her own experience. This is not something she knows; it is only something she does in practice.

Kami was married at the age of two to three-year-old Karma—a wedding ceremony of which neither of them has the faintest memory. Karma's father was a renowned acharya, Acharya Jnanadeva, and that was how Karma's name came to be Karmadeva. Kami's father was beside himself with joy when, thanks to a relative who mediated the proposal, Kami was blessed to be married to the acharya's son. Kami's mother was worried that the boy and his parents lived so far away. She felt it may be better to find a match for Kami in their village. However, Kami's father had decided and there was no way to change his mind. Kami's mother's only consolation was that Kami was to stay with them till she came of age. So it was only when she was thirteen that she moved in with her in-laws.

Kami is happy in her new home; she has a good friend in Karma and a new mother in Ahalya, her mother-in-law. Ahalya had wanted a baby girl after her firstborn was a boy. However, she had to abandon the idea of having a baby after three miscarriages. She showers Kami with all the love she can and is happy that Kami loves her back.

It is only her father-in-law that Kami is somewhat intimidated by. He is a very respected person in the village and a great scholar—overall a formidable personality. A part of that image is created by deliberately maintaining a distance from people, especially from those inferior in class, caste or age. He hardly ever addresses Kami directly and, on the few occasions when he has to, he does so by calling her as she was originally named—Kamalakshi.

Meanwhile, Ahalya is sensitive to the fact that Kami is only a child. She plans the day's work in a manner that Kami has time to rest, play or simply idle. Ahalya is also aware of Jnanadeva's short temper and takes all the effort needed to shield Kami from those fits of rage. On those two or three occasions when Kami has had to bear the force of Jnanadeva's wrath, Ahalya lost no time in taking Kami into her arms and comforting her, imploring Jnanadeva to exercise restraint. Ahalya had herself come to live in this home when she was barely twelve and her memory of her own experiences from that time helps her comprehend what Kami may be experiencing. She does all that is possible to ease Kami's life in the marital home.

When Kami came to live with them as a thirteen-year-old, Ahalya knew that she was not yet ready to explore the physical dimensions of her relationship with Karma, even as she was aware that Karma himself, not yet fifteen, was hardly ready for it. However, Kami is now seventeen and Ahalya wonders whether she has kept Kami away from Karma for too long. Karma, who had, for years, been too engrossed in his work to let his mind wander, seems to be showing a special interest in Kami more recently, which makes Ahalya realise that they need to spend more time with each other now.

However, she worries that Kami is still childlike, her innocence written all over her face.

On the fifth day after the new moon every month, people from the village gather at Jnanadeva's home late in the evening to listen to him read from the *Srimad Bhagavatam* and provide his analysis of the text. Singing of bhajans and dancing follow these sermons and late in the night the villagers feast on the delectable sweet rice that Ahalya makes for them. Kami looks forward to these evenings and, even if Jnanadeva's sermons bore her sometimes, enjoys the singing and dancing. When she dances to the beat of the dhol she feels herself getting transported, as if she were in a trance of sorts. That happens to her only when she allows herself to enter the space of the dance completely. However, when she does experience that feeling she has a strange sense of her body. It feels light and ethereal, on the one hand, and on the other, she has the sense of being aware of every part of her body, leaving her with a very tangible feeling of its materiality.

Tonight, Kami has that feeling of distance and proximity, ethereality and materiality co-exisiting in her even more sharply. When the singing starts she is, as always, mesmerised by the dhol and starts moving to its beat. However, tonight the songs seem to speak directly to her as they narrate stories of Radha pining for her lover, Krishna.

My heart is heavy, my body aches for my Lord!
I am a patch of parched land waiting for the rain.
Love is no arrow, I know that
Yet my being is waiting to be pierced, Madhava.

When Jnanadeva talks of Radha's love for Krishna, he talks of it as the desire of the self to become one with the cosmic being, the Jivatma's yearning to merge into the Paramatma.

Kami can make no sense of this. What she can feel is the love Radha feels for Krishna. That for her is real.

She looks at Karma who is sitting next to his father, bare-chested as he always is for these prayer meetings, his eyes closed and totally immersed in the devotion that the singing and dancing evokes. He is sitting erect and his bare body shines in the light of the lamp next to him. The sacred thread hangs diagonally across his torso and, while she has always felt the thread to be silly, tonight it appears to be adding to his charm.

There is always a lot to do in the kitchen after the meeting is over and Kami likes that part the least. Tonight, however, she is not too bothered by the work. She is thinking of Karma as she finishes her chores in the kitchen and the work seems light compared with the weight of her desire. After she is done, she splashes some cold water on her face and heads towards her room. It is only over the last few months that she and Karma have a room to themselves. Karma is lying on a mat on the floor and, even in the dim light of the room, she can see he is lying on his stomach. She lies down next to him and lets her hands move down his back, slowly starting from his neck and moving down his spine and reaching his waist. His gentle breathing tells her that he is asleep and she hopes that her caress will awaken him. He stirs a bit and she holds her breath. It is not that their bodies have not been in close proximity before; yet tonight the closeness seems different. It feels as if they are being held together in an envelope of fire. The fire is lit only on one side, however. Karma stirs again, moves to his side and is fast asleep again.

Kami is still asleep the next morning when Karma leaves for his day's work. She opens her eyes, realises it is late and remembers that she has a lot to do in the kitchen. Ahalya is already hard at work when Kami gets there. She reminds Kami that the rice that had been soaked and dried earlier needs to be powdered. Kami settles down with the stone grinder in the veranda and gets to work. Jnanadeva is also seated at the other end of the veranda. He has finished his work early and kept himself free for a friend who is to visit him. When his friend, Keshavacharya, arrives, Jnanadeva is very happy to see him. Kami has never seen him like this before.

When they have settled down and exchanged pleasantries, Keshavacharya says, 'I am happy we were able to meet. I am here only for two days and will then proceed to Sri Kshetra to live near the Jagannatha Temple for the next two years or more. Knowing the crowds of devotees the Jagannatha temple attracts, I will be able to make money if I spend some time there performing poojas. I made the effort to come here as there is something I needed to ask.'

'What is it?' asks Jnanadeva.

'Jnana, I have travelled cities and have spent time in places like Kashi and Gaya. However, Khilji, the emperor of Delhi, died last year and there has been a lot of chaos since his death. That is the reason I left Kashi and came back here. If we go to Sri Kshetra and work there for a few years, we can earn money to take care of everything till we are alive. In a few years, this land may also get affected by what is happening in the north. If we do not make money now, we will regret it later.'

'Go to Jagannath or Kashi or wherever, Keshava. Leave me alone. I have no desire to make money. I was never swayed by worldly desires.'

'Jnana, it is not worldly desires that are making me do this! We need to be prepared for the years when we are old.'

'Old age worries me too. However, I have Karma to take care of me and Ahalya,' says Jnanadeva.

Despite his words, Keshavacharya can see that Jnanadeva is yielding a bit.

'And where will Karma make his living? Times are changing, Jnana, and we will repent later if we don't change with them.'

'Keshava, even if I were to want to leave I cannot move the idol of the Lord from my home. It has to remain here and I have to perform the special pooja for the Lord on Janma Ashtami. How can I leave my home then?'

'All right. Begin by coming to Sri Kshetra for a few months and come back home for Janma Ashtami. That way the Lord can stay here and take care of things here. Janma Ashtami is less than five months away. That is not a long time.'

Jnanadeva looks at Keshavacharya for a bit and says hesitatingly, 'Karma learns from me . . . '

'Bring Karma along. We will benefit by having him there. He will be a real help.'

Keshavacharya sees that his friend is close to making a decision and adds, 'Jnana, I am saying this for the good of everyone. It is not a decision we will regret. Let's leave early on Friday morning. The days are getting hot . . . '

Kami has been following the conversation disinterestedly till almost the end. It is only when Karma's name is mentioned that she pays close attention. When Keshavacharya talks of leaving on Friday, she realises how fast everything is moving.

'Karma is going away in two days' time and he will be away for months,' she thinks, as a drop of tear falls from her eye and settles down on the rice powder.

By the evening, Kami is inconsolable, while Karma and Ahalya try in vain to soothe her. Ahalya takes her in her arms and in the warmth of her embrace Kami finds some peace.

'He is not going away forever, my child. Karma will be back before Janma Ashtami. And I am here. We will both have a lot to do together.'

Later that night, Kami holds Karma tightly as she lies by his side. She finds Karma is awake tonight—as awake as one can be. The night is magical: their lovemaking has none of the gawkishness that revealed itself on the few earlier occasions. Tonight, their rhythm matches perfectly to the beat.

Tired and sweaty after their exertions, Karma goes to sleep almost immediately. Kami, however, lies in bed still relishing the taste the night has left on her lips. She came close to experiencing ecstasy tonight—she knows that it was her body that felt it. Now when she feels the glow of the aftermath, it is still all that the body is feeling. She moves her fingers over the length of her body, drawing imaginary lines of confinement to contain all that feeling within herself. She does not want to think of Karma leaving her, she does not want to think of the months of separation. Tonight, she only wants one thing: to keep the feeling of the night to herself.

'When is Janma Ashtami?' she asks Karma when he awakes the next day.

'Five months away. The rains will still be here at that time.'

'Ma said so too. I can't get a sense of how long that is.'

That night Karma gives Kami two cloth bags. One is clearly empty and the other feels heavy in her hand.

'What is in this?' she asks.

'Open it,' he says.

'Tamarind seeds?' she says, examining the contents. 'What is this for?'

'This bag has as many seeds in it as the days to Janma Ashtami from now. Take one seed a day from this bag and keep it in the empty bag. It will be a way to keep track of when I will be back.'

'There seem to be so many tamarind seeds,' says Kami, her voice betraying the sinking feeling in the pit of her stomach.

The slow transfer of the tamarind seeds from one bag to another, over the past two months, has been made even more intolerable by the mad heat. It is late afternoon and Kami is sitting in the veranda of her home. She has stopped going down to the river to play with her friends. She does not climb trees with them either. Since she is alone at home with Ahalya, she sleeps in her mother-in-law's room at night. However, she does not lie down close to her and hold her as she did before. She is no longer a child, she is a woman.

She is lost somewhere in the processes of her mind when she feels a raindrop gently prodding her back to the world. She looks at the sky to see that it is dark.

'Rain!' she says, excitedly. The rain comes down heavily. Kami walks into the rain, allowing her body to be drenched by it. The heat and grime of the past two months seem to have settled in every pore of her body and she wants the showers to soak her being and cool it down.

Who can feel the rain, Madhava?

Who is wet with the water? Who is the one drenched to the skin?

My body, Madhava, my body!

The next morning Ahalya's brother comes to meet them. He lives in a village not too far away and drops by once every few months. He is older than Ahalya and she always treats him with a lot of respect.

This time he seems to have something very definite to say. 'Jnanadeva did not even think of asking me once before going off to Jagannatha. When he is not here, I am responsible for the safety of this home,' he says, somewhat annoyed.

'He wanted to. He had no time. They had to leave very soon,' Ahalya stammers.

'No good comes from making this kind of haste, Ahalya. His friend, Keshava, is not someone I hold in high regard. Neither does Jnanadeva, in fact. How did he leave only on the basis of Keshava's advice?'

Ahalya remains silent.

Her brother goes on: 'These are very bad times. There are big wars going on in the north. The soldiers of the defeated armies are escaping the battlefield and coming down here to loot and rob people. Every day there is news of people being attacked or even killed.'

Ahalya notices the look of fright on Kami's face. She asks after her brother's family and manages to divert the conversation.

When they are alone later, Kami asks Ahalya, 'Will they be safe? Will they come back before Janma Ashtami?'

Ahalya holds her close. 'Don't worry. They will come back safely. Lord Jagannatha will take care of them.'

Kami remembers that Ahalya had said the same thing to her brother: 'Lord Jagannatha will take care of them.' To which her brother had replied, 'I am worried if there is anyone to take care of the Lord himself. I have been hearing stories of how enemies are planning to attack Sri Kshetra and raid the temple's coffers. And if they do that, no one in that town is safe.'

That night as Kami takes the bag of tamarind seeds in her hand for her nightly task of transferring a seed from one bag to the other, it slips from her hand and falls down, scattering all the seeds on the floor. She breaks down crying: 'How did this happen? What does this mean? Lord, take care of my Karma.'

She is not able to sleep for a long time after this incident and when she finally does, she has a long, terrifying dream. She sees soldiers on horseback and men on foot chasing people with spears. She sees Karma being chased by two men brandishing swords. She falls at their feet begging them to spare his life. Jnanadeva is sitting at the back watching this whole scene indifferently. He has people sitting at his feet listening to his sermon. She can hear a dhol from behind. She looks to see that it is a procession carrying a dead body. Karma is dead.

Kami is screaming.

'Kami, Kami!' She hears Ahalya's voice and awakes, realising that it was a dream. She holds Ahalya and sobs inconsolably.

Many days go by. Kami does not know how many. She has stopped keeping track of time with the tamarind seeds. She is resigned to her fate. She believes now that whatever has to happen will happen. Nothing can change it. Lord Jagannatha's chariot moves inexorably, nothing can stop it. Strangely, she feels calm in her resignation. She still misses Karma terribly. She still worries that he may never come back. The difference is that she does not let her mind dwell on it.

The rains are still here. Kami sits in the veranda and watches the rain come down, listless and enervated. She does not feel like getting wet.

One day, as she looks down the road, she sees, in what is something of a haze, a cart coming towards their home. As it comes closer, she sees a man get down from the moving cart and sprint towards her. She still cannot see clearly in the rain who it is. He comes closer. Her heart skips a beat when she sees it is Karma.

21. S

Winter – 486

Ratna and Tuli had returned that morning after a week-long trip. 'Did you have a good time?' Ajita wanted to know.

'You know how fond we are of your mother, her home and everything around there. We had a very good time,' replied Ratna.

'When I am there, I don't feel like I want to come back,' Tuli told Ajita. 'I find it very calming.'

'How are my mother and uncle?'

'Your uncle and the family are all fine. But I am worried about your mother, Ajita,' replied Ratna.

'Why? Tell me, what happened to her?'

'Nothing in particular. But your mother did look weak and pale. Your uncle told me that her cough can become worrying.'

'I have been feeling the need to go there and take care of her. I cannot delay it any longer.'

'I don't think you need to do anything that urgently,' Tuli added.

'I believe I have to. I have not gone there to meet her for over a year now. There will be no demand from her ever but I cannot treat my own mother like that. I will leave tomorrow and will be with her for a week. The mountain air and a change of pace will do me good too.'

'I agree that you have been overworked for quite a while now and you need to take a break,' agreed Ratna.

On the way up the mountain where Dhvani lived, Ajita felt the quality of the air change. With every breath, he felt calmer and more relaxed. He halted halfway at a pond to get a drink of water and it felt unlike anything he had ever had before. He knew too well that it had to do with how overworked he had been and how much of a toll that had taken on him. He decided that he would put away all work for the time he would be here.

Dhvani looked weak but her health, on careful examination, did not appear too bad to Ajita. He gave her a tonic made from an herb that he knew would help her regain her energy. He had another medicine which he knew could cure her cough. Her condition did not worry him.

That Ajita had come to be with her worked more effectively for Dhvani than any herb or medicine and, in about a week, the colour returned to her face, her health improved and her energy returned. But by then, Ajita had begun to enjoy the bucolic life and he decided to continue to be there for a while longer. He had much to talk to Dhvani about—about Japa, in particular. Dhvani wanted to know why they did not want to get married but did not make any hue and cry about the fact that they were not.

'When you come here next, why don't you bring her along? I would like to meet her.'

'And I would like to bring her. But Japa cannot leave her work and come for long. We will plan it, though, and try for a quick trip.'

'I want to meet her once before I die.'

'Why do you talk of dying?'

'I am getting old, Aju. How much longer will I live?'

Ajita looked at her. 'Maye, you know how much I love you. I cannot let you go.'

'You will have to. And did you not talk to your father and me about the inevitability of death and about death being the end of everything? I thought you would accept the fact of my death too.'

'Maye, when I talk like that I am being the thinker that I am for the larger public. I believe all that from the depth of my being but even then, when I am talking in front of people, I feel I am performing. I may believe the truth of death but my unmoved acceptance of it may be a performance that I put up for them. I felt it very forcefully when Tath died. I never could really accept it. Why would it be different with you? It will be even more difficult, if anything.'

Dhvani held him tight. 'You are and will ever remain my little one, no matter how renowned you become.'

'I eagerly awaited your return,' Japa told Ajita, 'but, looking at you now, I feel you could have extended your time there. You have benefitted hugely from your holiday. You look healthier and more at peace.'

'I loved being there but then, after a fortnight, I needed to get back—to you, to our life here and to the beautiful city we live in.'

Japa held him tight. 'I really would not have managed to be without you much longer.'

Over dinner, Ajita talked to Japa about Dhvani. 'I do hope I get more time with her. My mother talked about dying but I don't think I can ever be prepared for it.'

'Your mother will not die now, Ajita. There will be a time for that when you will be more prepared. Don't worry about it now.'

'By the way,' Ajita interjected, in an attempt to change the mood of the evening, 'on my journey back home, I went back to thinking about the tricky problem of ethical action that Gautama had pointed out. I had been thinking about it from the time he talked to me about it. But I have been too occupied for a while now and haven't had the time to give it much thought. On the long journey back, I had a lot of time to think about it carefully. I have arrived at a way of looking at the whole matter from a very different point of view. I am not certain that it will appeal to many people. But I am now convinced that it may be the correct way to think about the ethical problem.'

'I am eager to hear your reply. Tell me.'

'If you remember, Gautama had argued that if a doctrine or an ideology can offer no ultimate goal for a follower then it will be doomed. The ideology, Gautama argued, will have to invoke God, heaven, the afterlife or karma or any other ultimate goal due to which people following that ideology will be motivated to act with good intention. If I offer them nothing, why would they perform work in a good and ethical manner, Gautama wanted to know. I found that I had no quick and ready way out of the conundrum. But when I got time to think through it carefully, it occurred to me that the idea of 'good action' may be the problematic feature and I decided to look at that attentively. The notion of good or ethical cannot be, according to me, inflicted on a mode of action externally but the motivation for the act ought to be determined internally.'

He continued, 'Let me take an example. Imagine a young man telling a friend, "You know, I very much want to come with you to the dance tonight but my old and ill mother will need to be taken care of." For the young man, what would be the right thing to do? To remain at home to take care of the ailing mother or to go to the dancing girl? If we approach the whole thing from the point of view of external morality then we would definitely feel that the young man ought to remain at home and take care of the old mother. In that externally validated view, the act of taking care of a mother will get rewarded and the fact that it will get rewarded will make it "good". But if we give up on the idea of a reward or an externally inflicted ethic then "taking care of the mother" or "going to the dancing girl" become equally acceptable. The man will now know that no virtue will derive from one action nor will any crime be committed by doing the other. The young man will decide knowing that the two are on par. In life, we often find that we are at a critical point where our action will be determined by a choice that we make. In exerting our will to make that choice, we find the meaning of ethical and moral action.'

'I can't help laughing, Ajita,' Japa replied. 'A little while ago you were talking about your mother and how you love her. If your mother were ill you would be with her all the time—I have no doubt about that. But when you talk to the world you are a different Ajita. I don't know how you reconcile that Ajita with who you are.'

'Japa, I don't think I am trying to project an image to the world. My love for my mother cannot be the foundation of a whole morality. But examining and evaluating my own conduct can help in doing that. I do not think of my behaviour with my mother to be "good" nor do I do it for any external reward. More importantly, what I feel for my mother and how I am with her have to be perceived within the context of my conditioning. I am not doing it to gain a reward in a future heaven or in the afterlife. I am making a choice that would be more valuable to me.'

'And if you were to go to the dancing girl?'

'That would be my choice too and for which I ought not to fear any retribution. If I were to make that choice, it ought to be free of fear, guilt and culpability.'

'I have no idea whom you are talking about,' Ajita told Maitreya. 'Tell me all about him before you tell me what we ought to be doing.'

'I am amazed that you have not heard of Kutadanta, a well-known Brahmin yajnik and a rich, powerful landlord of a town called Khanumata in Magadha.'

'A Brahmin landlord? How did he come into that much wealth?' Ajita wanted to know.

'The munificence of the emperor of Magadha—the father of the current emperor. Kutadanta performed a magnificent yajna for the old emperor and he, very happy with him, gave him the village of Khanumata. Luckily for Kutadanta, Khanumata had a large amount of natural wealth and grew to become a town—a thriving town at that, frequented by every travelling merchant.'

'He may be a wealthy Brahmin. But why would we worry about him?'

'Other than being a great yajnik and a wealthy and powerful man, Kutadanta would like to become the protector of the ancient religion. The challenge that we have all collectively put forward to the old dharma convinced people like Kutadanta that they ought to exert their power more blatantly. Every yajna that he performed became bigger than the earlier one and with each performance he brought in more people to participate, and eventually gained control over them. With a huge following now, Kutadanta announced that an important yajna will be performed at the end of next week. We have learnt that about a nine hundred head of cattle will be brought and butchered at the planned yajna. Makkhali and Mahavir feel that every attempt to perform the yajna ought to be thwarted. They are planning an agitation and I think we would do well to join them.'

'Without a doubt, we will join them in the agitation,' reiterated Ajita. 'Forget the people doing the yajna but even the people allowing it to be done are barbaric.'

Taking a moment to think, Ajita continued, 'You mentioned Kutadanta had the old emperor backing him. But what about the new emperor?'

'We were all wondering about how the new regime and Kutadanta relate to each other. From what we know, the emperor did not have time up until now to think of a minor entity like Kutadanta. But with a mammoth yajna waiting to happen, even the emperor will have to take note. Anyway, we will go along with our Ajivika and Jain brethren and do all that we can to put a halt to the yajna.'

'Definitely. Let me know when we are leaving to go to Khanumata.'

'We will leave early next week, Ajita.'

Maitreya had been given complete charge by Makkhali and Mahavir to plan the agitation. Maitreya had been told by an informant that the food grain, the cattle and the other material required for the yajna would be delivered in advance and he had, therefore, planned that they would be in Khanumata for a three-day period before the ceremony. Even though a thriving town now, Khanumata did not feel like anything but an overgrown village to Ajita. In a larger city like Rajgriha, two or three hundred people could enter without attracting attention but that could not happen in a tiny place like Khanumata. Makkhali had indicated that they may have more than three hundred people joining the agitation. Maitreya decided that they would occupy the open land around Khanumata and without even entering the town they would block each entrance to it and, in that way, prevent any of the yajna material from entering the town. He had to arrange for food to be carried with them and, not knowing which way the agitation would go, he had to prepare to counter any violence. Only an expert planner like Maitreya could anticipate what would be needed and plan ahead.

Following the plan that Maitreya had detailed, a big group of people arrived in Khanumata and occupied the area beyond the boundary of the town. Maitreya had worked out in detail the way people were to be grouped to monitor each and every entrance to the town. People were trying to keep up the morale of the group in the face of uncertainty: one would play the flute, the other would beat a drum, a third would chant or dance while a fourth would play a melody on an ektara.

In time, a big delivery of rice and ghee arrived only to be greeted by a long human chain blocking the entrance to the town. The delivery men had no idea how to deal with it; they were not prepared for it at all. The crowd, though firm and determined, appeared to be friendly. The men tried to explain to them that they only wanted to deliver the material and leave and did not have anything to do with the yajna. But the crowd would not allow them. The deliberation went on for over an hour but the human chain would not break and did not allow them to enter the town. In the meantime, one more delivery arrived—a large wagon carrying cattle. But they were not allowed in either. The delivery men tried to appeal to the men guarding the entrance but they knew they were hugely outnumbered and would not be able to do anything to the crowd. Defeated, they decided to inform Kutadanta about it.

Kutadanta, meanwhile, had no clue that an agitation to halt the yajna had been planned; again, Maitreya had taken care to keep the information confined to their own people. Kutadanta did not know how to deal with the confounding information that the guard had brought him. He had a younger brother called Nirmitra who he called upon for help.

Nirmitra immediately gathered a few men, each armed with a weapon, and went to the town entrance where he found Maitreya and Makkhali at the head of a crowd that looked much bigger than what he had imagined. He knew he would have to negotiate and buy time to arrange for more men.

'I am Nirmitra, brother of Kutadanta. I have come here to tell you to leave and to allow our yajna to be conducted in the manner my brother planned it. It will benefit all of humanity—in fact, not humanity alone but every life form on earth. Why would you want to interfere with it? We want you to leave peacefully.'

Makkhali could not help laughing. 'Nirmitra, we come here in peace too. But we cannot allow you to do a yajna where you will, without any mercy, butcher nine hundred head of cattle. We know who will benefit from the yajna—not every life form, not all of humanity, not even your little town but a handful of people like you and your brother.'

'We do not want any trouble. We do not want violence but if violence were to happen you are to blame for not having paid heed to our warning. I plead with you once more to leave. I will give you time till tomorrow morning. But if you have not left by then we will have to force you all out of here.'

When Nirmitra left, Makkhali turned to Maitreya. 'We have to be on the alert now, Maitreya. They are only trying to buy time to prepare for the fight. We have to, in the meantime, be ready and not get intimidated by Nirmitra.'

All through the afternoon, Maitreya, with the help of a few loyal men, worked to build up the courage of the people. He arranged for a few men to keep a watch on every entrance of the town, to be certain that Nirmitra would not get the delivery men to complete their work quietly.

By evening, Maitreya felt happy that he had taken care of everything. But even he could not have been expected to know what would happen in a little while. Tired after the work of the afternoon, he lay down on a green patch to relax a bit, when Ajita came up to him.

'Wake up, Maitreya!'

'What happened, Ajita?'

'You won't believe what I am going to tell you! Gautama arrived a little while ago. Makkhali wanted me to fetch you immediately.'

'Gautama? Why did he come here?'

'Exactly what I wanted to know too.'

If the journey to Khanumata had been long and tiring, one could not have known that by looking at Gautama. He looked relaxed and calm.

'I will retire early tonight and I felt it would be good to talk to all of you now,' Gautama told them. 'I got to know about the yajna and your agitation. I knew it will lead to a confrontation. I do not want any violence taking place here and would prefer a peaceful negotiation with Kutadanta.'

'We have tried negotiating but were only threatened in return. But we are trying to wear him down and get him to agree to end the preparation for the yajna.'

'But why will he be worn down when he can attack you?'

'We will not be cowed down by violence,' Maitreya replied. 'We can counter the violence they inflict.'

'But where will all that lead? To injury? To death? That cannot be the way. Look, I am happy to talk to Kutadanta. I will let him know I want to meet him early tomorrow. And I am certain he will agree to talk to me.'

'But what will the negotiation be about?' Ajita wanted to know. 'We don't want him to do the yajna and we will agree to nothing but that.'

'Ajita, I think if I talk to Kutadanta he will agree to not go ahead with the yajna.'

The three men had nothing to offer in reply.

Gautama looked at all of them. 'I take it then that you agree. I will let Kutadanta know to come and meet me.'

Early next morning, Kutadanta came to meet Gautama on a hillock far from everyone where they could have a private meeting. Ajita, Makkhali and Maitreya waited eagerly to know what would come out of the meeting.

When they finally came down, Gautama announced, 'I am certain that you will all be happy to know that our brother Kutadanta agreed to not perform the yajna. He can comprehend the cruelty of the ritual practice and he told me he will never perform a yajna. He had one entreaty, though.

Having bought a lot of food in preparation for the yajna, he would like to invite our entire group to a meal. I thanked him for it and accepted the invitation on your behalf.'

'How did that happen?' Ajita turned to Maitreya, confounded.

'When Gautama talked of meeting Kutadanta, I knew what would happen, Ajita,' Maitreya replied. 'Kutadanta would have known that turning down Gautama would offend the emperor and he would certainly not want that. And Gautama knew that if he clinched the whole matter in full view of the people gathered here for the agitation it would mean a big win for him. And he achieved that!'

22. V

February 753

Oran finishes mopping the floor of the shack and goes out to rest under the tree. It has been a long day at work and he now wants to go home. Pandit Madhusudhan is sitting under the shade of the banyan tree a little distance away from him. He is busy taking stock of his day's earnings—the coins, the grains and fruits that come his way.

'We had a good day, Oran,' says Madhusudhan. 'Your share is also substantial.'

'We got a lot but what is so good about the day?' asks Oran.

'That is all there is to a day, Oran. When I earn enough money and food, I think of the day as good. What more do you want?'

'Pandit, I don't need to remind you that my job is much tougher than yours.'

'I am not denying that, Oran. But you are also much tougher than others. I remember that young fellow who had started work here two years ago and didn't last a week. I like the way you do your job. You keep your distance and you do it dispassionately.'

Oran does not say anything in reply.

'I should be going now. You will, of course, wait for Chena,' Madhusudhan says, getting up.

The sun is just about setting when Chena comes.

'You are luckier than me, Chena,' says Oran, as the man approaches. 'This place is so much busier in the day. I am sure you sleep through the nights. But then, it must be unpleasant here at night with all the wild animals roaming around.'

'I grew up in a forest, Oran, and the dark doesn't scare me. Sometimes people do come in the middle of the night when I am fast asleep. I hate to wake up then and get to work. But, if you want me to, I am happy to work in the day.'

'No, I don't want to be here during the nights. I want to be home then with my wife and children. Okay, I should get going now.'

'Before you go, try some thoppi that my uncle sent. He brewed it himself and he usually makes a strong drink.'

The two men watch the sunset as they drink the thoppi.

'You will need to chop some wood today, Chena. We are running out.'

'Okay, I will do that soon after we are done with this drink. I guess it was a busy day then?'

'Yes, it was unusually busy today. There were six through the day. Two came together though, husband and wife. Most often I get two and on some days none at all.'

'That is why I prefer working in the night. I cannot do as many as you can. Each time I finish with one, I feel drained out and need to regain my strength before I can start on the next one.'

'I came to work here when I was so young, Chena. My father worked here too and I started coming in with him. I am used to it now.'

'Really? I don't see myself getting used to this work, no matter how long I do it for. I need to earn my keep so I will find the inner resources to do it but when I am done with the night and trying to sleep, the images from here come back to haunt me. When I came here three years ago, I felt that I would get past my initial distaste and soon get accustomed to this like any other work. But, no, that has not happened and I don't think it will. Thus I am more impressed by you. How do you manage to spend the day here and go back to your wife and children?'

'I don't know either, Chena. Either I am strong or I am heartless.'

'When I see you play with your children at home, I know that you are not heartless,' says Chena, putting his pot down as he gets ready to work.

'How is it that Chena relates so differently to the work we do?' Oran asks himself, as he takes a dip in the small pond close to his home. After an exhausting day like today, he would like to go to the stream which, though a way from his home, has so much water in it that it always refreshes him. But he is not allowed to use the stream, at least not at this time of the day. He goes there sometimes late in the night. For now, he has to be content with the brook.

Soaking in the pond, his mind wanders to the time his friend Dhama went for a dip in the stream early one morning. He had not seen anyone around and thought he would take a quick dip. But he had been caught. They had tied him up to a tree and thrashed him. The wounds healed but only superficially, Dhama always remembered the humiliation. He was a shadow of his former self after that incident and died a few years later.

Oran does not think about his exchange with Chena till later when, after his dinner, he is lying on the small patch behind his house. He is looking up at the sky and still wondering at Chena's reactions to the work they do.

'What is it that Chena really feels? Is it disgust, fear or hatred? And why does he feel it?'

He turns on his side and sees his wife Rasi standing beside a lamp and pounding grain in a mortar. She has her back to him.

'Why are you doing this at this time of the night?' he asks her.

Rasi turns and smiles. 'You are not the only one in this house who is busy. There is no flour at home and I need some for the morning.'

She gets back to her work and Oran watches her pounding the grain with such grace and rhythm that she could be dancing. Half of her back is left bare by her upper garment and her dark skin glistens in the light of the dim lamp. Oran can see a bead of sweat trickle down her spine as she pounds the grain.

When after finishing her work she lies down next to him, he holds her tight.

'You are always ready for this no matter how tired you are!' she says with a throaty laugh.

Oran is already too busy to say anything. The lamp has gone off and, in the faint light of the moon, all that is discernible are two bodies locked in each other's desire.

Rasi sleeps soon after but Oran lies awake, thinking. There are no perfectly formed questions in his mind that he is struggling with but he is beset by a sense of confusion.

'I want to ask you something, Pandit,' Oran says to Madhusudhan late next afternoon. 'You are learned and you will know the answers to these questions.'

'What questions?' asks Madhusudhan.

'I want to understand why people feel such disgust for all that we do here, for us who work here and also for this place. I am asking you this because I was surprised that Chena, who works here, was telling me how he finds it difficult. I think he feels disgusted by our work.'

'Well, it is not a pleasant place, is it?' Madhusudhan asks smiling.

'We are what we are because of our bodies. But then when a person dies, how does the body immediately become something to be shunned? Not just the dead body but all that is associated with it—the clothes that are used to drape it, the flowers that decorate it, the bamboos and the straw that are used to carry it, the pots that carry the fire, this cremation ground and us workers in the cremation ground. I guess it does not affect you as much because you keep a distance from it, say your mantras and do your rituals. You are not part of this world. But Chena and I are. And that makes people feel disgusted.'

'You are saying a whole lot of different things,' says Madhusudhan. 'With death, the body decays and that is why people want to do the cremation and dispose of the body as soon as possible. That is all there is to it. When there is life in a body it stays fresh like a stream in full flow. When the water stops flowing and stagnates, that is when it starts smelling foul. That is where the disgust comes from—because of the rotting body and its stink. It is natural to feel that disgust. Each of us find our own ways to cope with it and get the better of the feeling of disgust. But, frankly, I cannot understand why you are asking me all this. You are not clear what you want to know either. Neither are you really free of the disgust in reality. You only hide it. You cannot handle the day here unless you down your pot of toddy in the morning, can you?'

'Pandit, you are mistaken. I don't drink the toddy to handle any disgust. I drink it to handle my humiliation. I cannot take the way people look at me. I feel as if they are not looking at me at all. And if by chance their eyes meet mine, I can see disgust so clearly in their eyes. The toddy just helps me to not see them too clearly. And, of course, it is easy for you to talk about the flow of the stream. Your people don't allow us to use the stream, as you well know. We just make do with the stinking pond.'

'One should simply accept that some of these things are handed down to us from ancient times. This has been followed for generations. But you know that I am not like that.'

'I agree that you are different. It is all the others.'

'No, Oran. Each person is different. You can see that I am not like Narasimha, for example, though we come from the same background. We are distantly related, in fact. But, as I was saying, each person is different. So don't judge them the same way.'

Oran is quiet for a little while and then he says, 'Okay, let me ask you another question. You do all these rituals here, chant mantras and tell the family of the dead person exactly what will happen to the spirit. You are so sure about what you say. But, in spite of being here all these years, not a single spirit has been seen by me. You tell them it ascends with the fire or something like that. I can only see flames, smoke and ashes. I spend time collecting the bones and ashes of the bodies that are cremated here and I do not find anything like a soul in the remains. All I know is that a body is brought in here, it is put on the logs of wood that we stack up, the son or some member of the family lights the pyre and the body is burnt down to bones and ashes. Nothing else remains because nothing else existed to begin with.'

Narsimhacharya, who has come to help Madhusudhan today, manages to hear some of what Oran is saying.

'Come on, Madhusudhan. We cannot wait here all day. Let's go.'

As Madhusudhan joins him, Narasimhacharya says, 'I cannot understand why you sit and waste your time talking to such people. If we are to now start debating with people like these, then we are really doomed.'

Madhusudhan is aware that Oran has heard what was just said and, in an attempt to change the subject, he says, 'By the way, Narasimha, did you hear about the big feast that has been announced on the morning following the next full moon in Moharapura, in celebration of King Kumarapala's wedding to the daughter of Emperor Ama of Kanauj?'

'No! I did not know about it. Tell me more,' says Narasimha, his mouth already watering.

'Emperor Ama has a daughter called Ratnaganga and he has decided to get her married to King Kumarapala and put an end to the years of fighting that has gone on between them. We must definitely go because the emperor is known to be a generous person and we can hope to come back with some gifts.'

'And feast on the food!'

Soon the two walk away and Oran cannot hear what they are saying anymore. Neither does he want to. He is still seething at Narasimha's remark. 'Do these greedy men think that they are the only people capable of reasoning and thinking? First, they don't let us use the stream and now they want to dismiss what we feel and express? And they do not possess the courage to look at us. Let them face us one day and they will know. They will see things in us they could not imagine.'

When he gets to work the next morning, Oran is still angry. But the day keeps him busy enough. In fact, by the end of the day he is exhausted. The last pyre has been lit just a while ago—a man who, Oran thinks, looked peaceful in his death. His son, a young man, is totally shattered and when all the rituals are done he wants to stay till the fire has completely died down. His uncle, who seems less interested in spending his time there, tries to tell him that they need to go but the young man will not listen. Oran watches them sit by the pyre and is particularly struck by the look of helplessness on the young man's face. His uncle speaks to him kindly, trying to hold him together. But what strikes Oran the most is that for them he is non-existent. Neither the composed uncle nor the distraught nephew take any cognisance of his presence. Oran listens carefully to the uncle speak to the nephew and notices how gentle he is with him. But when they get up to go the uncle's tone is harsh as he turns to Oran. 'We will come back tomorrow morning to collect the ashes,' he says, his manner arrogant and rude.

When Chena gets in at the end of the day, Oran says, 'Chena, is there any of that thoppi left? I could do with some.'

'Yes, my uncle sent in two more pots last night. It is inside our hut.'

The two men sit drinking, watching the sun set at a distance. The smoke and specks of ash of the cremation ground obscure the sunset to make it look just perfect.

'The sun going down is beautiful, isn't it?' says Chena.

'The sun is going down but it will be up again tomorrow. When we see it set and rise day after day without fail, we get the feeling that that is how this world is going to be. Nothing will change. The sun will rise and set and rise again. But tomorrow when the sun rises, I want it to know that something is definitely going to change.'

'Why? What do you think will happen?'

'I will let you know later, Chena. But I wanted to ask you something. I will not come to work tomorrow so if you can stay here through the day that will be a great help.'

'Yes, of course,' says Chena.

That night, when the moon is up in the sky, Oran is, as always, lying on the patch behind his home waiting for Rasi. She comes in a little while and lies down next to him.

He holds her close to himself and says, 'I want to go away, to a land far off where we can start a new life for us and for our children.'

'Why would you want to go? And where? Our families are here, our people are all here. Who will we know in a new place?'

'I don't know. It is just something I feel I want.'

'We are happy here with what little is ours. Why would we want more?'

'It is not that I want more, Rasi. It's just that I want our children to not face what I do on a daily basis. The humiliation one has to bear here is suffocating.'

'But what will you do in a new place? How will you take care of us?'

'I will do anything but I don't want to work in a cremation ground. I can work as a wood-cutter or I can learn some farm work or to ride a bullock cart. But as long as I do what I am now doing, I will not be able to be free. I feel I need to hide all the time just to not get into people's way. I know from the look on their faces that that is how they want it to be. My presence disturbs them and they don't want to acknowledge it.'

Rasi does not reply but instead pulls him closer to her and gently caresses the back of his neck.

Oran is silent for a while and then says, 'I know that all this is a fanciful dream. Where can we go? Which other place will take us in? No, we won't be able to go anywhere else and I am not sure that it will be any different in any other place. I will accept that as reality. But I am willing to do that only if I can change the circumstances here. I do not want to go on bearing all the humiliation that is heaped on us. That has to change.'

'How are you going to change it?'

'By not pulling myself back. We need to ask for our space now. We need to ask for what is ours now. We need to feel that it is alright to do so. I want to be free, Rasi, not just when I am dealing with the world. But also when I am on my own. Or with you. When I hold you now, I feel I am being watched. I know you feel the same. I want to hold you without a care in the world.'

Early next morning, four young Brahmin men, all in their early twenties, go to the big stream for their bath and morning prayers. It is still dark when they take a dip in the stream. The sun has not yet risen. They come out of the stream chanting their mantras and settle down by the bank of the stream in their wet loin cloths to start their prayers.

'The water was quite cold today,' one of them says. 'It is quite hard to stay wet like this.'

'Well, we need to do our prayers and we cannot dry up before that. Let's finish up as soon as we can.'

'Okay, I think I will settle down here on that rock. I can see a bit of the sun there. It will keep me warm.'

He goes and perches himself on the rock. The sun is rising behind the clump of trees a little upstream from them. He looks up to see the sun as though the mere sight of it will help him feel less cold. As he looks in that direction he sees a man swimming in the water.

'Who is that? Is that one of us?' he says aloud but then he is not sure. He stands up on the rock and tries to see more clearly but he is still uncertain. He climbs down and starts walking up the bank.

'Hey! Where are you going? Don't you want to start your prayers?' shouts one of his friends.

When he has walked about half the distance along the bank to where the man is, he is able to see more clearly. The sun too has now risen. He is sure who it is.

He turns and runs back to where his friends are. 'Come quickly!' he shouts.

'What is it?' asks one of his friends who is annoyed at his prayer being disturbed.

'There, see! That's not one of us. That is the fellow who works in the cremation ground.'

His friends get up to look and they can see clearly now. 'You are right! It is that fellow, Oran.'

'Look at his audacity. How dare he swim in these waters and that too upstream from us!'

'We are polluted. We will need to bathe again.'

'Yes, but not before we deal with him. The prayers can wait.'

One of them grabs a stick that is lying around as they run to a spot on the bank close to where Oran is still swimming.

'This fellow needs to be taught a lesson. We should break his bones,' one of them cries.

'Let him come out first.'

'If he doesn't, we will drag him out.'

They stand at the edge of the stream and call out to him.

'Hey you! Come out of the stream. This is meant for us not for people like you.'

Oran is mid-stream at this point. He turns around and starts swimming towards the bank.

'He is coming,' one of them says, excitedly.

When he gets closer to the bank, Oran rises up and stands in the knee-deep water. The four men charge towards him.

Till they catch the look in his eyes. They are seeing him like this for the first time, his eyes ablaze with defiance.

They freeze.

23. W

Spring – 485

Maitreya and Ajita reached Shravasti after several days of travel. As they entered the city early in the morning, they could see the sun coming up behind the distant hills. The city looked grand in the morning light but neither Ajita nor Maitreya could really respond to the beauty; they had lost a dear friend and a man they respected as a guide. Makkhali Goshala had died.

For the last six months, Maitreya had been hearing from friends and travellers visiting Vaishali of the great penance Makkhali had undertaken: going through alternate phases of severely austere routines and riotous revelry for months. In the last month or so, all accounts of Makkhali's excesses suggested that he may not live much longer and Maitreya felt that he and Ajita needed to go to Shravasti to meet him once before his death. They travelled for six days at a stretch, by boat, up the river, for the most part, and by mule carts to avoid the treacherously rocky parts of the river course. In the nights, they stayed in places along the river—at times, in palatial homes and, at other times, in inns or small shacks—and the fact that Maitreya had friends in all these places never failed to impress Ajita. They had reached quite close to Shravasti and hoped to make it there in a couple of days, but before that could happen, they learnt that Makkhali had died.

'Death has managed to travel faster than us,' said Maitreya in a subdued voice. They remained silent in their grief and it took Maitreya some time to speak again. 'Ajita, there is no time to be lost. Let's travel all day and all night to get to Shravasti before daybreak to be there for the funeral.'

The journey by night turned out to be a special experience for Ajita. The golden sand along the banks of the Achiravati river, illuminated by the silvery light of the full moon, appeared extraordinary—an unforgettable image that remained etched in his mind for the rest of his life.

Tired after the long journey, they decided to refresh themselves before the funeral.

'Let us eat something before leaving, Ajita,' said Maitreya. 'The funeral may go on for quite some time and one can't stay hungry that long.'

As they sat in the open courtyard of their lodgings having their meal, Ajita said, 'From the time of my father's death, one thought has persistently troubled me: if there is one thing that completely defeats every system of philosophy, every grand system of thought, it is death. There is no system that comes close to understanding it and our conception of death or, for that matter, of life, does nothing to alleviate the pain one feels at the loss of a dear one. If there is a conception that could prepare you to at least handle death in a better manner than any other person, I might have conceded that there is some merit in our philosophies. The truth is that none of us—not you or me, not Makkhali or Gautama nor all the reputed Mimamskas or Sankhyayikas—understand the first thing about it.'

'I do not think I belong in the same league as any of the people you mentioned, including yourself,' said Maitreya, shrugging his shoulders. 'I am, in fact, a foot soldier in service of a cause that is bigger than my understanding of it. But, even then, I think you are right. All of us are ignorant about death and as I get older and death seems to be nearer, the mystery only deepens. Today, I am less sure of facing my death than in my youth.'

'The only positive thing to come out of all this reflection is that I have learnt that there is no room at all for arrogance. Our thoughts, our philosophies should only help us develop more humility,' said Ajita.

A spot on the banks of the Achiravati river had been chosen for the funeral site and Makkhali had explicitly expressed his preference for a cremation over a burial. As for the rest of his instructions, they only managed to create a lot of confusion. In his last months, given to delirious ramblings, Makkhali had told his disciples that they should bathe his body in perfume, apply sandal paste, array it in the finest robes and ornaments and mount it on a bier to be carried by a thousand men in a procession, through the streets of Shravasti, singing his praises, before going to the river bank for the cremation. At other times, though, he insisted that they should desecrate his body, tie a rope to his left foot, spit on his face and drag him through the streets of Shravasti, cursing him and declaring him to be a fake.

'In death as in life,' said Ajita, as Makkhali's disciples described his last instructions. 'He lived in the extremes and in death he sought the same.'

The disciples also told them that Makkhali, for several days before his death, drank and danced to the beat of drums and died in that state of ecstasy. Ajita looked at the dead man's face and felt that a moment of that ecstasy had frozen forever on it.

The funeral turned out to be a quiet and subdued affair—not approaching any of the extreme scenarios that Makkhali had suggested. But, after the ceremony, his disciples did their best to honour his memory by drinking and dancing for hours.

At the funeral, some of Makkhali's close associates had made short speeches, Maitreya being one of them.

'Makkhali lived a remarkable life and all his close associates realised his genius. His genius, as he desired, has been cremated alongside him. The future may never comprehend his greatness,' said Maitreya, choking as he spoke.

On their journey back home, Maitreya spoke very little. Ajita tried to talk to him but his friend had assumed a taciturn manner. On the fourth night of their journey, they decided to halt at Suguna's home. Suguna and Maitreya had been friends from childhood and in his joy at meeting Maitreya after a long time, Suguna laid out an elaborate spread for their dinner and some liquor made in his neighbourhood. The good meal, and especially the liquor, finally made Maitreya open up and he started talking about the issue that had been bothering him for the last four days.

'I am sorry I did not tell you this earlier but I had too many thoughts going through my head. I thought I should let it sink in first before I talk about it. I hear, from friends in Shravasti, that our confederacy is in danger. Emperor Ajatashatru is planning an invasion.'

'But he did that already three years ago. During that attempt, he found out that the Vrijjis cannot be overcome so easily,' said Ajita.

Maitreya shook his head. 'This time he is doing it very carefully. He is taking his time to plan.'

'Is there a reason Ajatashatru is doing this?' asked Suguna.

'Several,' said Maitreya. 'The Vrijji is a confederation of nine states. The Licchavis of Vaishali have traditionally been the dominant clan. Historically, the Licchavi rulers and the kings of Magadha have had a friendly relationship. But after Ajatashatru became the emperor of Magadha, things have changed considerably. After he imprisoned his father, he tried to kill his brothers and a couple of them escaped and took refuge in Vaishali because Cetaka, the ruler of Vaishali, is their maternal grandfather. That has enraged Ajatashatru and he has decided to seek revenge against his grandfather.'

'And then there is also the issue of the diamond mine, isn't it?' asked Ajita.

'Yes,' said Maitreya. 'The rulers of Vrijji have held exclusive rights for mining in a diamond mine for a very long time. This mine is located inside the boundaries of the confederation. But Ajatashatru claims that half the mine lies inside his territory and that he should be given his share. That is more or less the background of the conflict. But to get the full picture, one has to add Ajatashatru's ambitions to this situation. He has conquered and annexed many of the smaller kingdoms, but of late he has been turning his attention to the bigger ones. Vrijji is the one he covets the most but, after his first unsuccessful attempt to conquer it, he has realised that he has to do this more carefully. The failure of the first attempt has not made him give up. That is for sure.'

'So do you have any idea of his plans?' asked Ajita.

'My friends in Shravasti gave me some idea of the emperor's plans. Three months ago, Ajatashatru had sent Vassakara, an unscrupulous and vile man, to Shravasti to talk to Gautama about Vrijji. Vassakara met Gautama and managed to glean the secret behind the invincibility of the Vrijji through his conversations.'

'And the secret is ... ?' Suguna asked.

'I am surprised that the greatest of rulers and their ministers do not understand this simple thing: the secret is unity. Ajatashatru is self-obsessed and untrusting of people. He cannot understand this business of standing in unity. The Licchavis are completely different in their approach. They see themselves not so much as rulers but as participants in the process of governance. For them their people's interests have been paramount. This form of governance can be sustained only if none of them puts their self-interests above the interests of the confederacy.

'These ideas are beyond the understanding of rulers like Ajatashatru. My feeling is that he is going to use Vassakara to break the unity of the Licchavis and use that moment of their mutual discord to strike. In his last attempt, he used brute force against the Licchavis. He thought the battle machines he had developed could help destroy Vrijji. In his mind he is a modern ruler as he sees these battle machines, invented by him and his men, as a sign of modernity. But he is unable to adapt to genuinely modern ideas of a participatory form of government. In that sense, he is very old-fashioned and still believes in exerting his might to suppress and control people. The language he speaks is that of brute force. The first time around that force failed to defeat the Licchavis, so this time he is trying treachery.'

'And in all this, Gautama helped them? I cannot believe it!' said Ajita, agitated.

'No, Ajita,' said Maitreya, gesturing to him to stop. 'You cannot blame Gautama for this. From all the reports I have received, it appears that Gautama intended to explain to Vassakara the superiority of the system of governance in Vrijji. Gautama, as everyone has seen, is very fond of Vaishali and he is happy that the Vrijjis are committed to the form of governance that they have. I think he confided in Vassakara in good faith, perhaps hoping to open Ajatashatru's eyes. He did not have any idea that Ajatashatru aimed to use it against the Licchavis. I believe, though, that Gautama can still manage to stop Ajatashatru from going to battle.'

Summer – 483

'I am sure you have heard … ' Japa began.

'About Gautama? Yes. These are terrible times. Just eighteen months ago, Makkhali died. And Gautama yesterday!'

'It seems he fell ill because of the meat he ate.'

'I heard that too. The meat that a hunter offered to him in a forest appears to have been bad. If he had been close to a city at that time maybe they could have treated him. I heard that they had to travel a long distance and he died before he could be given any help,' said Ajita.

'You did seem to be more fond of Makkhali than him.'

'One can't say that. I admired them both. I think of myself as fortunate to have been around at the same time as these truly exceptional men. I became a disciple of neither, I accepted neither of them as a guru, maybe because I am too independent to accept anyone at all. But both Makkhali and Gautama raised questions about my system of ideas in our very first meetings. They both made me think more deeply than anyone else had and each of their questions helped me make my system more rigorous. In that sense, they are both my spiritual gurus. It is also true that Makkhali and I interacted closely, much more than Gautama and I ever did. In fact, Gautama and I had serious differences, but for quite some time, and especially after Makkhali's death, I have had reason to revise my stance about him.'

'Yes, I have seen that transformation and I am glad it has happened,' said Japa.

'I think I have Maitreya to thank for that. He opened my eyes to the fact that my critique of Gautama bordered on the personal and that I regarded him in a prejudiced manner. That really helped me change my perception of him.'

'I tried to tell you the same thing, but you did not listen to anyone at that time.'

'I made the mistake of being suspicious of Gautama's proximity to Ajatashatru and understood his motivations only later. The emperor truly relied on him for advice. Also, Maitreya told me that Gautama kept Ajatashatru in check, for had he been let loose he may have been much more destructive than he is. Gautama, for instance, realised that Ajatashatru planned to attack Vrijji and had sent Vassakara to him to get information about them. That happened a little before Makkhali's death and it has been eighteen months since. But Gautama made every attempt to dissuade Ajatashatru from attacking Vrijji but even then the emperor initiated the attack. After Gautama's death, there is no one to stop the emperor.

Autumn – 484

By the time Ajatashatru had intensified his attack on Vrijji, Vassakara had used his guile to infiltrate the courts and palaces of Vaishali and other Vrijji cities. Vassakara's task became simpler because he had pretended to have fallen out of Ajatashatru's favour and had circulated rumours about the emperor expelling him from his court. The rulers of Vrijji, tired of Ajatashatru's relentless aggression, felt comforted that one of his counsellors had, after a fight, left his court and come over to their side. This already made Vassakara's access to the inner circles of the Vrijji elite that much easier and, having once gained access, he used every possible stratagem to fuel conflicts among them.

'I have been keeping track of Vassakara and am trying to see if one can foil his devious plans,' said Maitreya to Ajita. 'But these are the times I feel I should have done something to gain the confidence of our rulers much earlier. I chose to keep a distance from the political system and rulers because I felt that may compromise our independence and autonomy.'

'As long as your reasons are clear in your mind there is no need to doubt yourself.'

'Yes, but I feel helpless seeing Vassakara going about damaging our systems. Using the resources that Ajatashatru has kept at his disposal, Vassakara has managed to coerce, force or bribe people in the system to do as he bids. Using the support of the vassals and the officers of the government, he is able to manipulate the Licchavi kings in the manner he chooses and they are already fighting amongst themselves like children. Gautama identified their unity as their strength, and Vassakara is all out to destroy that very unity.'

Maitreya sounded despondent but Ajita had faith in his ability to figure out a plan to tackle Vassakara. In less than a month's time, Maitreya returned to tell him about the progress he had made. He had an interesting story to tell.

Maitreya had got one of his trusted lieutenants to keep track of Vassakara's movements. Of the people in the administration that Vassakara contacted, Maitreya had instructed his men to identify officers given to a lavish lifestyle as it made them more likely to have been the ones to accept bribes. One of his men had identified a senior councillor called Yashapala and kept a close eye on him. Yashapala, it turned out, spent more time after he left his office in a courtesan's house than he did at home. To be a patron of a courtesan as famous as Soudamini, one's pockets needed to run deep, and it seemed unlikely that someone in the administrative service made that kind of money. Just ten days after he had met Vassakara for the first time, Yashapala agreed to help him in exchange for a sizeable number of gold coins. Yashpala had long dreamt of being very rich and, for the very first time, he had moved close to achieving that dream. But he did not think it safe to keep that much gold in his house: the surprise raids conducted by the royal guards had become more frequent and, if caught in possession of that amount of gold, he could lose more than just his job—his life may be at stake. He felt that it made more sense to keep the gold in Soudamini's house. He had become so close to her that he trusted her enough to give her the gold for safe keeping, hidden from the royal guards. Over a period of time, he planned to move the gold out of her place and keep smaller amounts of it distributed over several locations.

Vikarna, one of Maitreya's most enterprising assistants, having found out about Yashapala's frequent visits to Soudamini's home had decided to befriend one of the young girls serving in Soudamini's home. This girl, Devasena, easily charmed by Vikarna's good looks, told him everything he sought to find out about Soudamini. Devasena had overheard Yashapala telling Soudamini about the gold and duly conveyed the information to Vikarna. Yashapala had arranged to meet one of Vassakara's men, Rajindra, by the river to collect the gold and he planned to carry it directly to Soudamini's house. On hearing this from Vikarna, Maitreya decided to tip off the royal guards about the meeting by the riverside.

Yashapala and Rajindra met at the appointed hour by the riverside and even as Rajindra handed over the gold to Yashapala, the royal guards, hiding behind the trees, rushed in and apprehended both of them. Not only did they confiscate the gold but they also imprisoned Yashapala and Rajindra till such time that they could be tried by the court and punished. Maitreya could have asked for nothing more than these arrests.

'Vassakara's days are numbered,' he told Ajita, excitedly. 'Once the investigations and the court trials are done, and Vassakara is publicly exposed, our job is done.'

Maitreya could hardly have expected the turn of events that materialised. Rajindra managed to escape from prison, obviously aided by corrupt jail officials. He could not be traced in spite of a massive hunt set up to find him. The stories of him crossing the border to the safety of Ajatashatru's kingdom started doing the rounds. Even before Vaishali could recover from the shock of Rajindra's escape, Yashapala died in prison of a snakebite. For more than a month, much discussion and debate took place but then the investigating officers found nothing to go by and decided to bury the case.

The entire episode managed to break Maitreya's spirit; Ajita had never seen him so disconsolate. Also, Vassakara had figured out Maitreya's role in the imprisonment of Rajindra and Yashapala.

'I have never seen him so broken,' Ajita told Japa later, as he narrated the entire story to her.

'It seems like the convoluted plots of one of the plays that get staged at the annual fair in our city. Palace intrigues, corrupt officials, courtesans and riverside meetings to prison breaks and snakes—it has it all.'

'It is not the plot of a play and it is no laughing matter, Japa. You should see Maitreya to realise the extent of his fears. I think he is right. I also fear terrible days ahead.'

Ajita's prophecy did not take too long to come true. Late one evening, a fortnight later, one of Maitreya's assistants came rushing to his home. 'Maitreya has asked you to come immediately to our archives building,' he said in a panic.

Ajita and Ratna did not lose a moment in setting off for the archives. They reached the place to see Maitreya sitting on the ground, holding his head in his hand. The small building that housed the archives had been set on fire.

'The scribes ... are they all right?' Ajita asked, his voice quaking.

'Yes,' someone replied. 'They had finished their duties and left for their homes.'

Ajita sat next to Maitreya, putting an arm on his shoulder.

'It is over. All our records, all our documents are destroyed. It is over,' Maitreya said, crying.

The incident broke Ajita's spirit and he never quite recovered from it.

24. X

February 130

Angai lifts the pile of clothes in one swoop of her arm and holds her son's hand with her other.

'We have no time to lose. Hurry up,' her sister is saying, her voice quaking with fear.

'What did they say, the elders?' Angai asks. Aralai gestures with her hand, asking her to hurry.

Angai does not move. She wants to know the answer first.

'They said you should come with us. So just come now,' Aralai says.

When they step out, Angai sees that every house is shut and people are beginning to walk in the direction of the vihara. A few pikkus and pikkunis from the vihara are leading the group on their long walk.

Angai and Aralai catch up with the other women but Angai sees that they keep a distance from her. She deliberately slows down and walks with Ilampirai, her son, a little behind the rest of the group. The village could have been evacuated earlier had it not been for the fact that the women in the village did not want Angai to go with them.

'We can take her son but not her,' one of them had said. 'It is Aralai, her sister, who takes care of the child anyway. Why should that woman come with us?'

The opinion had been met with a cacophony of voices, but finally one of the village elders had quietened them.

'We cannot do that. We cannot leave her here for the soldiers to kill. Whatever you may think of her, she is a daughter of our village and we cannot abandon her.'

The compromise that had been arrived at was that Angai would stay separately and not come into contact with the other women.

It is just past noon and unbearably hot. Angai stops by a small pond to splash water on her face. She did not manage to get much sleep the previous night. Her sister had shaken her awake, saying they had to leave the village that instant. She gave her a jumbled account of which king was going to battle against which other king and Angai had made no sense of it. It was only at the village elders' meeting that she had been able to make out what was going on. It sounded quite simple, in fact: almost every ruler and chieftain in their land was at war with the young Chola, Karikala. From what she had heard of him, Angai had developed a great deal of respect for the king. She had no doubt in her mind that he would be victorious in this battle. But how long would that take? How long would this war last? For how long would they have to live in the vihara? These were questions no one had had any answers to.

Another question had troubled her and continued to do so—would the vihara be able to offer them safety? The village elders believed that the soldiers would not enter the vihara and thus the whole village was moving. But Angai does not want to remain confined to the vihara for many days. She prays for an early and decisive victory for the Chola king.

Angai notices one of the pikkunis deliberately slowing down to fall in step with her. She walks by Angai's side without saying a word. Angai ignores her for a bit but then her curiosity gets the better of her. She turns to look at the pikkuni and is stunned by her looks. She has the most beautiful eyes that Angai has known; they sparkle like two diamonds and look even brighter because of the dark shade of her skin. Her skin is glowing as though lit by a light of its own. Her head is clean-shaven and it looks like the last shave was recent. The bald head only adds to her beauty and Angai looks at her admiringly.

'I am Angai,' she says.

'Oviyai,' replies the other but then resumes her silent walk. Angai sees a bead of perspiration trickle down the dark skin of the front of her neck and wonders how it is possible for any person to be so attractive.

It is only when they reach the vihara that Angai realises that Ilampirai would be separated from her and kept in the men's quarters where the pikkus lived. She is distraught.

'He is only five,' she pleads with the stern old pikkuni who seems to be the person making all the decisions in the vihara.

'No male can stay in this part of the vihara,' she says. 'That is not permitted.'

'But he is a child. How can I leave him alone?'

'Our brother pikkus will take care of him. You can meet him once every day in the garden.'

Angai realises that the head pikkuni is unrelenting. She sees tears welling up in Ilamparai's eyes and she clasps him by his thin arms.

'You are brave, my love, brave like your Amma. You are not going to cry. And you are not alone. Amma is always there with you. Just close your eyes and think of me if you feel scared.'

Angai is separated from the rest of the women and given shelter under a small thatch, while the rest are put in a few huts that line the border of the garden plot. She is happy to be left alone. She has put up with the attitude of the villagers for too long and is no longer interested in being under the same roof with them. Aralai brings her food so she does not even have to see the others at mealtimes.

On the second evening, she is surprised to find Oviyai bring her food. 'I brought what I could. Let me know if this is enough for you,' Oviyai says.

'Yes, more than enough.'

'It must be difficult being alone here. And that too without your son,' she says.

Angai looks up at her.

'I would have liked to have my son stay with me, he is so young after all. Otherwise, I am fine here. I can't stand those women from my village.'

'I cannot understand why they don't want you with them. I tried asking your sister but she didn't say much.'

'They behave like my presence will pollute them. But I don't really care. We women have the ability to cope with every situation, don't we? When we come of age, they make us sit out of the house every month. Nobody comes near us, no one touches us on those days. We take that in our stride. This is just like that—only longer. But I can handle it.'

Oviyai smiles and looks even more beautiful when she does.

'I have to tell you that you are the most beautiful woman I have ever seen,' says Angai, unabashedly.

Oviyai shrugs.

'I have stopped thinking of all that. It is vain to think that one is good-looking and I don't want even a shred of vanity in me. I am committed to being a pikkuni, and on the path I have chosen there is no room for vanity.'

'I don't agree that it is vanity,' said Angai. 'You are beautiful and nothing can change that. Not even the fact that you don't think of your beauty.'

'I keep away from such thoughts. I don't want to get disturbed by them. Anyway, I have to go now. It is time for my prayers.'

'Alright. But do come back again, maybe tomorrow? I like talking to you.'

Two days go by before Oviyai shows up again. 'Where were you? I was waiting for you yesterday,' says Angai.

Oviyai smiles. 'I did come in the afternoon but you were lost to the world, deep in meditation.'

'Oh! I didn't realise you had come then.'

'Tell me more about your meditative practices.'

'It is probably not very different from what you do,' says Angai. But quickly changing the topic, she asks, 'How long have you lived here in this vihara?'

'A little more than three years.'

'And what made you come here?'

'It is the usual story. You have probably heard some variation or other of it. I was married to a man I loved but he fell ill very soon after our marriage. I spent several months taking care of him. But his health did not improve and eventually he succumbed to his illness.'

Angai looked at her and could see the pain in her eyes.

'Life after his death was terrible. My husband's brother wasted no time in taking over our property, cattle and money. And he also thought I was part of my husband's belongings. He forced himself upon me even though he had a wife living in the same house. If I had been stronger, I would probably have ended my life but instead I ran away and landed up here.'

'But why did you become a pikkuni? Did you want to be one?'

'You mean, why did I choose this path? That's because I believe this is the right path: the path of the Buddha. It has given me a lot of peace and helped me deal with all those injuries that my past inflicted on me. But enough about me, tell me about yourself. Why do people from your village want to avoid you?'

'I wish I had as simple a story as yours to tell.'

Oviyai smiled and said, 'You didn't see the effort I put in to tell a simple story?'

'Yes, that didn't escape me,' said Angai. 'I come from a family of performing artistes and the one thing I have learnt in life is to understand a story—about what it reveals, what it hides and what it leaves as a mere suggestion.'

'Then I am sure you will be able to tell me the story of your life in the most fascinating way.'

'Okay, I will but not today. Give me some time to think of how to tell it. Give yourself some time to prepare yourself to receive it.'

'Now you are deliberately making it sound mysterious. Like the hair on my head, I shaved off all the details of my life and presented you with the bald facts. You may have much more to talk about but that does not mean I have not seen life in its many forms. I have the stomach for anything you may want to tell me.'

'Just give me a little time,' says Angai.

A few days go by and Angai and Oviyai do not see each other much.

It is the night of the Marghazi and the cool breeze that blows across the garden brings the fresh fragrance of the flowers to Angai. It is already quite late and everyone is asleep but Angai is wide awake. In the light of the moon, she can see a human figure walking towards her and she soon recognises it as Oviyai.

'I could not sleep so I thought I would come down to see if you were awake,' she says. She bends down to place the lamp on the ground, and in its light her face is illuminated.

'If I had been a man, I would have married you,' Angai says.

'Even if you had been a man you could not have married me. I am a renunciate.'

'Do you not miss being with a man?' asks Angai.

Oviyai looks at her. 'No,' she says, finally. 'I have learnt to not get overcome by desire for anything at all. It is part of my meditative practice.'

'And you don't think that it is unnatural to curb what your body naturally feels?'

'There is so much that we may feel like doing but don't because we live with others in a community. We have to go by the rules and larger interests of that community. One doesn't always do what one feels. But it's not just that. There are also things we don't do, in the hope of bettering ourselves. I can abstain for my own reasons. But why am I the one talking? You were supposed to tell me about yourself.'

'Ah yes, my story! I guess tonight is magical enough for me to talk about my life. Like you, I also got married to a man whom I loved very much. I told you I come from a family of performing artistes. We perform plays and dances in temple festivals and fairs,' says Angai. 'The man I married was also a performer but not from our part of the world. He had travelled a great distance to come to our village. My parents were worried that he was not one of us but they knew I wanted to marry him and that I was in love with him. The trouble was I could never figure out whether he loved me. That he desired my body was obvious and within a few months of our marriage I had a baby in my womb. He stayed with me till my son was born and then one night he just disappeared.

'I hurt a lot, I wept, I suffered but soon realised that I had to get on with living. I had to take care of myself and my son. But the way our theatre groups are organised, it becomes difficult to get work if you don't have a husband. It was fine when I was a young girl but for women my age work is difficult to come by. The husband and wife work in plays together and here I was—an abandoned, single woman. I tried to find an unmarried man in my community, who would be ready to marry me, but no one wanted a woman with a child. I was getting work occasionally but that did not give me enough to provide for my son and me.'

'Oh, that sounds terrible,' says Oviyai. 'What did you do then?'

'For a while, I just tried to survive on scraps. Then I got some work with a dance troupe to perform at a festival in Puhar. I left Ilampirai in Aralai's care and went off to Puhar for about three weeks. And that is where my life changed,' says Angai.

'Why, what happened?'

'I met Kalan and we became quite close in a very short time. It turned out that Kalan also lived in my hometown and was in Puhar only for the festival. He really wanted me to become a part of their group and kept trying to convince me, in Puhar but also after we returned home.'

'He wanted you to join his theatre group?'

'No, not really. But it was not very different from a theatre group.'

'So, what was it?' asks Oviyai, unable to contain her curiosity.

'It was a group of Kapalikas.'

'What! Kapalikas! How could he even … ?'

'Yes, I was worried too but he promised that I would be able to earn money. The richer people in the group fund its activities and everyone gets enough to manage quite well.'

'So you joined this group to earn money?'

'Yes, for my survival and that of my son's. But the world does not like the fact that I am a Kapalika. People in my village know about it and that is why they do not want to associate with me.'

'But there is so much else you could have done rather than getting into a cult of this kind. From what I have heard—'

'What have you heard, Oviyai?' asks Angai. 'That they are a bunch of depraved people seeking ways to satisfy their lust? That they drink and indulge in orgies and perform strange rites?'

'Yes, in fact, all of this and worse,' says Oviyai, quite indignantly.

'You can't sit in judgement of something without really knowing what it is,' says Angai.

'So tell me what it is then.'

'The Kapalika quest is as much a spiritual quest as your own, Oviyai. And, like any other tradition, it has evolved its own set of practices—meditative and spiritual practices not very different from what you follow—at least not very different in essence. But the Kapalikas bring in a performative element which for me, as an artiste, is fascinating. The performances are done in a group and that kind of activity allows us to tap into energies that individual practice can never help us reach.'

'These don't seem like your words at all. The group seems to have drilled all this into you and you are not seeing the fact that they are doing this so that they can use you to satisfy their own base desires.'

'Yes, maybe if I had not come into contact with these people I may not have had access to these words. But that is what good company does to you. It lets you discover worlds and words that would never have otherwise been yours. I see no harm in that.'

'It is shocking to see how much you have let yourself be overcome by them. So much so that you are probably left with no sense of what is right and what is wrong! You say this provides you enough to take care of yourself and your son. But what are you offering in return? Your body? What does that make you then?'

'You may want to be moralistic and call me a whore. But, no, I am a Kapalika as much as I am a performer. I am not offering my body to anyone there but we all become part of that one ecstasy. You learn to see the act as a performance and you learn to distance yourself from your body and look at it from the outside. If you don't see a spiritual movement in that, you will see it in nothing.'

They are both quiet for a bit and then Oviyai breaks the silence.

'I don't want to be moralistic. But, try as I may, I can see nothing spiritual in drunken orgies. And I cannot treat them as mere performance.'

'One can see that you are not a performer, or you would not have described any performance as mere. But these rituals are, indeed, performances and not any less important because of that. Men and women of all castes and social standing are there as equal performers through the period of the ritual. Once the ritual is over, they are no longer Kapalikas. They return to where they are in life and perform their social roles from their location. But when they gather by the fire in the night, it is as though their identities melt together and they do not distinguish themselves from anyone else around. Very often the biggest obstacle in our spiritual journeys is our social standing, our place in life. It is an obstacle if we grant it too much reality and treat it as absolute. But if we were to shed that identity by the night then we are bound to treat it as ephemeral—like bubbles on the surface of water.'

Angai pauses for a moment and then continues, 'You think you are following the path of a renunciate but what is it that you can renounce? You did not have the courage to renounce life so you continued with it. You fast and deny yourself food but you cannot give up food completely, can you? You shave your head but what can you do to your beauty? It does not leave you. You cannot scrub it off and get rid of it. And what of your desire? You convince yourself you feel no desire. You pray and meditate when you think you may be succumbing to it, but can you truly overcome it? Can you renounce it?'

Oviyai is too stunned to say anything in reply.

'What I am saying, Oviyai,' says Angai, 'is that you and I are quite the same. Your path of negation and mine of acceptance seem as if they diverge but, in fact, they meet somewhere at a common destination.'

25. Y

– 473

When Ajatashatru went to war against the Vrijjis, no one could have guessed that it would be fought for such a long time. Had the Vrijjis not been such formidable opponents, Ajatashatru would have finished it in the short time it required him in his other conquests. Had the Vrijjis been less proud of themselves and loved their land less, it would have been possible to negotiate for peaceful settlements. Courage, valour, strength, pride and patriotism went against them.

In fact, there was a point in the long struggle when it appeared that Ajatashatru had no hope of winning and might end the war. But the emperor was never one to admit defeat. Pushed to the brink, he became a more desperate fighter. He goaded his people even harder and made his soldiers fight with more determination. He made sure that the spirits in the camps remained high, and when the soliders returned to the base after a battle, there was enough good food and drink to prepare them for the next morning. He also made sure that there were enough medicines and potions reaching the camps so that the injured could recover and fight again.

Ajatashatru took a personal interest in ensuring the proper disbursement of ammunition and ordnance supplies to his regiments. More men were brought in to work and produce weapons, but alongside he kept some of his most experienced weapon makers free to experiment and innovate. This constant pressure that he kept on his ordnance workers through the toughest times of war paid off at a time when it looked like he had no hope of success. Two new inventions that his men perfected at this time allowed Ajatashatru to take control of the war and move to a position of total command. One was a mechanical contraption that could be used to hurl massive boulders at adversaries. The Vrijjis, who had never seen a weapon of this kind before, were blindsided and suffered huge losses. The second invention, a chariot with blades attached to its wheels, helped further hasten the war towards its end. After that, it did not take Ajatashatru much time to win the war.

Except that when the war ended, the emperor realised that though he had won the war, he could not consider it a success.

Several full moons bore witness to the war and it had left the whole land ruined in its wake. One face of that ruin was also the manner in which the land had been altered: roads had come up to allow the movement of the warring soldiers, river courses had been altered and forests had been razed to the ground. Whole cities disappeared, leaving desolate ruins and broken memories behind. Life in its different forms—human, animal, bird or plant—was decimated. No one won the war because it was death that presided over its spoils, no one gained from it except the vermin that ravaged the land and the diseases that abounded. The fragrance of the flowers in the gardens of Vaishali was lost to the stench of rotting corpses, while the picturesque vistas had all gone up in dense smoke.

Spring – 473

After the war was over, Ajita decided it would be best for them to leave Vaishali for a while and move to his mother's old home in the mountains. Dhvani had died before the war, and when Ajita had gone to perform her funeral he had thought he would return and spend a length of time there. None of that had been possible during the war, but now, tired and defeated at the end of it, Ajita felt that a long stint in the mountains could work as a soothing balm.

Ratna also decided to go to the mountains with Ajita. He had aged, as had Ajita. In fact, he was a few months older than Ajita and his health had not been the best these past few months. He felt that the mountain life would restore his health. Tuli did not seem quite as old and was still her energetic self. For a long time now, she had been going to Ajita's mother's home in the mountains with Ratna. She never missed a chance to go there and this time was no different. Ajita was surprised though that Japa also agreed to come without even a moment's hesitation. Japa's situation in life now made it less difficult for her to think of leaving Vaishali for a length of time. It had been a while since her mother-in-law had died and her brother-in-law did not survive for too long after that. But the war had changed her circumstances to a great extent. While the war was merciless with the poor of Vaishali, it did not spare the rich either. Businesses of the kind that Japa ran were the first to be targeted in the attacks that the invading soldiers launched. Ajatashatru's generals had planned to attack the granaries and cut off supplies to Vaishali. Much of the food grains that Japa had in stock were either plundered or wasted. Her thriving business was reduced to nothing and she had little hope of restarting it now that the war was over. It was a fact, though, that she had enough personal wealth to continue living her life of comfort, so she decided that this would be the time for her to put her feet up and stop working.

In fact, the morning before Ajita invited her to his home in the mountains, she had spent some time alone, looking at herself in the mirror. People would still think of her as beautiful, she thought, or at least as someone who was once beautiful. But she knew her skin was no longer what it used to be. It lacked the lustre it once had. Her hair was no longer jet black and did age her, she thought. When Ajita asked her to come along, she somehow thought of that moment when she had looked at herself in the mirror and had realised that she was now old. She knew that their companionship mattered to her as it did to him, and she knew that the visible marks of age on her face were telling her that she should not be alone.

A week in the mountains was all that was needed to put them in a tranquil frame of mind. If a farmer or a hunter were to show up then it was possible to get fowl or meat to cook, otherwise it was the fish from the stream close to their home that was their food. Of the four, Ratna and Tuli were the most skilled at fishing, but even Japa was nowhere as hopeless at it as Ajita. In fact, with time, she was getting better.

One evening, as Japa and Ajita sat on a rock watching the sun set, Japa turned to Ajita and asked, 'Will we be able to go back to the lives we led in Vaishali—the business I lost? The work the Cārvākas had done?'

'I don't know … I don't think so,' said Ajita, somewhat tentative in his speech. 'How much time do we have left, Japa? We are old.'

Japa remained silent.

'I am still optimistic, though,' Ajita continued. 'Don't think I am not. Except that we are not going to be the individuals who will rebuild what we have lost. Someone else will do it. Some new business folk, some new philosophers. That is how the world goes on. But there is one thing I am sure about. What we as the Cārvākas put forward as a philosophical position will never die. For the moment, our enemies have silenced us and wiped out our archives. But it will re-emerge at some later point because, I believe, we got a glimpse of a vision of truth and that vision will be revisited.'

He paused for a bit and said, 'See there, the last bit of the sun is going down. It will rise again tomorrow. Of course, it will be a mistake to come and sit on this rock to watch the sun rise. It will not rise here but elsewhere, but rise it will.'

'But the thought that we will not be around, that we will be gone, isn't that frightening?' asked Japa.

'We don't need to fear death if we accept it in the correct manner. In fact, one can think of it as not something in itself but as the end of life. Just as an individual's life begins at some point, it ends at another. It is just life and its cessation. When I observed ants as a child, one thing that left a profound impression on me is that their death seems so commonplace and without the trappings of the theatrical. From the perspective of a superior being looking at us, like we look at ants, our deaths would seem as unexceptional.'

'Superior being?'

'I knew I would be caught there,' said Ajita, laughing. 'I meant "if there were a superior being" with the complete knowledge that there is none such.'

'So, our lives and our deaths are no more significant than an ant's?'

'I don't mean that. Human lives have the potential to be significant. How significant a life is depends on several factors, of course, but we can speak, think and love as humans and that is what gives our life its meaning. The end of life is not an erasure of that meaning.'

Japa held Ajita's hand in her own, her fingers curled around his, as the two of them looked at the darkening horizon spread out in front of them.

Ajita and Ratna had gone into the woods with a couple of men who lived in the neighbourhood to look for some medicinal plants. Japa knew it would take them a few hours to return so she decided to spend the morning working in the garden with Tuli. Tuli was an excellent gardener and Japa was also amazed at the range of things she could accomplish.

'I started working when I was a little girl, doing whatever work was assigned to me,' said Tuli with a smile. 'Of course, at that age one can learn things well and retain it for life. I had two older sisters and we went together to work in the fields and gardens. That is where I learnt all this.'

'And fishing?'

'Well, that was for our own food. We would catch fresh fish from the river and take it home. It was quite a feast! We also caught a lot of crabs. That was a favourite with all of us children.'

'There is so much I have to learn,' said Japa, with obvious respect for Tuli.

'Each of us has a lot to learn. I, for instance, know nothing about running a business.'

'But gardening or fishing is so real. One gets to work with one's hands. It is in the mountains here that we realise these things.'

'I don't quite agree with that. I would love to work in a shop and understand how a business works. I am hoping there will still be time for me to do that.'

Japa smiled. 'I am glad to see this positive attitude to life. But are we all not getting older?' she asked. 'Ajita and I were talking about death some time back and he was telling me how he thinks we need to have an attitude of acceptance to death.'

'I see him talking a lot about death. I keep listening in on the conversations he has with Ratna. But I think for Ratna it is different as it is for me,' said Tuli.

'Different how?'

'Well, I mean one can have these philosophical discussions about death when one is somewhat protected from the dangers that the world poses. I grew up watching people die—some of old age and some because of starvation. I remember I was about sixteen when a cousin who was a little older than me stole rice from the house he was working in. He got caught and the landlord he was working for beat and tortured him so much that he suffered for a week and then died. When one has seen something like that, one cannot understand what this business of a positive attitude to death even means. One knows that life is precious and fragile; it needs to be guarded but with the understanding that it can be snatched when one least expects it.' She paused and seemed to focus on a patch in the garden. 'I don't think this plant is getting enough sunlight. It will be better off out there in the open rather than in this clutter.'

It was getting close to winter and Ajita was beginning to feel its arrival in his bones. He knew it was time to go back to Vaishali—to warmer weather and to the comforts of his home.

It was the morning of their planned return and Ajita had a strong sense that he would never return to his ancestral home again.

'We will come back again,' Ratna said, sensing Ajita's trepidation.

'Come back here with Tuli. Several times, if possible. But I know that I won't see this place ever again.'

He walked across to the garden of his grandfather's home and sat under the shade of the peepal tree. The peepal tree stood in the garden in its timeless magnificence. So much around Ajita marked the passage of time but it appeared that it had left this tree untouched. As he sat there, Ajita remembered the hours that he had spent with his grandfather sitting under the tree. Much of what he learnt from his grandfather about medicine was under this tree, which stood over him and kept a strict watch to make sure he was being attentive. But, on other occasions, when he slept under it, the tree spread its shade and cared for him like a mother would. As he sat under it this morning, he knew that he still felt safe in its care.

In their absence from Vaishali, much had happened. Roads and canals were being repaired, homes and palaces were being rebuilt and people were back at work. It was a revitalised people putting all that was there at their disposal to bring their lives back on track.

Japa's business associates contacted her as soon as she was back in Vaishali and, while she did not want to get involved with the business to the extent she had been earlier, she did get back to work, even as Ajita and Ratna returned to their medical practice. On the whole, there was a sense of having recovered a good measure of the past.

A month or so later, two of Ajita's old friends, Bikrama and Manmadana, from the Cārvāka circle came to meet him.

'We would like to restart the activities of our group,' said Bikrama, eager to get to the point after the exchange of the usual pleasantries.

Ajita looked sceptical. 'I don't know if we can ever recover what we have lost there … '

'Don't be so negative, Ajita,' said Bikrama, interrupting him. 'It is never going to be what it was but having seen what we had in the past we know what we should be working towards. There are new people, energetic and enthusiastic, willing to work with us. We will miss some of our old friends whom we have lost during the war but we need to look ahead.'

'And, there have been some interesting developments,' said Manmadana. 'We were talking to one of the merchants who owns a piece of land not far from here. He is willing to help us build a small building that we can use for our meetings. We can even think of rebuilding our archives.'

Ajita's sat up. 'Our archives?'

'That's what I said. We can raise funds to get two scribes to work for us. In fact we should get started on it.'

'We must,' said Ajita, his voice choking with uncharacteristic emotion.

Summer – 471

With the regular meetings of their group, the supervision of the building of the new centre and the commencement of the archival work along with his own practice as a doctor, a headiness returned to Ajita's life—a headiness with which age could be both denied and defied. He was revitalised to the extent that those working with him, even the ones whose age was lesser than his, found it difficult to keep pace with him.

Japa was worried for Ajita because he was so occupied all the time. His mind was racing in a hundred different directions and that meant that he was not getting enough sleep or rest. She tried to talk to him about slowing down.

'I have not felt this energetic in a long time, Japa. This work is the secret that keeps me ticking. Once that stops, I think I will too.'

'I am working too but I make sure to have some time to do other things as well. Or do nothing at times,' Japa said. But Ajita's attention had wandered.

It was when he was walking back after a dip in the river one morning that Ajita fell down. All he remembered was that he had a sensation of giddiness and he stopped to splash water on his face but that he blacked out after that. A man going down to the river found him unconscious, recognised him and brought him home. In spite of Ratna's best efforts to revive him, he was not conscious for several hours and it was late in the afternoon when he regained consciousness.

'Will he be fine?' he could hear Japa asking Ratna.

'I think he will recover but it will take time. He will need complete rest for a while.'

'But he is so adamant. He refuses to listen. Look, he is stirring. He wants to tell us something.'

Ajita made an attempt to speak but he was not audible. Japa bent forward to be able to hear him better but he was too weak even to utter a few words.

For a week, Ajita's health seemed to be on the mend but he was still too frail to get out of bed.

'Let's make sure he gets all the rest he can. He will recover then,' he overheard Ratna telling Japa.

At best, Ajita had a vague awareness of what was happening around him. He knew that Japa and Ratna spent most of their time with him, taking turns to be with him and making sure that he was never left alone. Over a period of time the world came back in sharper terms to him and he was able to sit up on the bed and talk to Japa and Ratna.

'I am sure it will all be fine,' said Japa, in a tone that did not sound convincing to even her own ears.

'There is a lot to be done and I need to do it,' said Ajita.

'All that can wait. Nothing needs to be done now and no thought needs to be given to it at this moment,' said Japa, fighting her tears as she spoke.

But, even as he seemed to be recovering, in a dramatic turn his health worsened. He had a restless night and when he woke up in the morning, Ajita found it difficult to breathe. Ratna knew this was serious but he could not tell Japa.

'What is happening to him, Ratna? He seemed so much better last night,' cried Japa.

'I will prepare a potion of herbs for him. That should help. Be here with him.'

When Ratna left, Ajita asked Japa to sit close to him.

'Tell Ratna not to waste his time, Japa,' he said, in a feeble voice. 'I can see it is over.'

'Don't talk like that.'

'One knows, Japa. One knows when life is slipping out of one's being. And I am a doctor so I understand it even better.'

'No, I will not let that happen'.

'Who can stop it, Japa? In the acceptance of the end is wisdom and that is what we must do.'

He struggled a bit to breathe but when he recovered his voice, he said, 'This is the end of all that I am and all that is mine. There is nothing of me that survives. And nothing that will come back in some imagined new birth—because there will be nothing left to return.'

He gasped, his face contorted somewhat, he seemed to rise up a bit and then slumped back into his bed, lifeless.

26. Z

June – 524

Ajita is lying flat on his stomach on the ground along the wall of the kitchen. The seven-year-old has spent all morning in the garden following the trail of red ants who have now found a way through a tiny hole in the wall straight into the kitchen. It is a long trail. There are so many ants and there is so much happening that young Ajita cannot contain his excitement. He is particularly interested in two of them and is trying to follow them with his eyes to figure out how they are taking food from the kitchen and carrying it to their home in the garden.

'There they are, Gura and Dhura,' he mutters. 'Someone has told them to make sure the food is collected and put safely and quickly in the anthill. That is why they are moving so fast.

'I wonder what language they speak to each other. Is it a language I don't understand? Or even sounds that I don't hear? I am sure they can speak. How else would they know where the food is? That they have to follow this line and reach the kitchen? I wish I could hear them and understand what they are saying to each other.'

Even as his mind races, Ajita makes sure that his eyes are trained on Gura and Dhura. He does not want to lose them. At one point, he wonders if they could see him, like he could see them.

'Or am I so huge that they can't see me with their tiny eyes?' he thinks. 'Do they see tiny things with their eyes? Creatures so small that they are for Gura and Dhura as small as the two ants are to me!'

Ajita recollects his visit to the grand market in Vaishali on the first day of Margasirsah. His father often goes to Vaishali and that day he had taken him along. It was not Ajita's first visit to Vaishali; he had visited the city quite often when he was younger. It was just that he saw it then as a curious and awestruck seven-year-old and now he was savouring the city to its fullest. As they entered the marketplace, Ajita tightened his grip around his father's index finger which he had been holding. The expanse of the space and the sea of humanity around him were overwhelming, even if he was enjoying it all. He looked up sideways to see his father. Govinda was a tall man whose erect posture made him look taller. From that angle Govinda looked like he was the tallest person around. For Ajita there was no one quite like his father.

Ajita had noticed how, in spite of the crowds, there was an order in the way people moved around in the marketplace. People who were walking up the street stayed on the left and the ones coming down moved on the right. They walked past a fountain and the line of people naturally curved to go around it. He was really impressed with the fact that everyone knew what they should do to help maintain the discipline of the market. A huge cart laden with goods got stuck in the middle of the street, which caused some disorder. However, people appeared, helped move the cart and soon order was restored.

As he now sees the ants move in and out of the kitchen, their discipline reminds him of the people in the market and how orderly they were. If anything at all, the ants seem to follow their queues in an even more regimental manner.

He places a small stone somewhere along their path, making sure that he does not injure or harm any of the tiny creatures as he does so. Chaos follows. The neat order that the ants had set up is destroyed and they run around confusedly. However, all this lasts only for a few moments and soon order is restored as some of them seem to take charge. A new line is formed quickly—moving around the stone just like the people in the market had moved around the fountain.

'Do you think there are tiny creatures that we cannot see?' he asks his father later in the day.

'What tiny creatures, Aju?'

'Creatures that we cannot see. Like very, very tiny ants? Or … perhaps … sounds that we cannot hear?'

'Well, it is hard to say for sure, though I don't see why not,' says Govinda. 'Why do you ask?'

'I think there are creatures smaller than even tiny ants. Small ants can see very small ants and the very small ants can see the very, very small ants and so it goes, you know,' says Ajita, in the way of an explanation.

Govinda laughs. 'I don't know.'

Ajita seems convinced of his idea. 'And sounds?' he persists. 'Do you think ants talk to each other so softly that we cannot hear them?'

'I don't think they can talk.'

'Then how do they tell each other what to do, where to go, where to find food … ?'

'That is niyati: the order in everything—in things living and non-living. That is how ants know what to do. That is how a stone knows how to fall and the night knows when it is time for the full moon.'

'And people in the Vaishali market?'

'What of them?'

'When they walk in the market, is that also niyati?'

'That is different. We have minds. We can use that to think and do things. We can talk to each other and understand each other. We live together, make our own customs and laws which help us live together, and we follow those laws,' says Govinda with a sigh. Ajita's questions are never-ending.

'And the ants? They don't speak to each other or make their own laws?'

'I don't think so,' says Govinda, smiling. 'You know, we plan to send you next month to a Gurukula where you will start your education. And there you will find all your answers.'

The young eyes widens. 'I will learn all this there?'

'Yes, in a few years you will. First, you will learn to ask the right questions and then find the answers.'

'A Gurukula?' Ajita says to himself. 'It sounds so interesting.'

For the rest of the morning, he imagines the kind of things he might learn at the Gurukula. It is only when he cuddles up to his mother for his afternoon nap that he realises that he would have to leave home, his parents and all that is familiar. He huddles closer to his mother as the thought crosses his mind. He decides he would divert his mind and return to the question that had haunted him all morning.

'Do you think there are very, very small creatures like very small ants, Maye?' he asks.

'No, I think not.' His mother's answer is clear and unhesitant.

'Tath said he was not sure. Why are you so sure there are no such creatures?'

'If we can't see them, they don't exist.'

'Hmm. The other day Tath said that even if we can't see the wind, it exists. He said that to explain to me that the gods are there even if we can't see them.'

'That's true. We cannot see the wind, nor can we see the gods. However, we know that the wind is there when we feel it hit our face or our skin. Your teeny-weeny creatures, on the other hand, we cannot touch or feel them. So, there is no way of knowing they are there. I think it is the same with the gods.'

'That is not what Tath says ... '

'I know. I am telling you what my Tath told me when I was a small girl. We lived in the mountains, Aju. We had to walk long distances uphill to get water, food or wood. And all of us in the house had to do that so that there was enough for everyone. My father or his father never found the time to do yajnas and invoke the gods.

'Your Tath has grown up in the plains near the cities. Life is much easier here. Look at our home. We get water from the stream which is so close to our home, we grow our food in our garden and we can also get what we need from the market, which is not very far off. When your father performs yajnas for other people, they give him things that are useful to us at home. He can afford to spend all day with these rituals and, in fact, it helps him take care of our needs. My own feeling is that when you do these rituals all the time, then the gods whom you invoke start appearing very real to you.'

'What does that mean?'

'It's like this. You know the wooden elephant I got for you from the fair? It is only a piece of wood which is shaped like an elephant. It is not a real elephant till you start playing with it. Once you get involved in the game and you have made yourself a king out on a hunt and you set out with your soliders and horses, this piece of wood does feel like an elephant. If in the middle of your game I tell you it is only a wooden toy, will you agree with me?'

'So, you are saying that the yajnas are a game?'

'Like a game. Anyway, you should sleep now. You are sounding very tired.'

'Maye, I am scared. I don't want to leave you.'

'Oh, did your Tath tell you that we are sending you to the Gurukula?'

'Yes, Maye.'

'I will miss you so much, my dear one. I am not sure I want you to go at all. Having said that, you are our child. Strong and fearless.'

'I will miss you when I sleep.'

'I know. Though soon you will get used to sleeping on your own. And there are other students there in the Gurukula, so you should know that you are not alone there.'

'I am not scared of sleeping alone, Maye. I am scared of sleeping. That is why I hold you and sleep.'

'Scared of sleeping! I have never heard you say that.'

'Yes, Maye.'

'Why on earth?'

'When I am sleeping, I don't know where I am. It is all so dark and I feel like I am out in the night going to some place I don't know. So I worry that I will wake up in a new, strange place, without you and Tath. Where I don't know anyone. How do I know that I will always wake up in our home next to you?'

'You worry too much, my little jewel. Your mind is so full of questions. When you try to sleep, gently pat your questions to sleep too. Let them lie still. Then, just as you close your eyes, think that my Maye is with me. Your Maye is always with you.' Saying this, Dhvani pulls her son closer to herself.

The day Ajita has to leave for the Gurukula arrives sooner than it should have, or so Dhvani feels. She has tried hard not to let anyone guess the emotional turmoil that she is going through, least of all her little son. She has managed to get some strength out of the fact that Ajita himself seems to look forward to the Gurukula with great excitement, and in his little joys she always found the greatest comfort. Ajita has woken up with the sun that morning. While he is looking forward to the new world that lay ahead of him, he also wants to touch and feel his home, his parents and his friends.

He runs into the garden to greet one of his newest friends: a tiny mango plant. He had dug a hole in the ground with his friends Surjan and Ratna, and has planted a mango seed there not long ago. He was overjoyed when a small plant emerged out of the soil one morning. He had tended the plant with the utmost care and he knows he will miss it a lot. He has asked Ratna to look after it while he is away. He is still in the garden when he hears his Tath calling him. He has forgotten completely that it is time for his morning prayers. It was only two weeks ago that he had got his sacred thread and with the thread came the duty of praying thrice a day: in the morning, at midday and in the evening. Though, today he hopes his father would not keep him long at the prayers for he wants to run down to the pond to meet his friends.

They are waiting for him near the pond when he finally makes his way there. It is where they meet every day, play and run around, swim and swing from the trees to pluck the ripest fruits. Today there is no time to enjoy the pond and splash around. Ajita doesn't feel like it either. When he sees his friends the full realisation of his departure dawns on him. It is a teary farewell and Ajita realises that it has taken longer than it should when he hears his father's voice calling out to him from a distance.

'We have to leave now, Ajita,' says Govinda, as he comes closer.

As they walk home, Govinda says, 'You will find that the ways of the Gurukula are very different, Ajita. Though I am sure you will get used to them very soon. You will not have friends like Ratna there. It was alright for you to have him as a friend when you were young. Now you have grown up and you will have to move forward. You will have new friends there.' Ajita does not say a word. He has always known that his Tath does not like him spending time with Ratna, though he has not tried to find out why.

When he finally sets out with his parents on his long journey to the Gurukula, Ajita turns to look in the direction of the pond as the cart passes it. The area is empty, his friends have left and Ajita again feels something tug at his heart.

It is planned that, on their way to the Gurukula, they would go first to Dhvani's maternal home, so that Ajita could meet and spend time with his grandfather and his uncle's family. Owing to his indifferent health, his grandfather had not attended his thread ceremony and that was another reason to meet him. The journey is a long one. The fact that they go up the hill to his grandfather's house on mules is the high point of the journey for Ajita.

Ajita only has a few faint memories of his grandfather's home. So it is on this visit that he would get the chance to really know this home. It is quite different from his own, though it has a charm of its own. It is when he ventures outside that

Ajita feels the sheer power of nature overcome him: the huge rocks, the views of the mountains in the distance, the tall trees and, most of all, the silence of the woods.

He sits down under a large, shady peepal tree. 'I wish I could live here forever,' he thinks to himself. 'I would have so many friends here—these trees, these creepers—and I can't even imagine what animals I will find in this place.' He thinks of the mango plant in his garden and he wonders whether Ratna would take care of it. His thoughts then turn to Ratna and Surjan and he realises once again how much he is going to miss his two friends. This flow of thoughts is interrupted when he sees his grandfather sit down next to him.

'I am very happy you are going to the Gurukula, Ajita,' his grandfather says. 'I hope you will study well and make a name for yourself.'

'Did you go to a Gurukula, Aiyya?'

'No, I did not. My father moved to these hills when I was very young. I was not even a year old when I came to this place and I have lived here all my life. My father was a very learned vaid, did you know?'

'What is a vaid, Aiyya?'

'A vaid is a person who cures illnesses and makes medicines. We are a family of vaids and have practised medicine for several generations. My father was, however, more interested in studying medicinal plants that grow in these mountains. So he decided to come here and spend a life studying leaves and plants. He knew so much—in one glance, he could distinguish the good medicinal plants from the poisonous ones. So many vaids from the plains used to come up here to discuss with him and take his potions and preparations. He was a very generous man and shared his knowledge and his medicines freely, never demanding anything in return. Some people would offer him something of their own accord; he would then accept it graciously. Though I have seen quite a few vaids who only took from him, he never had a complaint on his lips. He was a great man.'

'I wish I could have met him. I could have made friends with so many trees and plants with him around.'

The old man smiles and says, 'I am sure he would have also loved to share all that he knew with you. That is what my education was—walking through these forests with him and learning from him. Of course, he had much more to offer than my mind could deal with.'

'Why can't I stay here with you and learn from you all that your father taught you? Why can't I make this my Gurukula?'

'No, Ajita. You are on your way towards greater things. You will learn a lot in the Gurukula and you will learn very well, I am sure. Years later when people speak of you as a famous agnihotri and you are called upon to conduct the great fire rituals, I will feel great pride.'

'Aiyya, don't you do any fire rituals?'

'Some small ones … well, no. Not really. Growing up here and living here in these mountains means you have other things to attend to and you cannot spend time doing rituals. We have to do everything here on our own. It is not like living in a village like yours where you can get help for everything. Last year, there was a great storm and a part of the roof of this old house got damaged. Your uncle had to spend a whole week working on it to get it restored.'

He pauses and then continues: 'My father was properly trained to perform rituals. However, after he had spent time here, he also did not do any of them regularly. He told me often that the forest was our altar and the trees were our fires, and that we had no need to perform sacrificial rites. I grew up with that way of thinking.'

It is getting a little cold outside so they decide to move in. As they get up to go, Ajita's grandfather says, 'In the end, Ajita, it does not matter whether you are a great agnihotri or a simple vaid. What matters is to have a deep sense of what you are doing. It is not so important to do great fire rituals as it is to understand their significance. And when you understand that, you will find there are so many other ways of finding that same meaning. You may find it in the mighty mountains or in a tiny leaf, you may find it in chants or in silence or, like a very old friend of mine, you may find it in singing.'

When he leaves the hills to go down towards Vaishali, Ajita leaves with a heavy heart. When it is time to get into the cart, he starts weeping. He is going away from his grandfather and his home, and the hills and the forests. He is also leaving his mother who is not going to accompany him to the Gurukula. Govinda has to carry him into the cart and leave as soon as they can, so that he would stop crying.

It is a few hours into the journey that Ajita composes himself. However, he is still thinking of his Aiyya.

'When Aiyya speaks to me, I feel I can understand every word he says,' he thinks to himself. 'And it is the same with Maye. Tath is very difficult to understand, though. He uses words like niyati which I cannot fully understand.

'I need to go to the Gurukula to study. I will not just understand what Tath says, I will speak like that myself.'

He looks out of the cart and feels a gust of fresh air caress his face. He closes his eyes and inhales deeply.

Acknowledgements

It is often said that writing is a lonely activity and writers, more than anyone else, derive a vicarious pleasure from this self-image. But writing, like everything we humans do, is nourished by the warmth and care of fellow humans, and conversations with them. These are some of the things I want to acknowledge here.

The first nebulous ideas around *Ajita* were formed several years ago in my mind and took shape over the early years through conversations with several people. Of these, the significant conversations that come to mind about philosophy, literature and Buddhism, in particular, were the ones with Amiya Dev and Ipsita Chanda in Calcutta, Bijoy Mukherjee in Santiniketan and Romila Thapar, whom I met in Bombay. But one of the people I am most indebted to for conversations around these themes is Mukund Lath when I met him a few times at his home in Jaipur, and also when we spent time together in Guwahati. I am grateful to all these people for their time but also thankful that I could be part of a conference in Santiniketan which Bijoy Mukherjee invited me to and where I presented a paper which contained the seeds of *Ajita*. It is sad that Bijoy Mukherjee and Mukund Lath are not here with us to see *Ajita* finally published.

I would also like to thank Prashant Varma because of whom I could spend time in Deer Park, Bir. That visit to Bir and Dharamshala has mattered to this novel in important ways.

It was around this time that Giacomo Polesello and Fawzi Boudjema, my physicist friends, introduced me to the literary movement, Oulipo, and as I discovered more about this movement the more convinced I became about the formal aspects of my novel. This commitment became stronger through conversations with friends in London—Boika Sokolova, Elliot Leader and Jerry Sokol.

I am hugely indebted to Nalini Malani for so generously offering an image she had created for the book cover, for reading the book and for showing immense patience through all the delays that happened with the book.

I would also like to thank: Mitra Mukherjee-Parikh, for being there throughout the creation of this book—reading, commenting and discussing; Soni Wadhwa, for doing a careful reading of the first draft of the manuscript; Sujeet Bhatt and Priyanka Vegad for being the first readers of the completed manuscript.

Immense gratitude to so many who stood by me in this journey:

Prabodh Parikh, Dharen Chadha, Ashok Vaidya, Sanjukta Wagh, Reshmi Mitra, Rhea D'Silva, Apeksha Vora, Smriti Ravindra, Himani Dehlvi, Vaseem Dehlvi, Leena Abraham, Ravi Subramaniam, Surabhi Altekar Jamal and Ben Allanach.

Antara Dev Sen, for her encouragement and advice.

Paula Mariwala and Ravi Mariwala, who have been wonderfully supportive friends, for hosting a reading of *Ajita* at their home.

Sudhir Vempati, for organising a reading of *Ajita* at the Indian Institute of Science, Bangalore.

To my publishers: Ajitha G.S., my first point of contact in Westland, Karthika V.K. and Sanghamitra Biswas for placing their trust in the book and commissioning it and, particularly, to Sanghamitra again who did a great job of editing what was not an easy book to edit, to Saurabh Garge for designing the cover, to Sonia Madan for shepherding the book through the crucial final stages and to everyone at Westland involved with the production of the book.

To my band of young loyalists who will stand by me no matter what (and even if they have no intention of reading this book!): Beena and Shyam, Yogesh and Neha, Pranav and Maya, Ananya and Nikhil, Oindri and Deepak, Indus and Sameer, Leher and Anmol, Chaitanya, Aashna, Drishti, Mehak, Alina, Tanvi, Aadvik, Vibha, Amara and Dhruv.

To Sudha, Shashi, K.K., Reshma, Girish, Sangeeta—for being family.

To Vidita Vaidya and Ajit Mahadevan, who looked forward to the completion of this project as much as I did (Ajit is missed so deeply).

To Mummy, Daddy, Amma, Appa.

To the newest member of our home: Utkarsh.

To Gitu and Iru, who have been the harshest critics and, yet, the greatest inspiration for this book. The quiet expression of joy I see in their eyes on seeing this book published is worth every bit of the effort I put into it.